smitten gate

Smitten Gate

Stan Goff

CLUB ORLOV PRESS

Smitten Gate
© 2017 Stan Goff

Cover design: Tatiana Villa

Publication date: November 10, 2017

ISBN-13: 978-1979660488
ISBN-10: 1979660484

Club Orlov Press
http://ClubOrlovPress.blogspot.com
cluborlovpress@gmail.com

To Laney and Jayme,
in hopes that fathers
learn to do better
by daughters.

Acknowledgements

Sherry is always first because she has had my back for twenty-five years now. God bless Sherry. Shout out to Rebecca Bratten Weiss for giving the draft a read and making invaluable suggestions, especially with regard to grad school culture, of which I have no experience. And to Dmitry Orlov for taking the leap and putting in the sweat to get this book published. Thank you to all my kin.

Certain truths are not represented by any mortal, living or dead. This story is likewise not intended to represent any real person, living or dead. It is a work of fiction. This never actually happened. Send the lawyers home.

Broken down is the city of chaos,
every house is shut against entry.

Isaiah 24:10

How much for this soup?

Dangriga, Belize
April Fools Day, 1990

GARIFUNA BOYS ARE swimmers, and Che Lambert was no exception. But he really *really* didn't want to swim in the mouth of North Stann Creek. All the sewage from Dangriga was concentrated in the mouth of that river. The prospect almost made him gag.

He could see the bag barely afloat, just a bit of black plastic showing, and the tide was coming in. A trash bag full of cash, and it would be battered, punctured, rolled up in the silt and lost.

Lost!

He had thrown it off Havana Street Bridge and had to get it back now. Without the bag they wouldn't spot him, he had calculated, so he had thrown it in the water. Now he weaved at a dead run through the market north of the river, stripping off his shirt and dropping it between the fruit stalls, leaping out of his tattered trainers. He angled toward the North shore of the river mouth, already disgusted at the prospect of wading into that shit water, swimming out in the shit water to retrieve the bag rocking in the waves above the sandbar. Water the color of milky tea, rippling sluggishly now against the incoming tide, the mixed fresh and salt water wearing the foul skin of the city's flotsam.

1

He scoped the market crowd. No Gibraltar there he could see. No Hobo Joe. Maybe he had lost them on Havana Street. Che took the rubber band out of his shorts on the run, tying his dreads back in a ponytail to swim, yes, but also to change his profile. They had chased a thirteen year old with shoes, an orange shirt, and a mop; now he was shirtless and shoeless with a narrow head. They weren't smart, he reminded himself. Both of them were kind of fat, too. They just oagli, mon. Real seed-of-evil, haggish an fraitnin, brudda. Catch ya and kill ya daid right dah. An me muma need dat moni.

ABNER DALE WAS twenty-two today. Born the first of April, he thought, and destined for foolishness. He had been here more than a week now...... he was losing track. Belize City wasn't so much to his liking, but Dangriga had something else. Funkier, slower, more musical. None of the frantic vacation parties with drunken expats.

Dangriga reminded him of New Orleans on a slow weekday. It had the heat and humidity, too. A film of sweat on him ever since he got here, he was habituated to it now, growing to like the way it surprised him with the breezes. No hotter than summer in Raleigh where he and sister Amy were raised by Grampa after Mom went mad.

This morning he had left the hostel looking for food and ended up in the market. The place was already abustle, men in trousers, short sleeves and ball caps, women in bright dresses and white straw hats, a drowsy hungover cop in his tan over blue, the vendor women plump from sitting under tarps and canopies nibbling all day. Market women with sharp eyes and quick hands, who could shift from scowls to laughter in a split second. He never haggled with them. The other expats and tourists were pretty obnoxious with them, though.

Some of the market women flirted with him. He was a little white man, but fit and striking with his black hair, aquamarine eyes, and unforced smile.

He felt like cooking, and the hostel had a four-burner gas stove. Maybe a big piece of snapper, fried, with an avocado, a lemon to squeeze on both, a couple of fried flour tortillas, and some of those little red fig bananas. He would need some flour for the fish and some coconut oil. He could use the rest of the oil later. No *123 Oil today*—that cheap shit! Axle grease manufactured for the poor to eat. Not today, because it was his birthday. He'd call his mom after breakfast, tell her thanks for giving birth on April 1st. She was somewhat lucid last time he called, then started to mutter about a sable filly with two white socks.

At least she sounded comfortable.

Stumbling through the market were a couple of painfully pink Pelican Beach tourists with red eyes, but mostly there were locals. He saw three nurses shopping together for their lunches in matching lime-green scrubs with toucans embroidered on the breast pockets. One light-skinned, one dark with long dreads descending from a white bandanna, one little muscular one with her hair cut short like a man—who was looking at him. He smiled at her, and she smiled back directly, showing off a gap between her front teeth that made him like her more. He lowered his eyes not to seem too forward, and heard her friends titter as they picked up on this little exchange.

A boy with tied dreads and no shirt came charging through the market, bumping the nurses, slaloming past him, careening between the stalls, trailing a wake of shouted rebukes. *Rude bwai!*

Dale was taking his snapper in a plastic bag moments later, looking around to see if he saw the nurses again, when he heard the scream. The whole market alerted, falling nearly silent. The scream was so plaintive and desperate, Dale dropped the bag with the fish and sprinted through the crowd. When he could see, it was a boy (was it *that* boy?) well out in the water, his screams now alternated with animal retching. Dale stripped off his t-shirt and kicked off his sneakers as he ran into the milky brown water, then executed a perfect racers dive. (A competitive swimmer in his first two years of college, he had given it up to concentrate on English literature and Spanish.)

He dug in so hard now he made a wake, raising his head every fifth or sixth stroke to breathe and spit and to orient on the boy, now gone silent and sinking.

He reached for the sinking boy when the hot knives hit him in the legs, groin, and abdomen. Suddenly gasping for air with the pain, he vaguely realized that something was stinging him as he clutched the boy by his pony tailed dreads and pulled his face clear of the water. Through the shocking sudden pain he side-stroked back, fighting the sensation that he was about to pass out and almost welcoming any relief from a pain that seemed to cover every inch of his body now.

What the fuck! He smelled the silt under him as he began to lose his orientation altogether. Then arms. People were plucking him and the boy out of the water. There was sand under him, in his clothes and on his skin, feet around him, and an odd noise that came out of him when he exhaled.

Men were talking.

"Bes' ting is to piss ahn im." Laughter. "Naw, f'sure, piss kill de stingahs."

"Tehn ya bahks, ladies…"

"Ye do no such ting," a woman's voice, authoritative. "Lemme 'av im."

"Dat's a mahn-o-wah, sugah. Da stingah's still bite." A man.

It was her, the little one with the smile, who replied, "Ah know what it is, brudda. Hol' 'im still and don tech de tentacle." She pulled a pair of hemostats out of one pocket, grabbed the end of a Portuguese Man of War tentacle and began gently pulling it off. He vomited, then passed out.

BETWEEN CAROLINA AND Duke blue. All around him, blue. Maybe a deep sky blue. Not quite dark enough for cornflower blue. Someone had scored a lot of this paint, because it covered the walls, the beams, rafters, and sheathing of the open ceiling. Even the ceiling fans were blue. The blue hurt his legs, hurt his back, abdomen, his left arm. But he didn't feel like doing anything about it. He felt slack, almost indolent, content to be very still. The pain was a shrike with its kills spiked to a hawthorn, observed at a distance. Birds, birds…… in a solid line midway around the entire wall were paintings of birds, framed in rough wood, dozens of different birds in a stream of riotous color.

"Whatcha say, sah?"

Lime-green. She was standing there in the lime-green scrubs, checking his IV, an old glass bottle.

"Hi," he whispered.

"Hi, yahself," she said. There was that smile that made him like her. "Ya said somethin' jes' now, bote a… strike? Was ya dreamin'?"

"Shrike... it's... it's a bird..."

"Ya know birds?" (Like 'beds'.)

"I know about that bird. It's cruel, but not on purpose."

"I love da beds, sah." She passed her hand over the room at the line of pictures. "Mebbe we talk. Rest a bit. I be bahk."

"God, I hope so..." He drifted away on the sound of laughter.

"I'M VANESSA. SHE Kendra. De ahda nurse, she cahl Farah. An you cahl Abnah, no?"

It was the nurse with the dreads. She told him he was in the Blue Clinic, what a surprise. Kendra was the light-skinned one. They brought him a steamy bowl of *escabeche*, a garlicky chicken soup with hot peppers and a whiff of vinegar.

"Abner's my name. Most folks, they call me A.D. For Abner Dale. It's a funny name in the States. Makes me the butt of jokes."

"Why dey neem ya dat, den?" asked Kendra.

"My grandfather's name. What did you give me? I hurt, but I don't seem to care much."

"Mahphine, sah. Ya goata beeg dose," Kendra told him.

"Call me A.D. Please."

"Eatcha soup, A.D. Mek ya bettah."

They explained to him that Farah was taking a nap and getting changed before she came back. This was their clinic. They were nurse practitioners, all three of them. The Blue Clinic was run by three nurses. They had all gone to school together.

He had been stung, badly and multiply, by a Portuguese Man of War. The boy he had dragged out of the river was stung, too. He was in the regional hospital, being questioned by the police. They had taken a skiff out and found a trash bag full of money, several thousand dollars. The suspicion was that the boy, Che something, had gotten the money from someone who was involved in something sketchy, and that he had thrown it in the river to get away. Farah had made the decision to treat A.D. at their clinic. He owed them some money, Kendra told him. Hoped he could pay.

"How much?"

With the morphine and a gram of IV Rocephin to prevent infection—he had been injured in water full of shit, after all—it was already past four hundred dollars. He tried not to wince, then they reminded him that was Belizean dollars, exchanged at two to one with US dollars. He owed them just over $200—bargain as far as he was concerned.

"How much for this soup?" he asked, provoking an outburst of laughter.

FARAH GILLET ENTERED the clinic to find A.D. sitting up in the bed with one arm holding up a sheet, inspecting the raised lesions that lined his arm and abdomen.

"Ya likely got a new tattoo." He looked up, red-eyed with residual morphine, and gave a weak smile.

"Tattoo?"

"Leaves a mahk fah good lotta time. Ahm Farah. You'd be A.D., da sewah swimmah, rescuah ta bad bwais."

He took her proffered hand.

"Hate ya seein' me like this," he said.

She laughed at that. "Mistah Dale, ya look fine now. We seen da wohst of ya. Bathed ya, dressed ya lesions, put dat catheta in ya."

He blushed at that and tugged up at his sheet a bit.

"Can I lose this?" he said, nodding down in the general direction of the catheter.

"Dis minute, if ya like." He blushed again, and she followed up. "Ya want someone else t' do it?"

"It's just... I remember you, before this. You were in the market. Would it surprise you if I said I was about to speak to you before the boy got in trouble?"

"Weh ya?" she asked, smiling that smile.

"I was gonna ask you if you'd like to get a coffee or somethin'. Now, you've watched me puke, washed nasty water off me, measured my urine output... kinda takes the glow off, doncha think?"

"Let me get dat cathetah out," she replied. "We'll release ya soon as ya like."

He was looking down again, nodding slightly. "Thanks."

"Ahl be done 'bout six dis evenin'. Pay ya bill when ya leave, be back hya six o'clock, an' I buy ya little bottle of beah. If ya feel up to it. Ahm givin' ya some pills f' da pain."

He was smiling back at her now, until she said, "Now, lay back an' getcha mind ready. Dis not gonna feel so good."

Green on blue

July 13, 2010
Kabul, Afghanistan

CAPTIVE ANIMALS CRIED unnoticed. The afternoon street market smelled of hot garlic, cilantro, raw sewage, and sweat. Greasy sunrays infiltrated quivering columns of cooking smoke. Loud voices haggled over prices, quieting down as people came within earshot of them... then he saw it: the solitary American military truck—a hulking armored troop carrier—moving at a snail's pace through the dusty congestion.

Jahid was stirring sugar into his *chai* when he caught the truck with a turn of the eyes—just the eyes, but not the head. American, a combat truck, an up-armored MRAP—mine-resistant armor protected, a locomotive engine on four great wheels—nosing through the market crush. Jahid set down his spoon on the stained rattan table in front of the *chai* shack, thumbing his rifle sling higher onto his shoulder and grunting at Rafik who was sipping from an incongruously beautiful Chinese cup. Rafik looked up. Jahid pursed his lips toward the approaching truck. Rafik set down his *chai*, keeping his eyes low.

Americans never came to this market. Doubly remarkable, this armored truck had entered the market surrounded by people and unable to move freely—alone. Omar, the third militiaman, came out of the tea shop with his cup in hand, halting too as he caught sight of it, falling in with their dis-

9

simulation by averting his eyes.

The MRAP's motor clattered through decelerations, the thunderous diesel engine revving and falling. Like an ox wading through a flock of egrets, the MRAP crawled ahead, leading with its square snout, wheels coated in ochre dust, the side windows sealed. The driver was a wraith behind the dust, abrasions and glare in the windshield's ballistic glass. The truck advanced by short lunges, a meter or two at a time, past the tea shop with its blanket door and cheap street tables, past makeshift awnings of many colors, past bicycle carts, butcher stands, smoking stove fires, fruit displays, storefronts with discounted clothes lined up on wall pegs, potato crates, plastic wares, pots and pans... past two sheep. Past people, mostly men, who moved reluctantly aside, averting their gazes as the truck passed, as if avoiding the eye of a belligerent bull. The truck's backplate was up. There could have been men inside; but when *amrekayan* troops were moving, they dropped the upper backplate for a machine gun on the rear, for security.

The three men's objective today was to kill an American— or two—as an object lesson. They had fought alongside the *amrekayan*. They had been trained by the Americans, armed by them and equipped by them. They worked on an American base. Nonetheless, this had to be done. With Benham's shocking revelation, it was an inescapable matter of honor to their minds, as Afghanis, as Pashtuns and as Muslims. Jahid, Rafik, and Omar had been headed to the Intercontinental Hotel to locate a target; but here was one creeping providentially down the street... perhaps. Galil assault rifles like theirs— paradoxically Israeli-made—would not begin to penetrate this armor. Nor would their grenades. And this street was very crowded, too crowded, a cacophony of shouts and murmurs, metal banging, horns, roosters and feral boys.

Someone would go to the *amrekayan* and exchange information for money if they were incautious. Good money. Euros and dollars. They needed more space to make a quick getaway. And to avoid killing other Afghanis.

Not only did the truck have no escort and no rear security, there was no gun mounted in the turret. Completely buttoned up, it moved like a crippled tortoise. A quiet word passed from Jahid to the others to follow the truck. They waited, these three unremarkable men in olive ISAF uniforms and patrol caps, taking a tea break—allies in the eyes of this unknown driver. Keeping their movements casual, they nursed their *chai* until the truck was nearly a soccer field past, then fell in trail, Galils still safely slung. Short, chubby Omar lit a PTC cigarette with a yellow Bic lighter from the Camp Virtue Base Exchange. They worked at the big base outside of the city. Jahid heard Rafik just behind him, quietly praying. The truck was repeatedly stopped by the crowd's encroachment, forcing the men to dawdle. They pretended to browse over sweets and soaps.

The truck began a slow left turn, and they picked up the pace, weaving between people on the street with more open deliberation. The truck stopped. They stopped, too, and watched, close enough now to hurl a cricket ball, hearts battering. The opening in the street was wide enough to make their move. The door cracked, then closed, then cracked again and their pulses followed. Jahid spoke to the other two, and they began to angle toward the back of the truck to cover it. The door opened now, and a filthy American soldier stepped out with nothing but a sidearm, wearing no body armor and no helmet. He was short for an *amrekayan*. His eyes were startling green-on-blue and rimmed in red, his short salt and pepper hair disheveled and plastered in dry sweat and dust. The American soldier circled around the front of the truck and approached a food vendor enveloped in fragrant smoke and steam. The driver was about to buy a meal. Jahid drew a long, slow breath to quiet his nerves. He had never seen anything like it.

"*Allahu akbar*," Jahid said to himself, and unslung his Galil.

Saving Dr. Ryan

University of North Carolina at Chapel Hill
May 12, 2009

"THEY ARE THE same," Deangela told him, only because class participation was a grading criterion. She felt like an impostor, despising grades while depending on them. She disliked class participation in particular. *Give me a good lecture any day*, she thought. A well-conceived thesis, expounded systematically and ingested anonymously. Class participation made her feel like a subjugated hound compelled to "speak"— "Woof!"—for her Bubba Rose biscuit.

Dr. Ryan—her professor—knitted his brow reflectively. His weirdly small hand tugged at the gold bead posted through his earlobe. A sleeve-mosaic forearm tattoo peeked out of quarter-rolled shirt cuffs.

His weightlifting was on display when he jogged through the campus in his tank top and nylon shorts, all cut gym muscle rippling under elaborate, vaguely Buddhist tattoos. Female students, some at least, made giddy vocalizations about him—thirty-nine, prematurely gray, long classic face framed in a rebellious beard topped with a bad-boy buzzcut.

Deangela saw him as a peacock. It was animus at first sight on the first day of class this semester—Western Analytic Philosophy, a level-four, first-year graduate course, finals in a week, praise the Lord. She tried to conceal her contempt in part because she wasn't altogether sure why she detested him so immediately and intensely.

He was a genuinely knowledgeable and skilled teacher as well as a publishing juggernaut on a fast track to tenure. Brain muscles to attend to the body muscles—but that was only a part of it. He was a grandstander, she thought, full of himself, and she couldn't overcome the suspicion that there was some lightless toxic void behind the freewheeling, hip performance.

He was, she had to admit, nonetheless always courteous, even deferential to her—the odd girl, the biracial prodigy starting her graduate studies at the advanced age of eighteen. She felt a little unjust for her disfavor of him even as she felt justified, as if she were haunted by the ambivalences of her mother's Catholicism.

Cool damp outside air drifted in through the cracked-open windows, carrying in the smell of fried food and a barely audible conversation about avian flu from the sidewalk one floor below. She could hear birds—house sparrows, a blue jay mimicking a hawk call to frighten other birds off a feeder, robins... robin-red breast—from a grub's eye view the vision of violent death.

Her attention drifted while Ryan waited for his answer. Velocirobins, terrorizing grasshoppers and worms, even little snakes... hunting in the rain that floods the worms out of their tunnels... Her mother Farah had passed along to her and her father alike a fascination with birds. Longing to be outside, she grudgingly turned her attention back to the senescent classroom and the muscle-model whose gaze grew impatient.

Since she had to jump through the class-participation hoop anyway, challenging Ryan was always irresistible. The question had been, "What are the key differences between twentieth-century philosophers Rawls and Nozick?" Her response—"They are the same"—was clearly provocative since Dr. Ryan had been portraying distinctions between them for the past two sessions. Leaning back against his desk, he waited for the rest of what Ms. Dale would have to say.

Her fellow students had turned toward her, but then they always did. She was the mutant among mutants. Philosophy grad students can be tedious, but they are not "tedious of the twice told tale." More like the confabulated tale, or the over-processed tale, or the agonizingly arcane tale, she mused. Yet even within the closed system of their terminal geekdom, she observed, there were power struggles and dominance displays that gave her visions of stags pissing on each other's territory and crashing their antlers into saplings. In this class, the diminutive, horn-rimmed James attended to prim Methodist Angela, his crush, as he quoted a virile Nietzsche against his rival—the prematurely and attractively balding David, who clung to the more effeminate Kant.

Deangela herself seemed to set them all bobbling. A scary-smart homeschooled kid, she was suspected by many to be socially retarded. She didn't always comb out her tangled hair and appeared at times to be someone who lived in the woods on locusts and wild honey. She never wore makeup and had dense unplucked eyebrows. Rumor had it she didn't shave either, though she always wore tattered boy trousers and never a sleeveless top. They couldn't know that all her clothing was second-hand and that she happily did all her shopping at garage sales and thrift stores. Hirsute was okay for a stoned, aging hippie woman hula-hooping in front of Weaver Street Market, but in grad school, on this eighteen-year-old, it suggested carelessness, or cluelessness, or both.

Sometimes she showed up for class with dirty clothes, wearing scuffed and muddy Danner hiking boots, looking not like a Carrboro hula-hooper but someone who had just stolen a carcass from a pack of hyenas. The whole campus knew she was a gifted aberration, a young woman who had read Tolstoy when she was seven, her mother a Garifuna nurse from Belize and a white American father who was an Army sergeant.

She glanced out the window, still distracted by the jay pretending to be a hawk.

"Go on," said Ryan.

She turned her eyes back to him and sat up straighter, wiping her hair away from her face only to have it fall back.

"Well, they're both anti-Aristotelian, aren't they? They both see every person as a detached agent, as someone without history or cultural context..." Her voice was her mother's voice—fruit and whiskey, like Macy Gray. She picked at the edge of a book while she talked, eyes switching from book to Ryan to book again.

"...Then a group of these rootless guys gets together to form rules for a common good." Pausing again, she rubbed her index finger in short repetitive strokes now over the surface of her desk, like she was crossing something out again and again, her eyes aimed downward now as she consulted and retransmitted another persona.

"They only disagree on the basis for establishing just rules based on competing origin myths;"—her hand stops moving, her gaze on Ryan again—"Rawls with his amnesiac veil of ignorance and Nozick with an Adam figure who appears out of nowhere to pick up pretty shells on the beach and establish the institution of property"—right index finger now poking at two points on the desk, back and forth like a metronome—"but they both assume the possibility of universal norms apart from any named tradition... and yet they both consider male as normative and ignore that this male normativity, along with the other social goods that they narrate, is not universal but developed out of the masculine, Euro-American, bourgeois history that both Rawls and Nozick personally share."

Ryan steepled his fingers as she continued.

"Both of them are arguing from a highly contextual status quo and pretending that it's universal. They disagree on some particulars about the basis for justice within that status quo, but they're both proposing elaborate rationalizations for it."

She held his gaze for a moment, then looked down at her desk, her mad-woman hair falling back over her face. The other eight members of the class gawked. Seven of them were men, so maybe the gender dig got their attention; but Angela House, the only other female in the class, was staring at her, too, like Deangela had just stepped off an alien spacecraft. She looked so childlike!

Ryan stroked his beard a couple of times, then stood, smiling broadly, his perfect teeth eerily white against a suspiciously early tan. He walked in a half circle to face the class from behind his desk.

"Okay," he said dismissively, turning to pick up a dry erase marker and presenting his back to the class.

He made an "R" and circled it, then an "N" and circled it too.

"Let's talk about these competing notions of justice."

WHEN THE BELL announced the end of class the students gathered their books and papers. Out the door they went: Steve the mustachioed and determined local International Socialist; Randall the fat one who wore Hawaiian shirts tucked in like an old man, always reeking of Axe cologne; Angela the Methodist (*Why wasn't she going to Duke?*); bespectacled David —James's nemesis; and then Deangela.

Ryan had a sensibility about women, he believed, especially the young ones. He knew that women were captivated by him—many of them, anyway. He had sensed from the first day that this girl needed the kind of affirmation he might give her; that she camouflaged her attraction to him with this odd Aspergerish compulsion to confront. And she was undoubtedly brilliant, which made her alluring to him, kindling within him the ambition to domesticate her like an exotic animal. He had noticed that beneath her ratty clothes (another camouflage for her own desire, he suspected) she was well-muscled, wiry... fit. No matter how she dressed, she couldn't hide that hard little ass, he mused, the thick muscular calves, and the almost boyish small swell of her breasts. Even her reputed refusal to shave beguiled him a bit, as a counterpoint to the young women he had been with these days who all seemed to have undergone full-body waxes. He liked that—that smooth infantile thing; but he liked variety, too. Ms. Dale was undeniably different.

"Have you got a moment, Deangela?" he asked, stopping her.

James, Angela's horn-rimmed Zarathustra, went out the door; then Déshì from Taiwan; and finally—as always—Andrei, the enormous, phlegmatic second-generation Russian, who gave a kind of bow and mock salute to Deangela and Dr. Ryan as he made his exit. Dr. Ryan and Deangela were left alone.

She stood facing him, all five-foot-three of her angled up at his six, her pack slung over her left shoulder. Ryan canted back against the desk again, the backs of his legs now propped against the edge to put him and Deangela at eye level, his legs out behind her.

"Deangela, you're going to make your mark on philosophy, I expect. Have you thought about your future? Do you know about our Parr Fellowship?"

She didn't reply. *There's that Asperger thing again*, he thought, so he powered through it.

"I've looked at your final paper."

"Okay?" She shifted her pack higher on her shoulder.

"Interesting choice. Wittgenstein and the Body."

"It's an interesting topic... to me." She tugged with her free hand at one of her anarchic locks, stretching it and letting it pop back. "Is the paper okay?"

He saw that flicker. Of doubt? Of interest beyond the paper? The need for approval? The hair thing. Maybe a pleasure signal?

"I'd like to talk with you about it."

"I have to go. I have a meeting." She glanced at the door then back at him.

He smiled again, looking into her black coffee eyes, and shifted his eyes to her mouth. "Not now, of course. I have office hours this afternoon from three to five. Can you drop by?"

She did a little two-step with her head down, then looked up again. "Orienteering club."

He cocked his head like a hawk, still staring at her mouth, full like her mother's. She inherited her mother's diastema, but he could only see that gap between her 8 and 9 incisors when she spoke directly at him with her face up. "Really? What got you interested in orienteering?"

"My father," she answered, but offered no more, ducking her head.

He nodded absently, looked at the floor, then back at Deangela. "Well, how about tomorrow then? Do you have half an hour or so tomorrow morning?"

"Between ten and twelve," she said, looking out the window, then back at the door, then down at her feet, then back at Dr. Ryan. He had his hand across his beard, stroking downward. His hands were slight, narrow and knob-knuckled like a squirrel's paw, incongruous next to his veined, tattooed forearms and the slabs of gym muscle under his shirt. He was able to bulk up in the gym, but his hands betrayed a sly skinny boy peering furtively out from behind all that sculpted sinew.

"Excellent. Can you meet me on the way to work, at, say, eleven?"

"Where?"

"The Mediterranean? They have very good coffee."

"Yes. Do I need to bring a copy of the paper?"

"If you like." She stood silent. After a beat, he went on. "Then I'll see you at eleven. Don't be late for your meeting."

WORRY PUMMELED HER like a mental hailstorm. Something was cockeyed. Was something wrong with the paper? Had she confronted him one too many times? Was he hitting on her?

The subject matter was easy for her, God knows. Frozen as text, dissectable as grammar and logic. These people, though, at college, now graduate school, were worm bins of conflicting desires and agendas. These were grammars she didn't recognize—she could blame it on home-schooling if she hadn't already been here three years—even if her study of Wittgenstein had revealed their game-like character. She didn't know the rules, even as she appreciated that there was a great deal at stake in them. Her gifts were of no use to her here; and she was acutely aware, yet again, of her awkward youth, her atypical parents, her lack of siblings, her biracial status which placed her outside by another measure still.

She raked over her memory of the conversation hunting for clues. What was she expected to say to a comment like, "You are going to make your mark"? That was either true or false, time would tell, but was it intellectual flattery or was he hinting at something else, some project? And why did that frisson of revulsion ripple across her skin when he gazed at her? Was that leer into her eyes just his way, or was he going for soulful? And why did he stare at her mouth? It made her acutely self-conscious. She didn't know him, couldn't disentangle his mannerisms from his performances. Why was she so suspicious of him? Why did she feel patronized? What in the hell was this meeting with him over the paper about?

Thank God this class was nearly over—two more weeks. She pushed open the door to the Student Union. Ian, Brett and Oliver—the only other members of the vast orienteering club—were already seated around one of the coffee tables studying the map for an Umstead Park competition that was in one week.

DEANGELA HEARD DISHES bumping in the suds as she strode into the apartment and threw her pack onto the tattered olive love seat in the corner. Sam was washing dishes in the kitchen.

"Hiya," said Sam without looking up from the dishes. The apartment smelled like hot yeast and rosemary. Deangela flopped onto the backless garnet divan across the scantily furnished room. The cushion sank precipitously into the broken springs. She started unlacing her hikers.

"Hey, Sam." She set her boots on the white plastic shoe stand by the door, lined up with her Mudclaws, the dried red clay from her last orienteering practice still attached, her exhausted old Saucony runners, her cheap aqua-socks for wading and her scuffed purple Crocs. Sam kept her shoes on the lower rack, equally utilitarian: two pairs of Keds, one black and one white, a pair of Birkis, and a pair of nicked and faded Broges. *Women and their shoes*, Sam smiled to herself.

Most people assumed Samantha was a butch lesbian, but Deangela knew Sam loved Ted, her fiancé in Asheville. Ted and Sam were uncommonly contented together in spite of their long-distance relationship. Ted was a nurse, like Deangela's mom, though not a nurse-practitioner like her.

"Sam," Deangela said, climbing out of the sinkhole in the divan to carry her pack to her bed in the half-size room with a sloped ceiling. The slope made her dwelling feel happy the way blanket forts did when she was very small. "Got a minute?"

"What's up?" Sam called from the kitchen, setting her last plate in the plastic drainer and wiping her hands on the dish towel. Deangela returned and dropped onto the love seat. Sam dropped the dish towel on the DVD player by the TV, and took her turn on the quicksand couch.

"Something happened in Ryan's class today." Sam pulled her knees up and let her shoulders drop back onto the oyster wall. "Is that bread I smell?"

"Yeah. Mixed it last night. Dutch oven with rosemary."

Sam never tried to lose her country white-girl. From Western North Carolina, her accent was pure NASCAR, and it led people to underestimate her.

"Mmm." Deangela felt a pang of hunger.

"So what happened?" asked Sam.

"Dr. Ryan stopped me after class."

"Oh, shit."

"What?"

"Well, I've been wondering if you'd get a pass or not," Sam said with a two-handed stroke over her hair.

"A pass?"

"He hit on you, didn't he?"

"That's just it. I don't know. But it's kinda weird you went there before I explained it."

"Guy's a walking hard-on is what I hear. He likes to fuck his grad students. What exactly happened?"

Deangela recounted the exchange.

"I mean, meeting in the Med is safe, right? And he might actually not like my paper. He says he needs to meet with me about my paper... at Med Deli tomorrow."

"Hmm," Sam rose and stepped back into the kitchen. Deangela got up to follow. Sam put the tea kettle on, then pulled two cups down from the cupboard: one from Internationalist Books, the local lefty-new-age bookstore a block and a half away from the apartment, and one from UNC Law School, where Sam was pursuing her juris doctor. "You want tea?"

"Sure... Darjeeling straight."

Sam bent to retrieve the tea bags from a floor cabinet, her ginger frizz coming loose from the scrunchy. She grunted against her own girth, a big-boned woman, boxy and sturdy and self-assured in her own skin. Deangela, for all her redoubtable intellect, was eighteen and still casting about to figure out how she wanted to be. She adored Sam, and very much wanted whatever it was that Sam had—that self-accepting poise.

"De, sweetie, you might be the smartest person at this University..."

"Sam, I..."

"Jus' sec', you know what I mean. Hell, you might the smartest person in the whole damn state, for all anyone knows. What's your GPA right now?"

"Four, but..."

"No buts, De. You know as well as I do that your paper, whatever it's about, is prob'ly publishable." Aiming her ice-blue eyes at Deangela, Sam swelled up with maternal affection (Deangela was nine years her junior). Deangela looked down and picked at a callus on her palm.

"Okay," Deangela said, looking up again at Sam. "I don't wanna jump to conclusions. You know I dislike him, and I'm afraid I'm projecting somehow. I mean, I'm not some campus diva," she said, rolling her eyes skyward. "I'm the poster child for nerd-girl. I'm nerd squared. I don't send off spawning pheromones; I send off footnotes. And I feel pretty validated without that shit. Over-validated. No one tells me how smart I am at Orienteering Club. They say 'good run' or 'crappy attack point.' I like that." She laced her fingers into her hair, puffed her cheeks, crossed her eyes, and blew out a little jet of vexation.

"You ain't gotta signal him, baby," Sam explained. "Guy like him, your quirks are another invitation to conquest.

You're exotic to him. Li'l teen-age hard-body brown girl. Ryan's prob'ly intimidated by you, too. Half his age and already runnin' circles 'round 'im. That intimidation..." she scanned across the kitchen cabinets for the right explanation, "...his fear of inferiority and your being a very young female... well, it puts a match to his tinder. He's a dickhead, a control monkey. He's a fuckin' trophy collector, and he Does Not. Like. Women. Guys like that, they're turned on by the idea of your humiliation... he thinks he'll be in control once he gets you to spasm on his little pudenda-poker." Deangela laughed aloud. "That's his little power fantasy. He's a blue-ribbon creep and moonin' around while he dangles a paper in front o' you stinks of sexual harassment to me."

"You sure?"

"*Prima facie*? No, baby, ain't never a hundred percent sure. But ya heard alarm bells, and ya oughta listen."

The kettle started to whistle. Sam got up and cut the flame. The whistle died. She poured spattering hot water over the teabags in the cups, holding the tabs to keep them out of the tea. Deangela followed her. Sam clanked the pot on the back burner, handed Deangela her tea, and picked up her own. Deangela retreated with her tea to the love seat again. Sam followed, blowing across the top of her cup.

"Okay, what constitutes sexual harassment?" Deangela asked. "You're the law student."

Chapel Hill, North Carolina
May 13, 2009

THE DAY FORESHADOWED A North Carolina summer. The temperature was eighty-three by 10 a.m. and climbing. Yesterday's drizzle had settled moisture along the seams of the streets, and damp heat waves rose thick from open dumpsters and patches of city grass.

She was running late, so she threw on the same pair of baggy green trousers she had worn the day before and a washed oversize t-shirt emblazoned with "The Beatles"—two-dollar swag from Club Nova Thrift Shop down on Main Street. She gathered her hair back with a red handkerchief wrapped over her crown and behind her ears that formed a minor explosion on the back of her head and aired out a pebbling of mild acne on the northern boundary of her forehead.

At 10:50 a.m. Deangela left the apartment and strolled southeast to get off Basnight Lane and onto Cameron, a long cut. She hooked around onto Robertson to take Franklin. Going up Kenan was shorter, but she had been verbally accosted there once from less than thirty feet away by a tribe of drunken frat rats—white guys who hooted "brown sugar" at her while they clutched at their crotches and fixed her with predatory stares. Their malicious alcoholic gazes had pushed into her heart like unwelcome fingers. She never went up Kenan again. Ever.

The Mediterranean Deli was already feeding an early lunch crowd. Deangela opened the door and was engulfed by cool air-conditioned air and the combined aroma of coffee, grilled lamb and hummus. Her mouth watered. Dr. Ryan was near the back of the room at a tiny round table between two rows of dessert display cases. He was wearing jeans with no belt, loafers with no socks, and a gray polo shirt. Grinning like they were old chums, he tracked her approach over a still steaming cardboard coffee cup clutched in his little squirrel fingers.

She dropped her pack onto the chair opposite Ryan and said hi.

"Hi, Deangela. Need anything?"

"Yes Professor, give me a minute. Gonna get some food. I haven't eaten."

"David, please," he said, shifting side-saddle and aiming his shoulder and a sensitive smile at her. "In graduate school we're colleagues."

"David. I'll be back in a minute."

"Take your time."

Staring at her mouth again. *What the hell,* she thought. She ordered a lamb and beef gyro. Lutfi, the youngest son in the family that ran the deli—a slender Palestinian with big eyes and a day's growth of thick black beard—told her he would call her when it was ready.

She returned to her seat, zipped open her Bean pack, lifted out a water bottle and placed it on the table. Pulling out the folder with her paper in it, she dropped it next to the bottle, re-zipped the pack back and plopped it on the floor. She scooted the plastic chair back to sit. As she squared up to face him, Ryan swung one leg over the other, draping his left arm over the seat back, and tipped his coffee back to drain the cup. He parked the empty cup on the table and wiped his mouth with the back of his rat claw, all the while fixing his relentless gaze on her mouth.

"Have I got something in my teeth?" she asked.

"What?"

"You keep looking at my mouth."

Ryan dropped his leg back to the floor and his eyes to the table, flexing a bit, and interlaced his rodent fingers. She was seized briefly by thoughts of fleas and the plague.

"Do I?"

"Yes."

He began looking around the restaurant now, licking his lips and rubbing his hands together. He finally faced her and clasped his knobby paws on the table, causing it to rock on uneven legs, almost toppling her water bottle. Deangela caught the bottle and placed it firmly on the floor. *You can theoretically stand a pencil on its point*, she thought distractedly, *but it's easier to balance a marble inside a bowl.*

"Sorry," he said. She wasn't sure whether this was in reference to the bottle or staring at her mouth. "Nice save." She looked at him. "The bottle."

"You said you wanted to talk about my paper."

Before Ryan could reply, Lutfi called, "De, you're up."

"Excuse me," she said.

"Course."

Ryan felt he had to regroup. He had read that women were more sexually susceptible if you didn't face them directly—makes you appear needy when you mirror—and that they somehow experienced subconscious sexual "reverberations" when you directed your gaze at their mouths. Wrong-footed now, he surmised that her autism made her the exception and decided to change tack.

When she came back, she dropped her paper plate with the gyro on the table and scooted the chair back under her.

"You mind?" she asked, unwrapping the gyro.

"By all means, go ahead. Do you prefer De or Deangela? I want you to feel as comfortable with me as I feel with you."

She hesitated while unwrapping her food for a split second (she had this weird flash of an angry possum chewing on a fence wire) then inspected the contents of the gyro.

"Deangela," she said. "About the paper?" She bit off a mouthful and dabbed cucumber sauce off the corner of her mouth with a paper napkin.

"Yes. The paper. Well, you were pretty hard on Kripke. He draws a distinction between metaphysical and epistemic possibility."

God almighty, I'm exhausted by this already. She took a few seconds to chew and swallow, dabbing again with the crushed napkin.

"Not my issue. He's off-base because he's trying to transform Wittgenstein into a skeptic."

"I did a Master's Thesis on Kripke," he offered.

"On his interpretation of Wittgenstein?" She took a swig of water to prep for another bit of the gyro. Damn, she was hungry! She was always hungry, it seemed. Her mother approved of her appetite. *Empty crocus bahg can no stan' up,* Momma was fond of saying. *You gote t' eat.*

"No, no," he smiled and looked down. "On modal logic."

The way he was perched up sideways on his chair, she half expected him to fart.

"Kripke's not the main character in my paper." She took a greedy bite of her sandwich and had to chew with her mouth open. She exaggerated it a bit because she had a sudden puerile urge to gross him out. The old "see food" gag.

"True enough," he allowed, hesitating for a bit to watch her chomp on her food. "Do you have a boyfriend?"

She slowly placed her sandwich on the plate, swallowing, then dabbing her mouth again.

"I beg your pardon?"

"I just want to get to know you better. Sorry, didn't mean to pry? Huxley said that an intellectual is someone who's found one thing more interesting than sex." He smiled.

"What?" She was not smiling. She was hit with a gush of icy antagonism, and the last remnant of her anxiety fell like a muddy brick.

Just then Oliver, her friend from the Orienteering Club, walked into the Deli. He was a nineteen-year-old junior from Winston-Salem with uncombed blond hair. He was wearing cargo shorts that exposed muscular calves covered in pale down. She waved, sucking at her teeth. He waved back. She held up a finger at him, and Oliver nodded.

"Who is that?" Ryan asked her.

"A friend."

"Boyfriend?"

"Friend."

Ryan was revising his Aspergers thesis. She seemed comfortably social when she acknowledged her friend.

"Would you like to get together another time?" He queried. "Perhaps we could have dinner. You seem to enjoy food. We could discuss food as desideratum." He flashed an oily sex-shop smile.

Desideratum! The shit was on now!

"I don't think so," she said, wrapping her half-eaten gyro back in the foil. "Dr. Ryan, is there anything wrong with my paper that we need to discuss?"

"Well, I can't really say..."

"Because, I'm going to be frank with you, Sir," she cut him off. Then she worked a pinkie into the back of her gums to dislodge something. See food, asshole. "It's a good paper, which I can probably publish when this semester ends. I've already queried *Faith and Philosophy*, and they're interested."

"I'm sure..."

"Excuse me, Profess... David. I'm not quite finished."

"Well, go ahead," he said, looking cornered and put out.

"My roommate is a law student, and she and I reviewed Title XII and Title IX last night together, as well as the Education Amendments of 1972."

"Wha..."

"They cover sexual harassment, and while I am not intending to file a complaint against anyone, I believe you might be soliciting a relationship that goes beyond grad school *collegiality*."

"But..."

"If I'm wrong, I apologize in advance. David. But for the record, I have neither the intention nor the desire to sleep with you, now or in the future. So from this point forward, I will ask that our intercourse with each other be of the academic and professional kind. That means that any further attempts at seeking personal information or seeking personal contact with me will be unwelcome, and therefore fall within the scope of the law." Sam's legal verbiage sounded pretty tough, she thought. *The scope of the law. Oooooooooh!*

David Ryan had drawn himself up in his chair. His feet were flat on the floor now, his little hands clamped onto the edge of the table like a rodent at a bird feeder. His eyes had narrowed into slits, and his mouth—which she looked at now —was a straight, cold line.

"There's no need for you to be bellicose," he stated. "I'll certainly maintain a professional distance if that's your wish. We came to discuss your paper, which I think needs work. I know you have a perfect scholastic record, and I assume you want to retain it. I was just trying to help you do that."

"Dr. Ryan, I'm eighteen. I look even younger to some. Causes people to jump to conclusions. Mistake. I'm not worried about the quality of my paper. I know the grade it deserves, and I know you'll be fair. Because if my grade is questionable, I will formally challenge it, which will include a paper trail. I'll be writing a memorandum for record of this encounter today when I get home. It'll be witnessed by my roommate, the law student. I don't want to file an actual complaint. Not because I'm worried about my scholastic record, but because I'd worry about you."

"Is that a threat?"

"No, Dr. Ryan... David. I don't ever want to put anyone in the position of having been publicly accused of improper advances or threats toward me, because I'd be terrified that it would get back to my father."

She suddenly realized that this did sound like a threat, regretting it, like she was bringing her big brother to defend her honor, though her concern was exactly as stated. She never wanted her father involved in something like this. Oh my God, no!

"Your father?" He gave the impression of swelling up, the sleeve tats hopping, his gym muscles contracting, his lats spreading under the polo shirt. "What about your father?"

"I never want him to become personally involved in any dispute concerning me, especially one that might trigger a protective reaction from him. I love my dad. Very much. I don't wanna see him in prison."

"And who is your father?"

Brachial artery hit

Ojo De Agua, Yuscaran, Honduras
June 27, 2009

SUNSET BURNED THROUGH the lace of the western tree line. Peasants cast long flickering shadows as they ambled back from the fields carrying machetes and hoes along the dusty footpaths bordered with motley patches of green—cassava here, maize there, beans. One farmer stood in his boxers by a pump outside his one-room cinderblock home with a bucket of water, taking his bath before nightfall.

Through the binoculars the bathing man—middle aged by the look of it, with a wispy gray Indian beard—was like an actor in a silent film: Dale could see but not hear farmer sink the dipper into the bucket, lift a panful of sun-warmed water and pour it over his coarse hair, rinsing down a surf line of soap off his face, over his chest, into his skivvies and down his legs. He was wiry, brown and veined—sculpted by labor, sun and simple food. The man circled his face with a callused palm, wiping the water out of his eyes.

Dale killed time with dull voyeurism. *Other people at least have remotes.*

Maybe forty minutes until dark, the dying afternoon suffusing the damp air with a subdued citrine radiance. *Primera Brigada's* base lay in the valley, two klicks from his position just above Rio Cangrejal. Dale felt something crawling under him, jolted when he saw the beetle, and swatted it before it registered that it was harmless. *The illusion of control is always in danger of being unmasked*, he thought to himself, his heart decelerating. He settled himself with a deep breath, and dropped back onto his belly. Some day he was going to be done with this shit—with heat and cold and sweat and bugs and grime and the hundred other little physical miseries that make him a "good soldier" for putting up with them.

And with the rest. "It's the job," he repeated to himself, taking some resolve from the strength of his reputation. It was a con he pulled on himself. When the rest didn't make enough sense, when it was hard—very hard—he aimed at that external reward, outside that thing where he warmed himself on his own competence, a substitute for what was happening inside. Vanity, he knew, is the ultimate counterfeit currency. A grift you pass along to the next fool. *Reputation, the last refuge of executioners.*

These days he found himself more and more often skirmishing with self-doubt—that sense that he had never stopped being a little boy and so was a pretender. It was scant solace that he had at least fooled them all, these men, his compatriots, who admired and approved of him for doing his "fucking job." He was seized with the urge to shit, and he knew it was because the clock was running, fight or flight, his body rebelling, like the insomnia when you worry about not sleeping and the near irresistibility of sleep when you are forced to remain awake.

Dale took the greasy plastic container of DEET lying next to him, the supercharged thirty percent stuff that melted the black labeling off the army-green bottle. He squirted a stream of it into his palm, rubbed his hands together, and patted the toxic-smelling oil onto his neck. The fumes stung in his eyes. Mosquitoes were sharing his shade and whining next to his ears. He thought about malaria, about the protozoans, about the doxycycline circulating in his blood to prevent it, the drug's toxicity in his liver. About photosensitivity, melanoma... too much thinking, like the mosquitoes were pitching around in his brain. *More matter with less art*, the Queen said.

He pulled the long gun to his shoulder and lined himself up with it. He and the gun together were a system—like a man with a dog on a leash—one thing made of two, united by a purpose. He thought about closet doors, about opposable thumbs, about statues of angels, the flight characteristics of feathers, demolition formulas, a painting called "Piss-Christ," *Entamoeba histolytica*. *Madame, I swear, I use no art at all.*

Mosquitoes.

Through the Leupold scope he inspected the southern quadrant of the Honduran Army base straddling the valley below him. Most of the buildings he could see were vanilla white with red tile roofs, tank-cisterns mounted on rusty angle iron stands between them. The grounds were well kept by conscripts making less than three hundred dollars a month.

His building was painted a queasy official yellow. Built in the manner of the old U.S. World War II longhouse barracks, two stories were separated by a wrap-around eave of red tile, creating the illusion of a second roof that laterally bisected the structure. The sinking sun illuminated a spider's web under the frame.

The old barracks had been converted into office space subdivided inside by freestanding office panels. He could see through the windows before the sun had thrown reflections on it—desks, computers, a chubby female secretary in a calico skirt and a cleavage-heavy tank top, glasses on a neck-tether, black hair in a single ropey braid. Three sets of unknown legs appeared, disappeared, reappeared—one in uniform, two wearing jeans. Whoever else worked there had gone home. Now the windows were just eye-stabbing orange flares reflecting a falling sun.

Four window air-conditioning units, two up and two down, gathered dust in their intakes, their dripping condensation forming puddles on the ground. A half-dozen song wrens picked through a raked-up pile of leaf litter ten meters off one end across the driveway that bent around the building. A beat-to-hell white Mitsubishi pickup truck was parked along the driveway in the front of what he knew from his Intelligence Summary was the operations building, *Primera Brigada*'s G-3.

The last wink of the sun disappeared and the windows went from embers to ash, leaving the valley enveloped in a yellow-green afterglow, reminding him of tornado weather back in North Carolina. He started to check his watch, then stopped, pushing down the impatience... *surrender, someone else makes the next move.* He had begun to worry that someone would step on his hide: a wandering child maybe or a curious dog. He was occupying it for more than an hour now, his rental van parked more than three klicks away near the *Hotel Lenca.*

Three *soldados* stood around the Brigade vegetable garden sharing a cigarette. A tall, skinny young officer revved his smoky old Yamaha 250 in front of the Brigade Headquarters, then hummed away along the winding driveway to the main road. Looking dusty and unused, a lonely Chinook helicopter with the Honduran flag painted on its side was the sole craft on the airfield above the headquarters. The troops were away, transported in trucks to key points, he assumed. Something big was happening, he didn't know what; but this hide, this mission, were part of it.

Dale shifted his rifle scope back to the operations building. The door opened, and two men laughed at something together as they blocked the door, then jogged down the steps to the scarred and dented white Mitsubishi. The athletic one, with wide-set eyes and a week's worth of beard, wore pressed jeans and a t-shirt that showed off some muscle and had a .45 tucked into his waistband. There was something familiar about him, but this was a long way even with the scope. The other, who was climbing into the driver's seat, was squat, dark, with receding short curly hair and a mustache, wearing blue work slacks and a tucked-in checkered short-sleeve shirt buttoned down the front. Dale perked up and ground his belly into the layer of leaf litter to stabilize his position as the window closest to the door at the left end of the building went white. Someone had closed the blinds.

The roadblocks were about to go into place.

He reached forward into the Molle pack serving as a bench rest for the gun. He found the camera in the outside pocket of the rucksack, slid it into his left breast pocket and buttoned it in. Two kilometers distant the Mitsubishi coughed out a stream of oily smoke, then rattled away with both men. The truck was already in motion by the time the sound of the engine cranking reached Dale's distant position. Deep calming breath. This was it.

THE TRUCK GRUMBLED up a long, steep curve on the southwestern slope of what was "Hill 882"—the metric spot elevation noted on Dale's map. The mustachioed driver downshifted, gears grinding, to get extra torque against the last of the slope. The truck had just crested when Dale's first shot drilled him straight through the windshield and emptied his skull onto the back of the cab.

The body dropped forward, hollow head falling between the steering wheel and door. The passenger, eyes wide in shock, grabbed the dashboard and the back of his seat to brace himself as the truck angled slowly off the road on the gentle downhill slope. The front wheel dropped into the roadside ditch and the truck did a slow-motion quarter-roll to the left, coming to rest with the driver's side down. The passenger flopped heavily onto the body beneath him. Again, that little delay before the sound of the passenger's dismayed shout arrived. A 350-yard shot.

Through the scope the passenger looked unhurt but agitated, thrashing about behind the shattered windshield. Then he got his bearings. Dale could see it—that return of deliberating calm—*Oh, I have to get my shit together and get out of here...*—and then the passenger started climbing up through the skyward window, his cream-colored t-shirt now spattered with his companion's blood. The blood-stained passenger hoisted himself up through the window aperture with a tricep dip, his sidearm catching on the window frame. He wiggled the pistol grip clear and his hips had cleared the window aperture when Dale's second shot went through his arm and chest. The target went limp as a rag, rocking back, then flapping forward to drape over the edge of the window. His legs were still in the cab, the rest of him hanging out. Dale watched through the scope as a ropy stream of bright red arterial blood drained down over the hanging right hand and into a spreading scarlet pool in the weedy dust.

Brachial artery hit, Dale guessed, the focus on something clinical diverting him from thoughts of funerals, mothers fainting, children weeping, his own child looking at him, a cold-blooded if official murderer, with accusing eyes. He capped his lenses, stood up, shrugged on his Molle pack, slung the rifle and began picking his way through the brush.

HE SCRAMBLED CLUMSILY up the last five steeply eroded meters, losing his footing like a kid trying to climb up a playground slide. Finally, he gathered enough momentum to grab a thick root and haul himself onto a little perch that was covered in thorny shrubs, holding his rifle out to prevent damaging the scope or plugging the heavy barrel with dirt. He listened for the sound of vehicles approaching. The roadblocks were in, sealing him away from accountability as a double murderer, a killer of strangers. And now he was obligated to take confirmation photographs, up close. He caught the breeze-blown smell of brains, blood and shit.

He rose and stepped out quickly, dancing between the thorn bushes while pulling the camera out of his breast pocket. Then he noticed the gluey sap on his left hand. it was from the root he had used as a climbing handhold.

"Fuck. Fuck."

He wiped his hand hard against his trouser leg, then pressed his palm into the dust on the road shoulder to neutralize the tack.

"Fuck!"

He stopped to sling the rifle onto his back, raising the sling-strap over his head and drawing it across his chest.

"Goddammit!"

The flies were already on the blood: the agglutinating crimson syrup sent out a fly homing signal. Angling the camera through the shattered windshield, he twisted his sticky-dusty hand around to hold up the strangely off-kilter face of the dead driver, unsupported now by the back of a skull. Dale pushed down the nausea at the smell of brains—he hated that sweet marsh odor worse than the shit or the blood—and blew on it to disperse the flies. He snapped a photo. The flash went off. He took one more just to be sure.

Holding the camera in his right hand, he reached under the forehead of the passenger, his main target, grasped the heavy shock of black hair in his sticky palm, and raised the head to shoot the picture of the face.

Then Dale froze, staring into a familiar face, a face that denounced him, while a fat fly crawled onto one vacant, un-responsive eye. Dale didn't even wave away the flies that were now attacking his own face, leaving bloody footprints.

In the fading twilight the flash went off again. And again.

Catrachos

DALE FLASHED HIS black diplomatic credentials at the childlike sergeant who stood next to the airport scanner. The mustard orange diplomatic pouch he held in his left hand sagged under its ponderous metallic weight. The hand was still stained with sap, even after oiling it, rubbing it with alcohol and washing it repeatedly during his morning shower. Waving Dale around the scanner, the Honduran childlike sergeant tried to look flinty, a victim of his own youthful insecurity. This was plainly not his job.

As if this isn't fucking obvious, Dale thought as he was walked around the scanner, his guns in the diplomatic pouch. He had greeted the sleepless morning with the disposition of a crippled bull shark, skipping breakfast to make his flight. He headed now up to the mezzanine deck with the little restaurant, *Tipicos de la Costa*, and sat down, wiping sweat off his face with his suit sleeve. *Lugging fucking guns and fucking carry-on up the fucking stairs wearing a fucking three-piece suit!* He hated the stairs, hated the suit, hated the sun and the the moon.

When the *camarera* came over, a late-teen *mestiza* with crooked teeth and a reassuring self-confidence that re-

41

minded him of Deangela, Dale calmed down momentarily. He was polite when he ordered a *balaeda* with avocado on the side. Then he saw the first one walking across the terminal below him.

Tall and blond, looking like the big-boned Scots from the Sandhills back home, the new arrival was tanned and coiffed, wearing his spanking-new "casual" *guayabera. With a fucking badge, no less. A badge around his neck!* The logo was a blue and white globe, and the letters read: "AT&T. Dan Campbell." Dale could read it from up above. *Dan fucking Campbell was here from AT& fucking T.*

"Seriously?" he said to no one. *Must be a public utility for sale.*

He reached into his shoulder bag and pulled out his copy of *La Prensa* with its remarkably well prepared headline story for something that had happened only hours before. *Presidente Zelaya* was out, flown away to parts unknown under cover of darkness after being dragged out of bed in his underwear. *¡Adios, Presidente! And every fucking plane flies out right on time!* The U.S. Air Force's Sotocano Air Base was buttoned up *because they flew Zelaya out of there*, the reason Dale had to fly back commercial with his fake-ass diplomatic creds. Then he saw the second and the third. More tanned Arizona types with their "exotic Honduras" safari duds on and their conventioneer's badges. Unembarrassed by the shamelessness of it. *Did they need badges? Fuckin'-A, why not t-shirts screenprinted to say, "We're the gringo pricks who are going to run your fucking telecommunications, you catracho pipsqueaks."*

The camera was in the pouch, too, along with the disassembled sniper gun and his match .45. The guns and the "target"—a set of photos of corpses. He flashed on *Macbeth* and his sap-stained hand. *Out damned spot!*

He was calm in the most disciplined way possible now, moving himself from outside like a marionette. Eating like a person, he moved his arm, opened his hand, grasped the *balaeda* that the *camarera* set before him—"*¡Gracias, hermanita!*"— leaned in, took a bite, but there they were, in his peripheral vision, more coming. And Frank's face. Frank's dead face in the camera, with the nameless driver, the camera in the pouch, the pouch at the airport, and him due at the chalet tomorrow morning straight off the redeye. *How the fuck am I going to get through DC?* They would see, someone would see that he was a stack of sandbags being chewed up by silent machine gun fire—something dissolving, disappearing into chaos.

What have I done? Oh, Farah, what the fuck have I done now?

May 12, 1990
Monkey River Village, Belize

SOUTH OF THE Monkey River delta, they sat down in the darkness while the waves stroked the beach. Wearing only swimsuits, they nursed two sweating bottles of Belikin lager. A quarter moon played peek-a-boo behind a shifting patchwork of altocumulus clouds. When the moon was clear, it, he and Farah had luminous lavender outlines.

A howler monkey bellowed from the jungle behind them. Another answered. There was a splash in the ocean among the glassy flakes of moonlight. A low cacophony of frogs sounded upriver. The air smelled of bay cedar and low tide. A sprinkle of lights studded the village to their north.

Farah took his hand lightly and slipped it into her bikini bottom over the mound of rough hair. He felt a sudden burst of warmth. She didn't say anything. She was urinating onto his hand, and he found himself holding very still. Like they were sharing blood. She held onto his wet hand as she rose, wordlessly pulling him to his feet, and walked him into the warm waves until they were waist deep in the surging dark water. Farah pulled him to her and kissed him for a long time. They were breathing together. Her mouth was soft, hot, aqueous, and he felt himself disappear.

"Can I trust you?" she whispered after a while. He waited for a long time, feeling her belly against his, watching her dark eyes in the lavender moon glow, wanting to freeze time.

"I think so," he said. "I want you to."

She took his hand and led him further into the warm swells.

Semicolon

THE CHALET THEY called it, the CAG compound in Fort Bragg. It was once called Delta Force but the wide recognition and the embarrassment brought by Hollywood forced a change to something more anodyne: Combat Applications Group. Of course, everyone knew that now, too. The cover name back in the day had been Combat Materiel Evaluation Element (the acronym—CMEE—sounding like "see me") and the operators used the unofficial cover that they were civilian equipment evaluators for the army. Its founder, Colonel Charlie Beckwith, had warned the original members: "If you wanna keep a secret, don't tell anybody." He never foresaw the coming age of endless self-reference, of everyone feeling like they were captured in a camera lens, of the self-consciousness shifting of the focus from outcome to performance. Or maybe he did. Hell, even Charlie eventually wrote a book about it. There is a kid in everyone, apparently, shouting at a preoccupied parent, *Look at me!* while diving off the one-meter board.

When I was a child, I used to speak like a child, think like a child, reason like a child; when I became a man, I did away with childish things.

Dale carded into the headquarters and walked straight to Boss's office—Colonel Richard "Dicky" Baker's. Here, he was just "Boss," "Dicky" behind his back, even "the Big Dick" and after unpopular commands, "Dickhead." Baker was an Anglophile, a nut for English shit. The 22 SAS, Delta's British counterpart, used "Boss" for its officers, so Baker liked to be called "Boss." From time to time he even used the terms "bloody" and "mate," which to Dale sounded incredibly stupid in the mouth of a Yank. Dale was suddenly seized by the unsettling idea (or was it a realization?) that everyone he had been working with here for years, each in his own special way, had a screw loose. *Crazy as shithouse flies, all of them!*

So what was he?

He looked in the office. Boss wasn't there.

A.D. poked his head into Regina's office—Dicky's secretary's.

"Where's Boss?"

Regina looked up through her hugely thick glasses, giving Dale a squinty smile.

"A.D.! You're back! How are ya, sweetie?"

"I'm fine, you?" A.D. was feeling impatient, but he couldn't be rude to a Southern grandmother who looked like a bespectacled Shirley MacLaine, even if she did have a Top Secret clearance and worked for thugs and assassins.

"Oh, another day another five dollars, A.D.," she snickered. "Thanks for askin'. Colonel Baker's swimmin' his laps, hon."

DALE WAS STILL dressed in the navy blue Brooks three-piece he had worn from the airport. He went through the door of the indoor pool's locker room and was enveloped in a miasma of chlorine and ass cracks. His heart raced in anticipation of confronting his boss and he was already sweating like a quarter horse.

Between the acting of a dreadful thing
And the first motion, all the interim is
Like a phantasma or a hideous dream.

Always Shakespeare interrupting him. Breathe big breaths.

He took off his jacket as he approached Colonel Baker on Lane 3. A new guy from B Squadron was in 6, Toby Fritz from A Squadron was kick-turning in 7. Baker nearly missed Dale standing poolside at the deep end of the lane. The Colonel had started his kick-turn, then leveled out to tread water, pushing up his goggles.

Boss smiled, thinning hair plastered to the sides of his head.

"Welcome back, A.D." Crossed his wet arms on the gutter below A.D.'s feet. "I hear it went well." Boss looked up at A.D. and knew something was wrong when A.D. didn't smile back. *He's sweatin' like rats fuckin' in a wool sock*, thought Boss, knowing that very instant that something had gone sideways with his operator.

"We need to talk, Boss."

Fuck me, thought Boss. *Somethin's happened, and he's losin' the fuckin' thread.* He knew that look—when they couldn't separate the squares and circles and triangles any more. And A.D. was one of his best. Old as a tyrannosaur in this business, which was a good thing. Older guys, they didn't get impulsive on you. But now Dale had the look, like his compass was busted. *Shame. A goddamn shame!*

"What's that shit on your hand, A.D.?"

BOSS WORE HIS white bathrobe and a pair of forty dollar flip-flops he bought from Whole Foods in Raleigh when he and his wife, Nadine, went to the comedy club. He toweled off what was left of his graying blond hair, frizzing it like a deranged professor. His barrel chest was covered in thick hair exposed now above the fold of the robe. His cheeks were raw-looking from this morning's shave.

Two large framed posters adorned his office. One was a 22 Special Air Squadron (British Special Forces) assault team lined up to breach a door, with the caption, "Stand-by, stand-by." The other was a pen-and-ink military free fall parachutist in full regalia, oxygen mask and all, poised mid-air in a hard arch. Dale loosened his tie, his blue-green eyes locked on Boss in a challenge, shirt soaked, his left palm stained dark yellow. And that unhinged look!

"My target," said Dale, folding his arms. "You named him Reynaldo Gutierrez." Dale, a fluent Spanish speaker, pronounced the name without an American accent. Boss paused for a second and laid the towel on the edge of the desk, sitting back on the edge with his legs extended. *The look, and this, too! It's gonna to be a really truly shitty fucked up day.* Boss crossed his feet.

"Named him?" He didn't know why he even responded.

"His name was Frank Garcia," Dale said, his voice flat, "and I was with him in 3rd Bat. He was on the ground with me in Mogadishu. I just killed a former Ranger. What the fuck... Sir? Not to put an overly fucking fine a point on it!" His voice went brassy.

"He wasn't a solider anymore," Dicky said, wondering how this prior association had fallen through the cracks. *I'm gonna march right up intel's ass once this has been handled, and I'm gonna drop a fucking grenade.* "Not ours anyway. Not anyone's exactly. Fuck, A.D., what the fuck?" *That goddamn look! Nuts with a secret. Shitty fucking day.* And he had to take Nadine —*high-maintenance bitch!*—to Sherefe for seafood tonight, too.

"Why?" Dale again demanded in that curiously neutral voice.

Boss stood erect, rocked once on his feet, took a deep breath, let it out as he circled the desk, furrowing his brow as he dropped into his swivel chair.

"Why?" Dale asked again.

Boss reached in his desk drawer, pulled out a thick cigar, rolled it between his palms and bit off the tip. *This is the top secret Delta Force headquarters, and my fucking office, and I'll smoke if I damn well want to.* He spat it on the floor, reached back in the drawer and fished out an old fashioned Zippo lighter. He flicked on a great, lolling flame that made the room smell like lighter fluid, sucked until a good ember was established, and blew out a long stream of appreciative smoke that smelled vaguely like vanilla. He closed the lighter with a sharp metallic snap.

"Whadda ya want me to say, A.D.? Ya got a mission. Ya done good." Looking away for an instant, he muttered, "Goddamn."

"Why?"

Looking at the cigar, Boss said, "Dominican. Soaked in vanilla. Santiago. You can buy a piece of pussy there for the price of a Big Mac. Flavored fuckin' cigars." He laughed. "I was a wino in a past life. You could make a fuckin' fortune importin' these things." Then he looked Dale straight in the eyes. "Why. Why, why, why, you fuckin' drama queen. 'Why' can be a fucking noun or a fucking adverb. You studied English in college, right, Sergeant Dale?"

There was a warning in the use of his rank. Boss continued. "Noun: reason or explanation. Adverb: wherefore or what for." Subtext to the warning: I'm smart, too, motherfucker; and I outrank you. "Used in a sentence: Ours is not to reason why; ours is but to do and die." He made his eyes big and clownish, bobbing his head back and forth for emphasis. "Actually, that's a compound sentence without the coordinating conjunction. This would be signified in writing, I believe, with a semicolon." Boss puffed the cigar. "Heard that before? Huh? Not to reason why!" Their eyes were now locked.

"I killed Frank. Another man, too." Dale's voice rose, not to a parade field pitch, but it had brass in it again. "Two days later there's a coup? I'm comin' back through Tegucigalpa Airport and I see AT&T on parade? Wearin' fuckin' badges that say 'AT&T'? With that little fuckin' blue and white globe? Did I just shoot one of my former comrades for fuckin' AT&T?"

Coup, Boss thought. *Sonofabitch!* He really, *really* did not like that look—that madcap aura. Broken.

"A.D., two things, and shut the fuck up while I say them and listen. Number one, lower your fucking voice, or I'll beat your ass and we'll both go to jail. Two, you gotta lose that word. 'Coup.' You hear me? We're gonna get you some time off, Brother Dale; you need a vacation. Name it. But, *this*... this is a health warning like on a pack of cigarettes, hear? Smoke this and die. There is no such word as 'coup.' Honduras is having a 'constitutional crisis'. Don't star..."

Both fell silent while a hulking C-5 cargo jet swept overhead, low and loud. The sound faded slowly. Dale's eyes never left Boss's. Dale lowered his voice. "The elected President of Honduras was just pulled out of bed in his fucking tightywhiteys and put on a plane at *a United States Air Force installation?*"

Boss responded in his quiet voice to mirror Dale's. "You are not hearing me, Sergeant. Ten years in the Fort Leavenworth Federal Penitentiary says you will delete the term 'coup' from your goddamn vocabulary."

And so the conversation reached an impasse.

"I'm done, Boss," Dale broke the silence. "I'll have my paperwork requesting reassignment by close of business." Dale put one hand on the doorknob. "Got strong D-LAT scores. Dicky. Qualified for Mandarin if I want. Learn another language, maybe... get the stench o' this criminal fuckin' conspiracy offa me. Send me to DLI. ASAP. Then you can keep me quiet, like those little dogs with their voices removed by little doggie surgeons. Fuck you, Dicky, and everything about this place. You wanna beat my ass now? Have at it. Delta farce... we follow the flag, and the flag follows the money. Maybe AT&T will give us some free minutes on our fuckin' phones."

Dale didn't wait for a reply, and he didn't close the door when he left.

Dicky exhaled relief in a smoky vanilla sigh, smirking as he picked up his desk phone. A.D. will cool his heels at the Defense Language Institute for a year. Good save. Give him a medal before he leaves. Some motherfucker was in the hot seat for not researching who in this unit had served with that turncoat commie cocksucker, Garcia.

Bakhtawara and Storai

Afghanistan, near Kabul
July 10, 2010

STORAI SPOTTED ONE of the kids prancing toward the wadi. If the mother doe followed the whole herd would drift down, and she was too small to carry one of the kids if it slid down the escarpment. She palmed a stone the size of a pheasant's egg, bounced it twice for luck and snapped a throw. The stone kipped off a boulder in front of the wandering kid. The kid skip-turned, capering back toward the mother goat. Tried to suckle, but the doe turned away, and the kid followed, both tacking toward the rest of the herd. Three shaggy rams stood watch in a cluster, one black-and-white and two browns, the older brown one with the looping horns the un-challenged master.

Storai lived with her mother, a widow, in the sole house across the wadi from the rest of the village called Zama, with thirty-three souls living there. Three wadis converged just below Zama, edged dusty green with scrub cedar, thistle, and camelthorn. Their house was faded ochre, built of sun-dried mud bricks and mud plaster with cob roofs and high open windows to vent the smoke from the cooking fire. Every house there was smaller than ten meters square, roughly cir-cling the well in the center of the village. Storai's house was perched precariously on a short drop-off but well-founded on several layers of solid sandstone the color of dry ginger.

Up the bluffs from her house she could see the walls and concertina wire of the giant base of the *amrekayee*, the Americans, like a city-sized alien spacecraft that had descended onto the plateau above.

Two more stones and Storai turned the herd of fourteen further from the wadi and tugged her headscarf forward to shade her eyes again from the early morning sun. She glanced back at her mother to see if she had seen how well she could throw, but Bakhtawara, her mother, was intent on removing a stain from her uncle's *tunban* in a bright blue plastic tub of water, wetting it, then rubbing it vigorously between her work-thickened hands, then wetting it again.

Bakhtawara's yellow *chadar* was covered in fading red dots that looked like the footprints of a jackal, and Bakhtawara had flipped it over each shoulder to keep it out of the water. The wind fluttered the folds of her *shalwar* around her legs. Smoke mounted from the high window on the front of their home, and with it the smell of hot garlic in the *naan*, onions and coriander in the soup. Storai wanted hands like that, like her mother's—strong hands, capable. If she kept working hard, when she got older she would have them.

Storai was fourteen now and might be married soon. Her father was dead, killed in an airstrike two years ago when he was trading near Jalalabad, but her uncle had a good reputation, so there was still hope of a *kwezhdan*, a betrothal. She was pretty, so said her mother, and she was virtuous—pleasing to Allah in thought and deed—as well as a good singer. Her three older brothers were already married. Her sister was married, too, to a handsome boy named Pasoon, from

Chelozai, who was fighting now somewhere near Khost. *Inshallah*, she might someday have children. There was time. She had not had blood yet. Her sister had blood when she was thirteen, but died with her first child at sixteen. Her mother said Storai was stronger than her sister and that starting with blood later made a woman stronger.

Overhead, a cargo jet roared toward the landing field at the American base two kilometers away on the plateau, jet engines screaming so loudly as it passed that the goats started bleating and stamping their feet. As the jet receded, dropping onto the distant landing strip like a monk vulture, Storai gathered wisps of dry grass into her pockets for fuel and sang to the goats about the creatures in Ali Baba's garden. Her singing pacified the goats.

Camp Virtue Base Camp, Afghanistan
July 10, 2010

"SHE'S JUST STARTIN' to grow titties."

Pollard peered through binoculars at the girl herding the goats. He and Correa had drawn the short straw in the guard rotation and were the designees for the previous night manning the North-1 observation post. Both of them had removed their uniform blouses, draped them over the wall to air out before they were relieved and dropped their "battle rattle" combat vests and MICH helmets on the floor. There was a good breeze in that spot, a bit chilly in the morning because it overlooked a steep drop and caught the updrafts. Their shirts stank but the breeze dried them out. They sat on grimy plastic lawn chairs. Gene Pollard leaned his elbows on a formed concrete slab with a collection of well-used smut mags in the storage space below. Bobby—the acting Team Sergeant—sometimes jokingly challenged the rest of the team to guess which ones had his cum on them.

Kellogg, Brown & Root had built this observation post, just like they built all of Camp Virtue—just like they had built every other thing the military had overseas since Camranh Bay. There were a thousand hilarious riffs on that name: Camp Virtue, ha! A favorite: "Virtue is its own punishment." Or, "When Tao is lost, There is virtue. When virtue is lost, There is morality. When morality is lost, There is propriety. When propriety is lost, There is chaos and Colonel Boyd Thomas is assigned." Even Special Forces had its geek humor.

The bunker was of formed reinforced concrete with RPG screens on the side—as if anyone could get within range with a shoulder-fired rocket—with a galvanized roof over I-beams, with three layers of sandbags on top, and with busted plastic lawn chairs to sit on. This shitty little pillbox probably cost the taxpayers a couple jillion dollars, plus a thousand apiece for these cheap-ass Walmart patio chairs. They had painted the outside of the OP desert camouflage, funny enough on its own—as if no one could see this metastasized Masada of a base overflown by a giant bright red white and blue US flag... to give the hajji mortar crews a reference point by which to adjust fire—that was the joke. No mortars yet, though, not on this OP.

"No men?" asked Pedro Correa, who would cover up in the sun—a light-skinned Puerto Rican with a mighty aversion to becoming dark—but here in the shade of the bunker he could let the post-dawn breeze blow the stink off of him without worrying that his arms might turn a shade too brown.

"Not today," answered Pollard. "I think that one dude is her uncle or somethin'. Hadn't seen 'im forever." He passed the binoculars back to Pedro and took a swallow of his canned Coke, fantasizing about strong hot coffee. He rocked back on the back legs of the plastic chair, which bowed precariously, and lit a cigarette.

Pedro stopped focusing the field glasses long enough to complain.

"Fuck, dude! I don' wanna smell your tobacco!"

"I'm downwind, chill." He blew a stream of smoke straight ahead and watched the wind bend it away to prove his point. *Fuckin' health freak.*

Pedro peered through the glasses.

"Just a mouthful of titty," he said. "I cou' hol' tha' li'l ass in one hand, man."

Pedro liked to talk like he was a real Newyorican, but everyone on Detachment 649 knew that he grew up on Long Island with a well-to-do daddy in the insurance business.

"So, we doin' this?" Gene queried.

"Yo, my man on the gate got us covered. But we got a new team daddy comin'."

"Good," said Gene, studying the tip of his cigarette like there was a bug on it, then gazing across the valley at the stone house and the girl. "Bernie was a fuckin' slug."

"Bobby's okay, man. He's cool." Pedro put down the binoculars, picked up his shirt, smelled it and started putting it back on.

"Bobby's cool. Goin' to the ho-house. Runnin' these bullshit recons," said Gene. "But we can't get no missions with Bobby as a top. Bobby's got no ops experience. We're nothin' but humps for blood-n-guts Boyd." (That was the nickname for Colonel Boyd Thomas, their bombastic, foul-mouthed Task Force commander who was the subject of the last stanza of the bastardized Tao joke about Camp Virtue.) "Maybe if we get this Delta-boy, Dillon or whatever the fuck his name is, we can get some real shit."

"Dale, I think it is. And careful what you wish for, homey."

Progress

BAINES WAS CAREFUL of his uniform as he wiped down stacks of juniper-green metal storage containers using lemon Pledge and a rag. He couldn't remember all the whys or hows of finding himself backstage in this press room, *eating shit from Major Carroll, being this yellow mothafuckah's boy.*

He was supposed to be a light-wheeled vehicle mechanic. The plan was to get out of the *goddamn Army* and make thirty dollars an hour repairing cars back in DeFuniak Springs. They needed one really good black mechanic there, but by the time he had gone to Airborne School and worked for a couple of months at the SOCOM motor pool, he knew the Army had set him up with some bullshit. This was paint-by-number mechanics—just turn on the computer and follow the step-by-step instructions, *with pictures*, in a dash-twenty manual. This wasn't a skill at all, no more than you learn working at KFC. *Fuckin' Army!*

He wished he would never have learned the art of looking like a recruiting poster and reciting lines like a string doll. The perfect uniform right down to the last burned thread and a talent for memorization. Every guard mount, he always looked the best and he always aced their questions about

General Orders, Army history—all that happy horseshit. Every time he was supernumerary. That's what got him his sergeant stripes in the first place, but then he got the "job" as this redbone Tom's butler-boy.

"He'll be here in ten, Winston" she said, startling Baines. It was Anita Barber, Major Tom's office flunky. A Staff Sergeant, she was always acting like Winston Baines was her ace, but in that weird, rehearsed, mechanical kind of way. Something was not right with her, he knew. She's here, but she's aimed somewhere else, like a candidate for town Mayor, always on guard, trying not to leave tracks. Cute though, for a frosty.

"Got it," he replied, returning to his dusting. "Thanks."

INSIDE THAT PERFECT *uniform is an ignorant, ambitionless, embarrassing country fuck.* Major Carroll braced himself to inspect the press room and face his subordinate, Sergeant Baines. *An embarrassment... a kind of stubborn refusal to see anything beyond the horizon of some small town in the Florida panhandle, a pig-headed inclination to remain the stereotypical Negro wearing a well-pressed uniform.* Carroll tried to anchor his resolve to be civil to Baines, feeling confused and a little guilty at how easily he found himself losing his temper with Baines' seemingly unfocused existence. Today he would be charitable with Baines, find something to praise him for.

When Carrol came out of his little dressing room backstage the curtains were uneven. His water pitcher was on the left side of the podium, and the glass on the right. His notes were lying on a storage container! The press was already filing in, *God damn it!*

"Sergeant Baines," he said ominously, calling Baines out of sight of the four reporters. The press reps were already drinking coffee at the refreshments table, dribbling it on the white tablecloth and gulping down canapés while two of their cameramen—one white and one Asian, both looking like bored teenagers—were setting up their tripods and aiming their lenses at the empty podium.

"Sir." Here it comes, Baines thought.

"This should be very simple by now. My papers go on the damn podium, this way." He tapped the edge of the papers onto the little stand he indicated, squaring them up. "The curtains are exactly six feet on either side of the podium center. My pitcher is on the right side of the podium, my glass on the left."

"Yes, sir." *Why you talk so white, mothafuckuh? 'My papers go on the damn podium.'*

"Don't yes Sir me unless you understand, Sergeant."

"I understand, Sir." *Understand you got that Colonel's dick in your mouth.*

"Then why wasn't it done?"

"Sir..."

"No! No excuses. They're already out there."

Baines was silent, expressionless, standing now at attention.

"Well, get it done, Sergeant."

Baines went to adjust the curtains, concealing the storage area backstage, pulling his humiliation in close to him like a hungry baby. Through the open door of the dressing room Anita Barber could be seen checking her appearance in a mirror hung over a sink, tucking an escaped strand of dark hair behind her ear. Baines switched the glass and the pitcher of water on the podium, carefully stacking the four pages of notes in the center. *So this yella ass fakin' jack can read his mothafuckin' lines.*

Five more noisy reporters entered the room whooping at some inside joke. Two of them, cameramen, naturally, headed to the front row of perfectly aligned folding chairs and began assembling their kits. The other three—a fortyish man who could stand in the prop blast of a C-130 without it stirring a hair on his gelled head and two self-consciously blue-jeaned women, one a skinny bottle-blonde and the other a redhead with a high-in-the-back yuppy cut—headed straight for the gourmet coffee and the canapés. Major Carroll knew the redhead, Rosemarie something, stringing for Fox. She always looked at him like he was a slice of spiced bread with mango jelly. The blonde was Connie Mason—a stringer, too, but she got her name in the *New York Times* more often than some people who were on staff. The gelhead was George Yowell, from TCN International—a twit, thought Carroll, but an important twit. No one's stringer, he was a bona fide news personality "reporting from the front lines." The man had an audience, including now and again the Commander-in-Chief. *Be nice.* George was going to be in Kabul for the next week to consolidate his chops as a "war reporter."

They couldn't care less about the fuckin' curtains, Baines mused angrily, watching from the wings as reporters crammed smoked salmon and goat cheese into their mouths and masticated like cattle.

Now Carroll was in the dressing room, checking himself in the mirror. Baines watched from the wings. *Vain yella bastard.* He had this job because he was pretty, slender and athletic without seeming too scary-black. *Like maybe a tennis player or one of them friendly, harmless homos.*

Three minutes.

Will Carroll went to stand in the semi-darkness off-stage right behind the curtain, Anita Barber on the left. They had done this countless times, or so it seemed. Four more reporters filed in: a very serious-looking white guy who looked like he belonged in a college classroom teaching political science, and two darker guys—*Al Jazeera* stringers, maybe, or *Gulf Weekly*. Carroll had seen them before. They took notes and never asked anything.

But then he seldom said anything.

The last reporter to enter had the look of a man nursing a hangover—fifty-something, crew-cut gray hair, face hadn't seen a razor in a few days, wearing sandals with socks, shirttail out over a bloated gut and sweating circles into his armpits. He took a long pull on his cigarette and before Sergeant Roof at the door could tell him to get rid of it the reporter pushed the door back open and snapped the butt outside, exhaling a dense stream of smoke that drifted toward the coffee dispenser as it dispersed. *That commie prick from France, Gaston Villeneuve.* Carroll sighed. Villeneuve was what they called a "spring-butt" back at West Point. *Always got a damn question that's not in the script.*

Sergeant Roof, who manned the door, directed the reporters to the feeding trough for their canapés and coffee as if they didn't already know where they were. *Same shit, different week.*

A Master Sergeant came in with wrinkled ACUs, sidearm on, wearing his battle rattle, and carrying his M-4. He strode past Roof before he could respond and headed to the back. Special Forces patch, but Carroll couldn't see his name tag. *Fucking seriously? Who the hell is this guy? You can't just barge in on a press briefing. In his battle-rattle, carrying a weapon?* Older guy, Carroll guessed, in his early forties, week-old beard, black hair with gray on the temples, weather-brown over a naturally pale complexion, strangely blue-green eyes. Kind of short and solid without looking stocky. The E-8 went to the back of the room, stood his M-4 in the corner and dropped his chest rig in a heap. Then he strolled over and drew himself a cup of black coffee, strolled back, sat down in the very back of the room, crossed his legs all the way like women do and blew gently on his coffee, apparently ignoring the activity around him, including the two women in front who both fixed their stares on him.

One minute. Carroll would have to decipher this afterward. He looked up at Staff Sergeant Barber. She was already watching Carroll's reaction and shrugged her eyebrows to signal "I don't know." They held each other's gaze for a half minute, then he gave her a thumbs-up.

Anita Barber took a deep breath and advanced onto the stage with well-rehearsed false self-assurance, centering herself at the podium. The reporters began drifting toward their seats. She switched on the mike, gave it a light tap that reverberated thorough the room, waited another beat and put on a professional smile. A cargo plane came in close overhead and drowned the room in the familiar din, affording the journalists another moment to choose their seats. No one expected anything momentous. The plane receded, tires squawking in the distance as it touched down. Anita looked down for an instant, recovered her welcome-face, looked up and leaned almost imperceptibly into the microphone.

"Ladies and gentlemen, Major Carroll will be out momentarily. Please find a seat and make yourselves comfortable."

Her lines. Delivered.

As the final journalist was seated, several still murmuring, she nodded a kind of thanks, then retreated smoothly back behind the curtain stage-left. Carroll strode confidently to the podium. The journalists went silent. Carroll had presence. Rosemarie and Carol both suppressed lascivious smirks. Carroll's very serious mien as he initially pretended to review his notes was transformed into pure charm as he raised his face to his audience and his gravitas face was almost magically transformed into a welcoming, so-happy-to-see-you-all smile.

"Good morning."

"Good morning," the press corps muttered back, several instinctively returning the smile, Rosemarie crossing her legs extravagantly. Major Carroll averted his eyes a moment late and her eyes narrowed with satisfaction. His smile faded decorously as he launched into his presentation.

"I'm Major Carroll, Public Affairs Officer for Special Operations Task Force Bird, and on behalf of Colonel Boyd Thomas, the Task Force Commanding Officer, I'd like to welcome you again to our weekly operations briefing.

"This week, we have continued to train with Afghan Militia Forces and Afghan police as well as conduct local and joint reconnaissance operations West of Kabul. There have been no major incidents this week, and our work with local militia and the constabulary is progressing.

"Two minor engagements between local Afghan forces and suspected Taliban have resulted in one enemy K.I.A. and no friendly casualties."

Paused a moment to hint at another smile.

"I'm aware that such an uneventful report might disappoint our friends from the fourth estate..." Mild, polite laughter from the press corps, on cue. "...But we welcome this lack of theatricality as a sign that our joint operations are successful in maintaining stability in our sector."

"*Theatricality is a sign that our joint operations are successful in maintaining stability in our sector,*" mocked Baines under his breath, as he stood in the wing.

"So with that out of the way, my friends, what questions do you have for me today?"

Rosemarie's hand went up like a schoolgirl's.

"Rosemarie." Smile still plastered on.

"Thank you, Will."

Gaston Villeneuve coughed wetly and conspicuously, tugging at his crotch to relieve some apparent minor discomfort.

"I wonder how morale is among the troops right now," she asked, never losing eye contact. "Has the ambiguity of statements from Washington or the lack of recent combat activity taken the edge off them?"

"Thanks, Rosemarie," he began, the smile emerging and disappearing like little clouds crossing the sun. "Morale is great. As you know, aside from the government contractors who manage the installation and coordinating staff, Task Force Bird also has a Special Forces contingent, a Ranger Company, and Special Ops aviators. These guys are mature, quiet professionals. Our current stability is evidence that their work with Afghan forces is making progress, and our primary mission of supplying Forward Operating Bases has been running very smoothly.

"As to Washington, I'm not sure I'd characterize their statements as ambiguous. I think you'll find the administration is careful not to generalize about a complex situation. Next question."

Villeneuve's hand went up. *Fuck! Springbutt!* No smile this time.

"Sir."

Villeneuve's English was clean, but the accent was marked.

"Thank you, Major. Gaston Villeneuve with *Nouvel Observateur*."

Major Carroll acknowledged with a distinctly expressionless nod.

"This February the President suggested that NATO and American forces would begin leaving Afghanistan. You are also saying that this departure will coincide with a transfer of leadership from the Americans to the Afghans. This *progress*—that was your word, *progress*—toward transition is not as evident in the field as you suggest. Roadside attacks continue. Green-on-blue and green-on-green attacks are becoming more frequent. Kandahar is flaring up. And your President just fired his main commander. Aren't these claims of progress contradictory?"

"Sir, I'll begin by noting that I am a small Task Force PAO, and I am neither authorized nor inclined to speak on behalf of the Theater Command or the National Command Authority."

Carroll noted as he spoke that the Master Sergeant in the back of the room had finished his coffee, quietly geared up and was treading silently out the door, dropping the empty coffee cup in the trash as he left.

DALE STEPPED OUT of the press hooch and walked into the alley between rows of bunkers. His head had gone all wooly again, his heart pounding like a drum in his ears, and he had stopped there to let the breeze cool his face. He gazed up at the electric line running between the press hooch and the Task Force ops bunker. A green bird the size of a house sparrow perched there, tilting its head to watch Dale watching it.

A long slender black bill with an orange throat and pale blue lines under its eyes. Transfixed, Dale didn't know how long he stood there gazing at the passerine. The muffled drum receded. The breeze raised the bird's back feathers, then died down, then raised them again. He found himself wondering if the bird was consciously enjoying the wind when he was startled by a tap on the shoulder. He actually jumped a little, then noticed a gaggle of reporters climbing into a Chevrolet van. Though momentarily startled, he felt more tranquil now.

Major Carroll was facing him. The briefing's over already? How long had he stood there?

"Master Sergeant..." Major Carroll paused to read his name tag, "Dale. Master Sergeant Dale, would you mind telling me why you showed up uninvited to my press briefing?"

Dale gazed back into Carroll's eyes for a beat, brow suddenly plowed with lines, appearing to think very hard about the question he was asked, baring his teeth like he was straining to understand. Carroll's cheeks had begun to color when Dale finally answered.

"No."

They stood there, Dale still seeming puzzled about something.

"Well?"

"Yes, Sir?"

"Well, what were you doing with a rifle in the press room?"

"They just issued it, Sir. I'm headed to the range to zero it."

"But why were you in my press room? You weren't authorized to be there."

"Oh, I just peeked in. I saw the coffee and figured I could use a cup, Sir. I haven't slept for shit in days. Jet lag, maybe. Disorientation. Who knows why we can't climb back inside ourselves sometimes and just relax. Very good coffee by the way. I mean, wow. The canapés looked great, too. Are there any left?"

"Where are you assigned, Master Sergeant?"

"Oh, I just got here. I think I'm taking over an A-Detachment."

Carroll's face darkened even more.

"Are you alright, Sir?"

"Master Sergeant, my name is Major Carroll, and I'm the Task Force PAO. I suggest you begin to learn how we do things here before you take over anything."

"Couldn't agree more, Sir. Always good advice. Do you see that bird, sir?" He looked up, but the bird had flown. "Oh shit, you missed it. Well, you see 'em all the time, I reckon, but that was a blue-cheeked bee-eater. Gorgeous bird. A songbird. Never see that bird in the States."

"Sergeant Dale!"

Dale was silent, still apparently unperturbed yet curious about Carroll's agitation. He waited. Carroll waited.

"Sergeant Dale, you're not to enter any building on this installation without authorization. Do you understand?"

"Perfectly, Sir." Dale was tilting his head and gazing at Carroll's face as if contemplating the moon. "Very sorry. Didn't mean any harm. Won't happen again."

Carroll waited, unsure for what.

"Is that all, Sir?"

Another moment passed.

"Yes, that's all, Sergeant Dale."

Dale offered the Major his hand. Carroll looked at the proffered hand like it was a live Gila monster.

"Pleased to meet you, Sir," said Dale, apparently without sarcasm, keeping his hand extended.

Carroll looked around and grudgingly grasped the hand. Dale gave him one firm squeeze, then snapped to attention and rendered a salute.

"All the way, Sir." Then he caught himself and lowered his hand. "Silly me. Downrange, right? No saluting. My bad."

Wilbur didn't want food

Weymouth Woods State Park, North Carolina
June 29, 2010

A PASSING DRIZZLE had humidified the morning and the air was close: seventy-five degrees at dawn. By the time Deangela pulled the parking brake on her rattly once-white Echo at 8:16 AM eighty degrees felt like a steam room. The overhead haze was dissolving and the sun was still veiled in the trees. Her father hopped out of the passenger side before she had time to cut the engine, pulled his pack off the floor and slung it on his shoulder. She cut the engine and climbed out herself, pocketing the keys in her venerable baggy Levis.

The parking lot was otherwise deserted, the three trailheads marked with signs—shellacked maps of the trails bolted onto once treated but now mossy four-by-four posts. The pine barren rose around them in tall straight columns of blued bark, the ground still blackened from the annual controlled burn.

She folded the seatback forward and grabbed her own daypack, the very same black-on-gray Lowepro that Daddy had. He had bought it for her birthday three years ago, ordered from England, and got one for himself. These packs had nice padded compartments where you could separate binoculars, spotting scopes, cameras, field-books, drinks, ponchos, first aid kits and food. Deangela locked her door, shouldered her pack and rounded the car to double-check the hatch lock.

Her father watched her, head clearing a bit. Things were shifting more lately, like blocks knocked over, the spaces filled with something soft and dirty, something emptied from a vacuum cleaner bag. Then his skin would pick up a low-frequency buzz and he would need to breathe intentionally—like someone trying to stay calm after waking up in a coffin.

He had watched Deangela being born, when Farah was puffed up and sweating with exertion as the infant's head, body and feet slithered out on the blue umbilical cord in a flash flood of blood and water. He could see Farah in her even then, with her newborn's head still compressed like a peanut and puce skin as wrinkled as an old fisherman's.

"What?" she demanded when she caught him gazing. He looked down with a guilty smile. "Come on, Daddy," she smirked back. "The birds."

She lifted her Dollar Tree sunglasses from the flimsy pocket of her t-shirt—a thrift store find emblazoned with "HE₂ISENBERG"—and lodged them on top of her head, crushing down the mass of chestnut tentacles. She was short like his people but had her mom's skeletal angularity and soft African features under a honey complexion. Her carelessness with her appearance was a constant concern for her Belizean aunts, if not her mother, but Dale found it endearing. His mother never recognized her, but then she never recognized him anymore either.

"Daddy!" She interrupted his reverie again. "You're making me self-conscious! Let's go!"

"OH, I GOT one. Got it. Oh, it's a warbler, wait, it needs to turn a bit. Uh... Blackburnian warbler!" Four chirps and a longer *tseeee*, they both heard it. "Hear it?"

"Yeah yeah," he answered, holding his binoculars at the ready under his chin while he scanned, following the call. "I got it. I hear it."

Then Dale caught a flicker of motion and a flash of light. His sniper's eyes reached out and grasped objects like tentacles—not passive receptors but instruments of power, of death. *Full fathom five thy father lies... those are pearls that were his eyes.*

He raised his field glasses, trying not to lose his place among the foliage. Deangela had her glasses up, aimed and locked.

"Where?" he asked.

"Gum tree, third of the way up, thick bifurcation..."

They had committed list after list to memory together: birds, trees, leaf morphologies, anatomy and physiology, state and national capitals, table of elements, cloud types, weights and measures, the plays (and characters) of Shakespeare (Dale's special interest from his college days), dog breeds, greetings in dozens of languages, rivers of the world, heads of state, the one hundred county seats of North Carolina, makes and models of cars, butterflies and moths, constellations and on and on. It was something that was theirs, but it also augmented the endeavors of her childhood tutor, Theodora Hall, whose salary had consumed a goodly portion of his and Farah's for ten years.

"Got it!" He rolled the focus ring and pulled the outlines tight. "Pretty bird. Female." The white ring under the eye gave it a permanent scowl, its head popping in frenetic rotations. A gamboling squirrel startled the warbler. The bird disappeared from the optical field in a flicker of black and gold.

"Oh," Deangela lamented. "She's gone."

They rested their glasses in the leaves. The morning drizzle had softened the deadfall, making it easy to be quiet, to stalk. They had positioned themselves upwind of a minor swamp, hoping to avoid mosquitoes, and were bothered by only a few. The ground beyond them was pancake-flat and the forest soothingly monotonous in its piney uniformity. The little draws were what they looked for—boundary niches, hardwoods, understories. The scrub oak gave a lot of cover but they had trouble trying to find a place to sit without being blackened by the ground char from the spring burn. They lay down on their sides in a stump crater, facing each other like mirror images and twisting their bodies to scan for a few minutes, when Dale reached in his day pack and pulled out two thick sandwiches. He held one out to Deangela. "Hungry?"

"Oh," she emphatically truncated the expression like a cork popping, the Belizean way her mother had, and seized the sandwich. "I'm hungry enough to eat cat shit."

"That's good. I'm pretty sure that's what this is." They laughed a bit, then he looked around as if he had forgotten something. "Have you ever noticed," he asked, "that if you watch one of those TV comedies, and you start to pay attention to just the laugh track, how it gets really weird?"

April 2, 1993
Phoenix City, Alabama

"WILBUR DIDN'T WANT food, he wanted love. He wanted a friend." *Charlotte's Web*. It was Deangela's favorite first birthday present. She had peered into it, turning the pages forward and backward, backward and forward. Farah knew she was precocious. She had walked at six and a half months and chattered in complete sentences at seven, mostly about food, but "hold me" was also prevalent, as were the names of animals. Her favorite word then was the name of a nearby river —Chattahoochee—and she giggled when she said it.

DALE OPENED THE apartment door, a green gym bag over his shoulder, still in uniform that Friday afternoon. He was about to suggest pizza and a DVD when he saw Farah sitting on the gray sofa with Deangela in her lap. Farah's look arrested him.

"What? What's happened?" he asked, his voice with a hint of alarm.

"Put y' stuff away, lovah," she said in that Belizean-West-Indian accent, which became crisper when she was angry or excited, "and come sit wid us."

"Everything okay?"

"Ya sho, everting's okay, but you got t' see sometin'."

'What?"

"Put ya stuff away, lovah. Sit chaself."

He turned into the master bedroom—a funny way to think of any room in a cheap two-bedroom apartment—the bed complaining with a squeak when he dropped his bag on it. He strode back to the living room with a look that combined concern and curiosity.

"Sit with us, Daddy," the one-year-old said.

"What, Baby Girl?"

"Sit, Daddy."

"I'm sittin', sweetheart. Here I am."

Deangela clambered into his lap and clutched his neck. Farah collected the book lying next to her and waited for A.D. and Deangela to exchange their greeting kiss.

"Deangela, shugah," said Farah, patting the book. "Show Daddy what's in dis book."

Deangela leapt onto the cushions between them, plucked the book from Farah's hand and opened it to page one.

"Start here, Mama?"

"Ya, baby."

"Wilbur didn't want food, he wanted love." Looking at Farah, "More, Mama?"

A.D. was standing.

"Sit, lovah. Go on, baby."

Deangela turned the page.

"He wanted a friend—someone who would play with him." Deangela looked up again and tittered.

"Did she memorize this?" he asked, looking like the moon just fell into their bathtub.

"I reed it, Daddy."

Farah flipped some pages over.

"Go ahead, Baby."

"'Why did you do all this for me,' he asked. 'I don't dee-serve it." She grinned up at him.

Weymouth Woods State Park, North Carolina
June 29, 2010

"HOW'S YOUR LOVE life?"

Deangela stopped chewing her sandwich, made a smack with her tongue and rolled her eyes.

76

"Hey, you're eighteen. Shit happens."

"Are you asking if I'm horny or if I have a beau?"

"Whoa!" Now he stopped chewing. "Maybe I shoulda re-phrased that."

"Or a belle?" she snickered.

"Oh stop! Okay, just wondering how things are at school. What you're up to."

"Fish out of water? They look at me like I'm a beetle on a pin?"

"Nice image. But you come by the fish 'n' water thing honest."

They were silent for a beat.

"Just focused on grad school."

Dale swallowed the last of his sandwich, wadded up the plastic wrap, poked it in the pack and wiped his fingers on his jeans. Deangela turned her half a sandwich and bit into the crusty side with a crunch. Dale made his Dagwoods with cabbage.

"Whatcha studyin' this summer?"

Mouth full, she replied, "Wittgenstein, Aquinas and Hume."

"Huh?"

"Philosophers, Daddy."

"Where's this goin'?"

"Dunno, Daddy. Maybe a doctorate in analytical or moral philosophy."

A bird called, ack-ack-ack-ack-ack in a tiny voice. They both alerted. Dale grabbed his binoculars. Deangela swallowed hard, dropping the last bite of her Dagwood to the ground to grab hers.

"Listen! Listen, hear that?" he whispered suddenly.

"White-bellied nuthatch," she replied.

Chlamydia

July 10, 2010
Camp Virtue, Afghanistan

CAMP VIRTUE BEGAN as an airfield, a big one. It needed 8,300 feet by the book for a C-5 Galaxy to land with a full belly, so NATO—or rather Kellogg, Brown & Root—gave it 11,000. Camp Virtue's virtue lay in being a printing press for money. Add another 500 feet on each end for a security wall, and the base ended up more than two miles long. In Afghanistan size wasn't just security; it was profit. Planes that landed there, in addition to other supplies, had to ship in 25,000 gallons of water a day—in half-liter plastic bottles and 500-gallon tanks that would have made overland truckers into ambush bait.

Troops running PT (physical training) could do three-mile jogging circuits, apart from the airfield, beginning and ending with the Morale Support Activities gymnasium on the southeast corner. The outside wall was a great rectangle, 11,500 feet by 6,000 with a margin of at least 200 meters between the wall and the buildings, which placed them outside the effective range of any enemy rocket-propelling grenadier.

Around three sides of the base there was a 100-meter ribbon of sand that was raked every day so guards could spot footprints that might appear during the night. The north wall vaulted above a drop-off, portions of it almost vertical, the bluff itself laced with antipersonnel mines that no one wanted to check.

It was seven in the morning, with just a hint of a fog line left along the base of the mountains. The sky was a washed-out blue and cloudless, white around the rising sun. Hardly a breeze stirred.

One C-5 was parked in the middle of the airfield like a giant carp. Off the runway were two specked-out Sea Stallions, three MH-47 Chinooks, a half dozen Blackhawks with FLIR bumps on the noses, and four "Killer Eggs"—AH-6 Little Bird gunships, two armed with mini-guns and two armed with two-point-five rockets. The choppers were spread equidistant and alternated up and down the field. Every so often, mortars would drop into the airfield—never very accurate—but still, separating the birds curtailed the occasional damage and the additional hours spent on post-attack repairs.

Four long arched maintenance hangars rested adjacent to the black apron of the airfield, surrounded by earthen berms. There were people in flight coveralls ambling in and out of them. Three hummers were parked near the hangars.

KBR's buildings throughout the base had a strong, angular frame construction, everything one-story, with 12/4-pitch roofs that would support two layers of sandbags which smelled like rotten plastic and clay. The greenish buff of the pressure-treated wood was color-coordinated with the arid terrain.

Above everything, the wrinkled skyline of the snow-capped Hindu Kush showcased wild contrasts with illuminated ridges and dark shadows in the vertical crevasses, the rosy AM sun making it look labial, like a Georgia O'Keeffe.

Two motor pools were equidistant from either end of the built-up area paralleling the airfield, great open spaces delineated by yet more earthen berms, like giant slugs on the landscape, and guarded along the sides with straight rows of squat olive Conex containers. Twenty-two up-armored hummers, three Strykers, two HEMMTs, some deuce-and-a-halfs and five-ton trucks, assorted trailers and a dozen "water buffaloes"—400-gallon cisterns mounted on wheels—were sorted and aligned inside both motor pools like the playthings of an obsessive-compulsive child. Each motor pool had a maintenance shed on one end: linear arched structures, like the hangars but only half as high.

The buildings for headquarters, staff offices, operations, ten-point showers and two DFACs (dining facilities) were arrayed in side-by-side formations that would suddenly and arbitrarily alternate 90 degrees, a Tetris-looking patchwork from the air. Alleys ran between the rows, connecting to one main road that ran the length of the built-up area.

That main road was called Main Street. There, troops in tan fatigues and green body armor, their heads covered with Nazi-looking MICH helmets, drifted back and forth, weapons slung, headed to chow or to take a post-prandial shit. Mess hours were from six to nine for breakfast. Twelve short chains of ten portable toilets (cost: $15,000 each) punctuated Main Street, their plastic doors making hollow bangs over the hum of dozens of generators.

One space the size of a football field on the eastern side of the base was designated for burnable trash. A hulking heap of garbage mixed with fractured pallets, it stank like hell when the wind changed and seemed to smolder perpetually even when no one was there. This morning there were already four fat vultures picking through the putrid vapor of rotten meat and burnt plastic.

Troops lived in GP Large tents pitched on raised concrete slabs because someone had argued successfully against the CHUs—Containerized Housing Units—the aluminum box dorms used on many bases. Most tents had one or two fork-lift pallets on the ends for the rare occasions when it rained, and to keep the dust down inside. Most tent sides were rolled up, part way on some, all the way on others, leaving just the mosquito netting for walls. Sandbags were stacked to forty inches around each tent to protect sleepers in their cots from mortar shrapnel.

You could tell which tents were the women's, all four of them, because they kept the walls down against the greedy gazes of the men and ran air conditioners with five-kilowatt generators, the latter a source of resentment among those same peeping toms.

At night some of the women travelled to the crappers and showers with a female buddy or a boot knife because there had been more than one assault in the nineteen months since they moved the troops in, none of them investigated too aggressively, with the women who made accusations finding themselves reassigned. A Navajo woman, though, an E-4, had stabbed a masher PFC one night last year, right in his scrotum. Fortunately for him, both testicles survived, and in that particular case, he was the one reassigned, with a Purple Heart for "wounds received in action." The Navajo woman's name was Maria Haskie, and a lot of men called her a lesbian after that—which happened to be true—but no one fucked with her anymore.

Contractors lived in town and commuted back and forth from the Intercontinental Hotel in MRAPs—bulky desert-tan armored vehicles that looked like Roid-Legos. The contractors' salaries and perks—the rooms and the vehicles—were another chronic source of discontent among male *and* female troops. The troops travelled in up-armored Humvees. A few of the contractors were actual high-technicians of sorts—avionics people, computer geeks, and other brainiacs—but most were former Special Ops guys who looked and acted like garden variety macho-alcoholic Western mercenaries.

The North DFAC where Special Forces A-Detachment 649 ate was positioned around 150 meters from the team's tent. Only aviators and their support folks ate at the smaller South DFAC. The North DFAC was divided into a large main dining room and a smaller dining room for the Afghan Militia Forces who had their own cooks and dietary restrictions. The entrance to the North DFAC had a broad awning that supported a professionally hand-painted sign ($9,333) announcing "North DFAC, Camp Virtue, Task Force Bird" with a great eagle claw reaching from clouds bordered by a red circle. Every other window was fitted with a 6,000 BTU Frigidaire AC unit powered by a truck-trailer 1,500 kW generator.

Seven members of 649 approached the dining facility in a gaggle, wearing chest rigs and slung M-4s, all variously bearded in accordance with the relaxed grooming standards designed to allow them to better fit in with their Afghan counterparts. *What a fucking joke*, they all said, but the boys enjoyed growing out their beards and looking like characters from *Cowboys versus Aliens*.

Bobby—Sergeant First Class Robert Milano—was the acting team sergeant and the team's strange attractor for the time being, an affable guy who cut up for laughs and to maintain the general morale. He played at being dumber than he really was. What got him into hot water from time to time was that he didn't have a cop in his head that most people do that directs traffic from the mind to the mouth. He would say the first damn thing that popped into his head. He was chattering up the detachment gaggle, them laughing around him, as they headed into the chow hall, MICH helmets hanging off their battle rattle instead of on their heads as a sign of rebellion—a tradition of nonconformity in Special Forces that went all the way back to World War II.

Each breakfast cost taxpayers $41.97. Lunch and supper were $48.53. There was a rumor afoot that lunch would soon be cancelled, replaced by an MRE ($6.66 each, no apocalyptic numerology intended) to save the Department of Defense some money.

Opie was first in the chow line. It had started with his initials for Orrin Pibbles, O.P., which became Opie, sometimes just Ope. Staff Sergeant "Opie" was talking with Bobby, interrupting himself to tell the E-4 server he wanted an omelet "all-the-way" with sausage on the side. Opie was six-three and bony. His head was enormous and seemed to stoop him at the shoulders. He had acquired the habit of slouching when he was young and taller than anyone else. The junior weapons man on the team and the team's primary sniper, Opie had the features of a hawk, a thick mop of auburn hair and a little goat-like beard that made him appear even younger than his 26 years. He had married his high school girlfriend, Mary Sheets, and joined the army a week later. Originally from Modesto, California, Opie and Mary lived in Fayetteville off Raeford Road in a beige tract-house they bought last year and had a three-year-old daughter named Cecilia after her paternal grandmother. Opie hated Afghanistan, even though he admitted that sometimes it looked like places near Modesto. The problem with Afghanistan, said Opie more than once, was the Afghanis.

Bobby constantly and paternally humored Opie because when allowed to fester Opie's chronic discontent infected the team and disrupted the general morale. They had only been here for seven months and were scheduled for twelve. Opie struggled to accept his situation, killing an occasional "suspicious" farmer with his sniper gun to make things more interesting, but the effort at acceptance cost him. He was a beehive of bizarre facial tics—one-eyed blinking, pursing his lips, and unaccountably opening his eyes as wide as he could, giving the impression he had gone all Charlie Manson on you. He didn't appear to have any idea that he was doing these things, which people found a little disturbing. No one poked fun at Opie because he had a reputation. He had beaten a man nearly to death two years ago over a minor insult outside a Fayetteville restaurant after a memorial service for a former team member. Three other Special Forces buddies dragged him away before the cops came, but the story circulated through "the community," including the detail that Pibbles hadn't had so much as a single drink.

The dining facility was framed wood, spacious inside at forty-by-forty feet with a salad bar in the center the size of a canoe, equipped with a half-dozen four-slot toasters and stacked for breakfast now with trays of white, wheat and rye bread, sliced fruit, cottage cheese, pastries, pancakes, French toast and three kinds of hot syrup atop Sterno burners.

The hot serving line was to the right as you entered from outside, with a framed, green plywood partition separating the line from the dining hall and the stainless steel service dock was parallel to the wall where the pots, pans, stoves, and grills were manned by three highly paid American contract cooks ($91,000 a year, plus room and board, medical and per diem) who were in a flurry of motion.

Blue padded stackable chairs were positioned along rows of six-foot folding tables covered in plastic tablecloths with tacky flower prints. The rows of tables were three long to form walkways throughout the dining area, allowing the whole detachment, as was the custom, to sit together at one row, separating themselves from most of the other diners. Long ago Detachment 649 had claimed a row in the corner farthest from the front door and adjacent to the passageway between the American and the Afghan dining areas. These unstated claims by each unit were respected, establishing little territories within the dining facility. The exception was when Air Force aviators occasionally dropped in, but they mostly hot-footed it over to Kabul to lounge in hotels.

The walls were decorated with flags from every member of the NATO alliance, even though this was strictly an American camp, and along the suspended wall over the doorway were framed unsmiling portrait photographs of the entire chain of command, beginning with President Barack Obama and ending with Colonel Boyd Thomas, the Task Force commander.

Bobby ordered a cheese omelet with bacon. The server was a Phillip Maro, like Bobby, a young Italian guy from New York.

"Phil, my man," greeted Bobby, "We're playin' Seattle today, well... tonight here."

"Fuckin' home game for the Mariners, Bobby. Hope Vasquez can hold 'em for the whole nine."

"His fast ball is slow this year, *paisano*, but the boy still has a curve 'at breaks like an A-10."

"Got that right. Have a good one, Bobby."

"Thanks, Phil. Back 'atcha."

Bobby was an ex-weapons man who had attended the Operations and Intelligence Course at the Special Warfare Center and was—after the departure of the previous Team Sergeant and before the impending arrival of Dale—the senior noncommissioned officer on the detachment. Married twice without kids, this time to Carolina, the half-Japanese daughter of a retired Air Force First Sergeant. The oldest of six siblings, Bobby had learned the art of leadership through comedic diplomacy. He was the detachment's funny man, but also otherwise fairly well-organized. His efficacy, however, like that of his commanding officer, Captain Robert Dunny, had been compromised long ago by fraternization with the detachment: drinking with the men in violation of a General Order and their regular collective patronage of a bordello in Kabul that specialized in very young girls. Bobby was a pretty boy, accustomed to the attention of women on the prowl, which gave him a reputation on the team as a stud.

Peter Townhall, aka "Pete" or "Chief," was 649's Warrant Officer, or "tech," an assistant to the team commander, Captain Dunny, but not in the practical chain of command. Pete had attended Warrant Officer Candidate School as a Staff Sergeant not long out of the Special Forces Qualification Course, called the *Q-Course*, and he had very little operational experience. He had joined the army late, after his divorce in 2004, and was thirty-two. It was an open question whether the team distrusted him because he was shifty or whether he was shifty because the team distrusted him, but he lived up to it in both ways, stubbornly embittered by his exclusion. From Bear, Delaware, he was a man with a small frame—he had passed Assessment and Selection as well as the Q-Course by the skin of his teeth—and his general nervousness was never a good fit with the buccaneer spirit that enlivened most A-teams. He had a luxurious black beard that seemed incompatible with his narrow shoulders and slender hands, and his shiftiness was accentuated by horn-framed glasses with photochromic lenses that gave him the somewhat sketchy look of a jazz musician or a bookie. He compensated for his inability to make friends by taking refuge in rules, policies and regulations, for which he could quote book, chapter, and verse.

He nodded at Maro with slowly clearing lenses and requested two eggs over-medium with "well-done" bacon.

Fall was next in the queue and ordered an all-the-way omelet, meaning everything: two cheeses, onions, bell peppers, jalapeños, mushrooms, spinach and tomatoes. "Fall" was diminutive for Faulhaber, his surname; first name James. He was a Sergeant First Class from Terre Haute, and the senior weapons man on the detachment. His hair and beard were ash-blonde, though his mustache, pushed forward by an overbite, was dark. Squat as a fireplug, and a bit soft around the middle, with blue eyes and thick stubby hands, he was inexplicably attractive to certain women in bars, which is where he had met his girlfriend, June Buczek, a sergeant in Civil Affairs who was back at Fort Bragg now.

Fall was listening to Sis, Royal Sisson, the senior communications man trailing Fall through the chow line. Sis was complaining about his junior communications man, Pedro Correa, not back yet from all-night guard duty on North Observation Post 1. Fall had started hanging out with a contractor lately, and everyone knew he had a money-itch over the hundred-K-plus those guys were banking every year for doing less than the detachment guys did. Most men in the Group suspected that the gravy train wouldn't last forever and that contracting wasn't as smart as going for the pension; but Fall was full of schemes, investment ideas and whatnot. Fall held Sis up long enough to get scrambled eggs with cheese alongside bacon *and* sausage. Meat lover.

"That's a lazy motherfucker, man," Sis complained. "Lift weights for two hours at a time but won't pick up after himself."

"You're his senior, bubba," said Fall. "Put his fuckin' ass to work."

"Fucker's got more sham scams than a fat baby got farts. You end up working harder to make him do his shit than doin' it yourself."

Sis had a baby face with a wispy beard that looked worse than none at all, and because of it his complaints always sounded like whining. Black hair sticking up in a cluster of cowlicks, he was wiry and slender, further contributing to his childish aspect, though he was a twenty-nine-year-old Sergeant First Class. Sis was from St. Charles, Missouri. Like Opie, he hated being in Afghanistan. His reason was different, though; he was engaged and cockeyed in love with an elementary school teacher back in North Carolina named Diane Painter. They Skyped every chance they got and she sent him scented letters every day that he read ten times apiece, provoking some of the guys to heckle him about being pussy-whipped. Sis ordered an all-the-way omelet.

Next in line was 649's tall, chubby senior medic, Sergeant First Class William Hillman, called "Woof," because he raised dogs, read about dogs and talked incessantly about dogs, finding a way to turn almost any conversation into one about dogs—*his* dogs. He had a wife and two young boys, and no one on the team could tell you the name of any of them, but they knew when his dogs—currently a Jack Russell named Peewee, an Alsatian named Molly, and a pointer called Shotglass—got their last distemper shots or had their anal glands expressed. Woof ordered over-easies and bacon.

Behind him, lagging back a bit, were his junior medic, Staff Sergeant Hector Fermin, and the junior engineer, Staff Sergeant Eduardo "Eddy" Cuellar, both Mexican-Americans, though Eddy was from San Antonio and a deep-down Chicano while Hector, called "Baby Doc" on the team, was from a little town in Michigan called Tecumseh, third generation. They hung together not because they were Latinos but because neither of them was quite as boisterous as the other members of the team and attempts to include them in the general noise made them both a little nervous. Baby Doc spoke halting Spanish while Eddy could supervise a construction crew in Veracruz even while gutter-drunk. The other thing they shared was a genuine interest in their respective specialties—engineer and medic. Baby Doc was the distinguished honor grad during his Phase Two training and Eddy could compute explosive charges or building materials in his head. Baby Doc was single while two years earlier Eddy had married a convention center banquet cook named Inga Nisly, whom he affectionately called "Inga *la gringa*."

The team meandered past the salad bar loading their plates, then settled around their table.

Baby Doc and Eddy sat together at one end of the table and the rest clustered at the other, leaving a one-seat gap. Baby Doc was the last one to the table. As he pulled out his chair with a squawk on the wood floor, a black female Staff Sergeant entered the DFAC, last name Howe according to her name tag. She was dark with prominent eyes, hair wound tightly across her skull and pinned back securely, symmetrical, full features and a high forehead. Tall for a woman— around five-ten—she showed hints of muscularity through her uniform. Detachment 649's table went silent as all of them watched her pick up her tray and disappear behind the green partition to collect her breakfast.

Bobby broke the silence with a smirk.

"What's your name, little girl?" he asked in a theatrical granny-voice. Replying to himself in the affected voice of a child, he said, "Chlamydia." Woof barked with laughter, as did the rest, with the exception of Eddy and Doc. Even Chief gave a suppressed snicker in spite of himself. "That's a pretty name," Bobby continued his little vignette as the inquiring adult. Again in the childlike reply, "Mah mama gimme dat name."

The boys were having a difficult time suppressing their laughter. Still, they kept a watchful eye on the partition. No reason to give direct offense, after all. Sis leaned across to Bobby with a lascivious grin.

"Bobby, you ever do that?" He nodded toward the partition. "You ever do a black chick?"

Woof groaned, knowing he was, at least in part, the target of Sis's inquiry. Woof's aversion to black people was legendary and his antipathy to interracial sex was a familiar button for the rest of the boys to push. Woof chewed slowly as he stared down into his runny eggs.

Fall piped in, "Bobby used to be a stripper, didn't you, Bobby?"

"For a while, when I was stationed in Lewis."

"More pussy than Brian Pumper," Fall went on. "Didn'tcha, Bobby? Got used like a cheap sex toy." All eyes on Bobby, and Bobby didn't pretend he didn't like it. He laughed in anticipation of what he was about to say.

"Just before we left Bragg," Bobby began his story, leaning in, "I met this redbone over at Bennigans..."

"Aww fuck," interjected Woof. "You mean a nigger chick."

"Light-skinned nigger chick," Bobby corrected, leaning in to say it quietly. More laughter.

Sergeant Howe emerged from behind the partition and carried her tray to the salad bar, walking within ten feet of their table. The table went silent, and the boys returned in earnest to their food, smirks aimed at their plates.

When she settled safely on the other side of the room, next to Sergeant Baines, the PAO flunky, Bobby beetled back in to resume his tale, and his audience likewise slanted in to catch it, Doc and Eddy now quietly eating and pretending to ignore them.

"She was fuckin' hot," he said. "Ass you could set a cup on, and she comes up and says, like, you know, you look like some actor, and I'm like, yeah?" Bobby forked a load of omelet into his mouth, chewed for a moment, swallowed half of it, then talked around the rest. "Hussy was totally DTF, word. I took 'er home and gave 'er the big Italian sausage 'til three in the morning."

Fall giggled "Rock 'n roll, man," while Woof groaned. "Dude," asked Fall, "Where was your wife?"

"Oh, the Jap was visiting her mom up in New York. Next morning," he continued... there was obviously more, "I found her gold bracelet and shit on the nightstand. I was, like, fuck son, what if I hadn't seen that? Carolina coming home that afternoon."

"Oohhhh!" was the collective response.

"Seriously, Boo?" put in Opie.

"Serious as dick cancer, yo! Breezy's active duty, man. Some leg outfit over by COSCOM. I dropped her gold shit over at 'er CQ desk before work."

"How d'ya know she won't come back to your house like a dumped dog?" Opie interjected again. He punctuated the question with an involuntary procession of winks.

"Oh, when I took her to the house and back home, I drove all over North Fayetteville," he answered, provoking a hoot of laughter from most of the table.

"Fuck you jungle fever cocksuckers," muttered Woof, dropping his fork onto his plate and shaking his head.

Chief spoke unexpectedly, and all eyes turned his way.

"How do you know you didn't get AIDS, Bobby?" It was like the whole table was hit with cold water.

Bobby waited a beat, then smiled and ignored him. Fall broke the silence.

"Hey, is anybody gonna pick up plates for Gene and Pedro? They been on guard."

"I got 'em," Opie said, then tuned back to Woof, wanting to resume the thread. "Hey, Woof, you don't approve of splittin' the black oak?" This time, his tic was a side to side head bob and an exaggerated expression of curiosity.

Pete wasn't going to let it go. "You know, Bobby, that black women have AIDS at a higher rate than white women."

Woof answered Opie: "Hey, I don't breed a pointer with a German Shepherd, okay?"

Bobby replied to Chief: "Chief, I'll tell it to you like my daddy told me. 'It's my dick and it's my soap, and I'll wash it as fast as I want.'"

Another clap of laughter went up. Chief's cheeks colored crimson.

Opie went for Woof again.

"So, Woof... you never, *ever* fucked a black chick? What I hear, somma you southern boys don' know white girls got pussies 'til yer eighteen years old."

"You're risking your life, Bobby," Chief said. "Your wife's life, too."

"Cut me some fuckin' slack, Ope. Goddamn," Woof said, scowling at his eggs.

"How about a Chinese or Mexican chick?" Opie pressed. Eddy and Baby Doc looked up at Opie. They weren't smiling.

"Chief," Bobby said, not smiling either now. "Why don't you lemme worry about *my* wife and *my* dick?"

"Not the same," Woof said to Opie. "Fuckin' boofs are another species, man."

Bobby saw the tension begin to generalize, so he went back into his routine.

"What's *your* name, little girl?" Answering himself again in his little black girl voice, "Dry-humpa." The laughter returned, minus Chief and Baby Doc. Bobby reverted to the first voice: "Tha's a pretty name, baby."

ACROSS THE DFAC Captain Bob draped his battle-rattle over the back of a chair at an empty table. He was Robert Dunny, Captain, his source of commission ROTC at the University of Ohio, from a town in the same state called Sylvania, around an hour from Baby Doc's home town in Southern Michigan, married, with a two-year-old boy.

The boys started calling him "Captain Bob," and it stuck.

He was twenty-eight, good-looking in a bland way, blue-eyed with thinning blonde hair cut very short, athletic, with a thick mustache over a well-groomed beard. Captain Bob

94

emerged from the chow line, passing the boys' table en route to the salad bar, and greeted them.

"Morning, 649," he said, eliciting a flurry of "Mornings" and "Hey, Captain Bobs." Dunny loaded his plate at the bar then carried it to his table.

The dining facility door opened and Dale entered. The boys went quiet again at a strange face in an SF uniform, old guy, maybe in his forties, but fairly fit. Unremarkable haircut with a newly-started beard. Not very big. Black hair, some gray on the sides. Pale blue-green eyes. Dale gave the food line a pass, picking up just a white porcelain coffee cup. He drew a cup of black coffee from the stainless steel machine and headed straight to Dunny's table.

He saw 649's table, and surmised from the sudden chatter and the eyes that followed him that this was the team on which he was the new Operations Sergeant. The Ichabod Crane-looking one was making faces at him, or was he? He looked like a giant goat and opened his eyes as far as he could three times in succession, like he was signaling an 'O' in Morse Code.

Hovering with his tray at Captain Bob's table, he announced himself.

"Captain Dunny. I'm Dale. Believe I'm your new Operations Sergeant. May I sit?"

Dunny wiped his chin with a napkin and swallowed his food, standing with his hand extended.

"Omigod, yes. Hi." He gave Dale a firm shake, looking him in the eyes. "Wow, it's good to meet you. You're not eating?"

"Time table's off, Sir. From the flights over. Not hungry really." His accent was pure North Carolina, Dunny noted; eastern North Carolina, with that ghost of Scottish.

Sitting down, "Bob, please. Or Captain Bob. S'what the boys call me. Mind if I call you Top?"

"Not at all. Name of team sergeants long as I remember."

A C-130 resupply bird approached, the big turboprops emitting an ear-splitting groan. Dale took a cautious sip from the steaming mug. The plane passed by and they could hear the engines reverse after it touched down.

"Really glad you're here," said Dunny. "You're very well spoken of."

Dale looked into Dunny's eyes for longer than was comfortable until Dunny blinked, knitted his brows, and waited for a reply. Dale seemed to have checked out, looking through Dunny by way of his eyes.

Then, as if there had been no pause, "By whom?"

"Huh?" said Dunny.

"You said I was spoken well of. By whom?"

"Oh," Dunny tried to get back on track. "Well, just people." *That sounded stupid.* Dunny sighed. "Colonel Thomas talks you up. Talks up your background, your time across the fence. With the Rangers, too?" Dunny inflected up, like he was asking a question. Something about Dale made him feel wrong-footed, like a kid caught breaking a rule. "With Group? He believes your background will bring in stronger missions. You've got a hell of a lot of experience in operations. Didn't you just come from CAG?" (He pronounced it "kag.")

"No, Sir... Bob. Left in June last year. Went to Monterrey to study Farsi. I was a Spanish linguist before."

"Farsi, huh? You test?"

"Three-three, Sir... Bob. I was there almost a year. Aptitude for language, I guess. I suck at math though." He smiled, but the strange unblinking gaze took the warmth out of it.

Bob whistled. "Three-three. Pretty impressive."

The conversation ran into an impasse. Bob wolfed two big spoons full of cottage cheese, then took a bite from a glazed doughnut.

"Master Sergeant Bernays," he began again, chewing doughnut. "The last team sergeant, he was a ROAD Top, retired on active duty. I just took the team three months ago. I could use a strong hand. Bernie left the detachment pretty rudderless. Nice guy, but a fuckin' slug."

Top did another long pause, staring again through Bob's eyes like he was sleepwalking, increasing Bob's sense of dismay. *This guy is fucking weirding me out here*, he found himself thinking. *What the hell did we get? Must be some Delta Force psyops shit.*

Dale dropped his doll-eyed gaze and took a swallow of the black coffee. Looking up again, he was re-engaged.

"I'd like to have each of 'em sometime after chow," Dale said, "for initial interviews, if that's workable. Can I use the Ops hooch?"

"No problem," said Dunny. "Can you take Correa and Pollard first? They were on O.P. all night. Need some rack."

"That's..."

The explosion just outside the DFAC rattled their internal organs. Dishes smashed on the floor, tables rocked and dust blew in through shattered windows and cracks in the fractured door. There was a long scream, then some shouting. People crawled around on the floor like bugs, trying to put on their helmets and combat vests. More dust streamed in, as if pushed by a second gust of wind.

Somewhere in the distance a fifty-caliber machine gun chopped out six-round bursts.

Outsourced

Weymouth Woods State Park, North Carolina
June 29, 2010

"WHAT'S THE DIFFERENCE?"

"In what?" Deangela asked.

"Moral and analytical philosophy," said Dale.

The nuthatch had spent more than two minutes like an upside-down dart inspecting crevices in the pine bark before flying off. They lowered their field glasses. He had a pretty good notion, having been exposed to Aquinas, Aristotle and Plato in the course of studying Shakespeare, his favorite, in college. It seemed like another life and his memory of it was hazy. But he loved hearing her speak, more so when she got on to something that absorbed her.

"Hmmm," she collected her thoughts. "Okay, analytical philosophy deals with what *is*. Just that, what is reality, or being." She stopped to worm a finger into her molar and dislodge some of her sandwich. "However that's constructed. What is reality, being? That kind of thing. Moral philosophy begins with the same question, but tries to impute from its own metaphysical assumptions what we *ought* to do, what kinds of norms and rules we need to live together in a way that makes people and societies flourish."

Dale was gazing at her, into her eyes, but he suddenly seemed to be somewhere else. He had gone silent. Deangela waited. And waited.

Just before she asked him what was wrong, he returned. With humor.

"Are you mine?"

With a surprising sense of relief, she said, "Hundred and ten percent," and just as suddenly found herself sad. "Daddy, what's going on?"

"Wanna walk a ways?" he asked.

"Sure," she said, frowning with curiosity.

They stood and shouldered the packs. She pulled her compass out of her shirt pocket, attached by a lanyard around her neck.

"There's a nice, dry stretch along a fifty degree bearing," she said. "You game?"

"Lead."

She saw him reading maps when she was eight, when she was already being tutored at home by Theodora. Deangela asked him to show her what he was doing, and he already knew that she was capable. He began by explaining what a map was—"a two-dimensional representation of the earth's surface, drawn to scale, as seen from above." He taught her how that surface was divided into grids along north-south and east-west axes and the different ways to measure and read these grids. Within two days she was plotting coordinates, calculating intersections and identifying elevations and terrain features from 1:50,000 military topographical maps. She wore him out asking for more problems. Free weekends were soon devoted to orienteering together, giving Farah a welcome break from De's incessant interrogations.

Dale had moved out the following year, though they had never officially divorced... or annulled. Farah was a practicing Catholic, and Dale never seemed inclined to push it. Not making anything official also kept Farah and Deangela on full benefits as military dependents.

"Are you okay, Daddy?" She was looking back as she ascended a slight rise, and stumbled in a hole.

He rushed forward, but she had already recovered, shaking it off.

"Alright?" he asked.

"That's what I just asked you," she replied, stopping now and facing him from uphill, wiping leaves off her legs.

There it was again. He was doing that silent staring thing. What the hell, she thought.

"Sounds sticky," he said. She furrowed her brow at that, and he smiled. "Analytical philosophy. The 'what is' part," he explained. "Don't we all have our own little abbreviations for that?"

She started laughing.

"What's funny?"

"You, Daddy. You ought to study philosophy, I think. You just summarized the philosophical dilemma of modernity."

He gave a shake of the head.

"Modernity," then grunted. "Lead on."

"Daddy, I asked you a question. Something's on your mind."

"I'll get to it," he said. "Let's just walk a bit."

She turned, then he interrupted her.

"Okay, one more question," he announced.

Deangela waited, thumbs hooked into her pack straps.

"Okay," he began. "You said, 'I ought to study philosophy,' right?"

"Mm-hmmm."

"Well, that's an ought, right. Moral philosophy."

She rolled her eyes and turned to head over the crest of the small rise.

"Okay, wait," he said again. "Jokin' aside, I have a moral philosophy question." He raised the bottom of his pack to adjust his waistband. "So, on the question of what one ought to do, what's moral, right? Can that be outsourced?"

She studied his face like it was a riddle, then her eyes went wide.

"You're asking about the army, about what you do."

"I suppose I am," he allowed. "Probably an unfair question. I guess if it can't be outsourced, my professional life has been unjustifiable." They both sat silently ruminating on that for a bit, their gazes drifting down to share a spot in the dead leaves and pine straw. "Your mom. She believes in God." Deangela looked at him again. "I don't mean she consents to the existence of God as a proposition, okay? I mean she *believes*. She'd have a conversation with God like she's sitting across the kitchen table. God's as real to her as you and I are to each other, like this, right now. That's magic to me, how she does that. I wish I could... I can't get my head around it, even if I just think about God, like whatever came before—whatever came before the Big Bang, you see? Whatever is there on the backside of infinity. How could God say yes to all this when it ends up with us. Billions of years and we're the only creatures there are that think about God, and yet we ourselves are bursting with these... possibilities. Transcendent possibilities. Terrible, unspeakable possibilities." A pause. "But then again, there's shampoo that washes body in, not out."

December 30, 2009
Monterey, California

THE TRIDENT ROOM over on University Circle was known for frosty tap beer and tasty appetizers and had over a thousand different mugs hung from the ceiling. For a few of the students from the Defense Language Institute it was a favored after-class watering hole. Dale was nursing a beer by himself in the corner and trying not to listen to the animated chatter at a nearby table. Three young Special Forces students, fresh from the Q-Course, were half-drunk and ranting about a bombing attack that was in the news. Seven CIA agents had been killed in Camp Chapman, Afghanistan by a suicide bomber who had been working with the Americans. A so-called "green on blue" attack. The talk turned to "fuckin' hajjis," and why the only good one is a dead one.

"If there's a rag on its head, it needs to be dead," rhymed one of them to surly nods in assent. The poet was shaved bald with black eyebrows and a recessed chin. One of his companions was eagerly tossing him questions about his time in Iraq —where the older student/poet had apparently been a Military Policeman in the Reserves, only later going on full-time active duty and volunteering for SF.

"I was at this prison camp, man... you always hear about Abu Ghraib, but we had more. Right there at Baghdad. We was workin' with the spooks, the boys across the fence... all of 'em. We got this bitch one day... maybe fifteen, with a hot fuckin' body." His colleagues hooked into the story, leaned in and smiling, making noises like they were in the first stages of a tent revival. "Me n' muh boy, guy named Bledsoe, we were totally in charge... we broke that bitch in like a mustang." Hoots of laughter, a bit nervous. "So we fucked her twice apiece, even though Bledsoe couldn't come the second time, and it pissed him off. So he starts wailin' on the bitch, an' I tell him hold up, dude. We can pimp the bitch out if you don't fuck 'er up. So we start bringin' in motherfuckers from all over camp—on the down-low, man—and we charge twenty-five bucks a pop." He was slurring his words a bit, teetering between buzzed and bombed, and his story was kind of flowing out of him now. He wore a half-smile, like he was reminiscing. "We made almost three hundred dollars in a coupla hours. That night, we find the bitch dead. Hung herself in the cell with ripped up clothes."

"Why'd she do that?" One of his companions asked.

"Dunno," he replied, appearing to think it over. "She was unhappy?" This cracked the table up, though there was now a kind of edge between surprise, disgust, and admiration directed at baldy.

When baldy got ready to leave, one of his friends suggested a cab, but he waved him off.

"Ain't but three miles. I'm good."

Dale called the waitress over, a stocky tattooed youngster with spiky yellow hair and hipster glasses. He gave her a twenty for his stuffed potato and a beer and told her to keep the change. She pushed the whole twenty into her apron.

Dale went to his car and took a pencil out of the glove compartment.

STEVEN RICKS FUMBLED in his right front pocket for his keys. The parking lot was perpendicular to the bar entrance, divided by a curbed island dressed with four poorly manicured hawthorn trees. The single security light was flickering, but the powerful fluorescents from the entrance to the saloon threw yellow bars of light across the asphalt and gleamed off the cars. Nautical pennants on a cross brace above the entrance of the bar, presumably to make it appear shiplike, fluttered in the chilly east wind. Ricks shivered. He shifted his car keys into his left hand and tried to zip up his Gore-Tex jacket. He was feeling pleased with himself. His companions would be talking about him right now, calling him a bad motherfucker, cold-blooded, crazy. *Fuckin' zipper won't line up.* There were levels of respect in this world of men and the highest level was always laced with awe and a little fear. And he really did enjoy the hajji bitch.

He turned when he heard light footfalls. It was that short turquoise-eyed guy from the bar. He had seen him around the Institute—taking Farsi if Ricks recalled correctly.

"Say," called the little guy. Ricks stood six-feet-one. The little guy was actually kind of old—fortyish—holding out what looked like a napkin as he approached.

"Yeah?"

"I think this fell outa your pocket in the bar," said the short guy, extending the piece of paper. Ricks looked at him, then down at the paper. When he took the paper and looked down at it, it was just a napkin. *A plain fucking napkin. What the...*

Just then the little guy punched him in the neck, fast—pop!—just like that. He was about to get angry when he was overcome by an icy lightheadedness. The color started draining out of everything. The little guy was standing there, not moving, just watching and holding a shiny black pencil. Ricks reached up slowly and touched below his left ear where he felt a hot sensation. Something was spraying hard like the jet off a pressure washer. The he felt himself hollowing out. He pressed his bloody hand against the car door and lowered himself slowly to the ground. The little guy was walking away now, and everything grew dark and small.

Interviews

Camp Virtue, Afghanistan
July 10, 2010

THE CLEAN-UP CREW wore plain helmets and body armor over civilian clothes. They were contractors—the closest to flunkies such as dining facility inspectors and gym managers —but they made more than $85,000 a year.

The generator and its trailer were pulverized. The RPG had scored a direct hit, a tactical miracle given its short range and the distance from which it must have had to travel from gunner to target. Similar odds to a child shooting an arrow into a faraway thicket and nailing an unseen rabbit.

A twenty-year-old Ranger fifty-gunner on the northeast claimed the rocket had come from a vehicle on the road nearest to the minefield, and he shot the shit out of a covered Hilux truck, but when a team went to investigate the wreckage it found nothing in the back except exploded watermelons stained with splashes of blood. Whoever had been on that truck made tracks out of there with the wounded. Getting hit with fifty fire was like having lightning bolts dropped on you at a rate of 500 a minute. They decided to call it as three enemy wounded-in-action, military-aged-males, and gave that Ranger-boy a Bronze Star for meritorious mayhem.

The chow hall was now officially no longer air-conditioned. It would take a week to get another generator. Knock a tenth of a point off troop morale. It had been almost two hours since the hit, and this time the laws of probability had spared them any injuries beyond ringing ears, headaches and maybe some invisible brain damage. Except for the generator, of course. That was clearly toast.

A C-5 screeched onto the runway and was reversing its engines, but it carried nothing that could compensate the loss of a cool and dry dining environment for non-aviation personnel. The DFAC crew was already opening windows as the mid-morning temperatures climbed past eighty.

In the 649 Operations Hooch, Dale stared at a yellow legal pad and dreaded the interviews. He had lobbied for a limp-dick job shuffling papers when he arrived at ISAF, but Colonel Thomas had already intercepted Dale through the grapevine and pulled strings to ensure he would get the former Delta operator onto his post. Thomas idolized Delta, though he had never so much as entered the compound, and he thought every operator there could juggle live chainsaws while they recited long passages of Goethe from memory.

Inside the ops hooch, Dale felt as if he was back in the States at the isolation facility in Aberdeen. White walls were covered in dry erase boards, presentation easels stacked in the corner alongside folding tables, two big sand tables in the middle of the room for terrain models, complete with drawers underneath to hold all the modeling props, including colored chalk powder, fit-together walls and lots of tiny toy soldiers. A whole section was set aside for a dozen open cots, three large safes and a bank of five computers. One whole wall was a bookcase full of field manuals and communications equipment. There was a cart with twenty folding chairs.

Two bands of powerful fluorescent lights made the window-less building feel like high noon daylight 24/7.

Top unfolded one table and placed two chairs across from one another. He sat in one, staring at the notepad, and wondered what to ask. He would go through the motions, but the truth was he had lost something between Ojo de Agua, the Defense Language Institute, Chapel Hill, and here. Giving a shit? That, yeah, but the other thing, too. Like he walked some place scratching a trail behind him, but by the time he tried to go back the wind had erased bits of it and he would circle around and around trying to find it again.

A year and a half before he was eligible to retire. *Fuck! A century! An aeon!*

It was more than burnout, more than post-traumatic stress disorder—*whatever the fuck that meant.* He looked back on his entire adult life, and aside from Farah and Deangela, everything that had animated him seemed no more meaning-ful than that pair of big red roaches that scuttled under the bookcase when he flipped on the lights. One minute he knew his lines, the next minute he was five years old with big cosmic question marks all around him. He thought back to Monterey and his head started to feel soft again. Soft and sticky, like cotton candy being ravaged by ants. He needed to sleep. He imagined that he was an enormous one-eyed fish flapping its way breathlessly up a stony mountain.

Today was Saturday. The last time he could remember sleeping was—he thought hard—the day he was with Deangela on the 29th? Was that a Tuesday? He had flown out on Thursday... maybe a week. He must have slept, but he couldn't remember when. Maybe a few snatches on the plane, wearing earplugs and tying a cravat across his eyes.

Pop songs he had heard in odd places, buses, airports, childhood—they were replaying constantly in his head. But the words had changed, lost their sense.

Someone rapped on the door.

"Come in," he called. *Deep breath, let it out.*

It was the guy who looked like a bookie. Dale stood and offered his hand.

"A.D.," he said.

"Pete Pownall," Chief said, taking off his MICH helmet and shaking the hand as his eyes cast about the room looking from behind his darkened lenses for threats, for disorder. *Bone-all*, the surname mutated in Dale's ears.

"Have a seat, Pete... or do the boys call you Chief?"

"Chief, yeah. Thank you." He unslung his M-4 and leaned it against the table.

Dale settled in and retrieved the notepad, jotting down "Chief Pete" and putting four outward facing arrows around it for no particular reason. He put the notepad in his lap and looked up. Chief's lenses were still dark from the sun and un-likely to lighten all the way in this fluorescent tomb.

"You want to be called A.D.?"

"Sure, or Top. Whatever's comfortable." *Did I say comfortable?*

Pownall folded his forearms on the table, thrusting his face close enough to make his eyes grow unnaturally large behind the gray lenses.

"I'm glad you're here, Top."

"I'm not sure I am, but thank you."

"No, I mean we need some guidance. A strong hand. This team has problems."

"I'm sure they do," Top said. "Never seen one that didn't."

"I mean discipline problems. Pedro, our junior commo guy, was on deck, but I asked to speak with you first. You need some perspective on these guys."

Dale wrote *dickhead* in very small letters by *Chief Pete*.

"Okay, Chief. Tell me about the detachment."

"They're a soup sandwich, Top. Bernie had no discipline. I keep written memos 'cause I need to cover my ass. They don't like me. They don't see a warrant officer as a real officer."

"Sorry to hear that, Chief. That they don't like you. But you *are* a tech, not a commander."

"I just want some respect. We got in this firefight two months ago, out south on a recon. I said 'break contact.' Protocol for recon. Right? Break contact. They killed two guys anyway. Now they think I was afraid."

"You weren't afraid?"

"No, Top!"

"Why not?" ... *What was that? Was it REM?*

That's me in the corner
That's me in the hot light
Losing my blue pigeon
Trying to sleep walk with you
And I don't know if I can do it
Oh no, I've said too much
I haven't said enough
I thought that I heard you staffing
I thought that I heard I-Ching
I think I thought I saw you fly

TWENTY MINUTES LATER he still hadn't thought of anything to ask them. He was glad to be rid of Chief, though. *Kind of a whiner. Definitely a dickhead.* The term *dickhead* suddenly struck him funny, and he could hardly suppress his laughter. *Boy, I need some fucking sleep!*

Another knock.

Deep breath, let it out.

"Come in."

A very fit guy with a trimmed black beard, wavy short black hair, just under six feet at a glance, with red-rimmed eyes. Hispanic, Dale guessed, *dominicano* or PUERTORRIQUEÑO, BUT A SELF-CONSCIOUS TRIGUEÑO WITH NO TAN LINES. His MICH helmet was under his left arm, weapon held between the magazine-well and forearm assembly.

"Hey, Top." said Pedro.

"Hey. You can ground your gear."

Pedro set his weapon against the wall, shucked his vest and body armor in one move, and plopped his MICH helmet on top of the heap. He turned and offered his hand to Top.

Top shook his hand.

"A.D."

"What?"

"That's what people call me. A.D. Or Top. Now. I guess."

Pedro smiled, seeming relieved. He wasn't sure what A.D. meant. Accidental discharge? That was a chargeable offense, but he had not accidentally fired his weapon. They weren't even allowed to have a magazine in while on the compound unless they were taking fire.

"Have a seat. What's your name?"

Pedro looked confused again.

"Correa, Top," he replied, running his finger across the olive green name tag velcroed over his left pocket.

"I mean your first name," Top explained. "You can sit down."

Seemingly relieved again, Pedro sat across from Dale and settled in. This was not the team's most intuitive member, thought Dale.

"Thanks," said Pedro.

A question, a question, I'm supposed to ask something.

"So, Pedro. Tell me about yourself."

Fucking brilliant. You're a real managerial masterpiece, Dale.

Within fifteen seconds he regretted the question.

Pedro was talking. *What was he saying? Focus!* Minutes passed before he found himself tuning back in, and Pedro's mouth was still in motion.

"...my thing is PT. I mean, I'm a good commo man... well, my code is a little slow, but I can make comms with a fuckin' barbed wire fence if you want. But my real thing, you know, is I like to take care of my body. I don't use tobacco or caffeine or sugar. Sugar is fuckin' poison, man... I mean... Top. And I think core work is the key, abs, obliques, lower back. Get a strong core, and your body is a weapon, man... I mean... Top.

"How close was that fuckin' rocket?"

Top had written: *Pedro. Dickhead.* More arrows, with meandering stems now. Pedro talked. Dale listlessly unwrapped a tootsie roll he found in his pocket. Where had that come from? In his head, a Human League cover... was being performed by Alvin and the Chipmunks.

Don't

Don't you haunt me?
You know I can't reprieve it
When I hear that you won't flee me.
Don't
Don't you haunt me?
You know I don't deceive you
When you say that you don't bleed me.
It's much too late to find
When you think you're strange and blind
You'd better change the pack or we will both be quarry.

ONCE BACK OUTSIDE, PEDRO MET the waiting team gaggle. They abruptly stopped shooting the shit to hear what Pedro had to say.

"Dude," he began. "He's not..." He struggled for the words. Tapping the side of his head, "He's weird, man. He don't say much." Still tapping his head, "Mu'fuckah's got a faulty circuit."

"TELL ME ABOUT yourself, Gene."

Gene was studying Dale's face.

"Can I smoke?" asked Gene.

"No."

"Okay," he put the pack of Marlboros away. "Okay. Yeah, okay."

Dale said nothing as he stared straight through Gene's eyes in a way that unnerved him. After several long seconds of silence, Gene spoke. He was sleep-deprived after guard duty and found himself wanting to spill ideas at Dale, saying things he would normally never say.

"Close call today, eh? Fuckin' hajji don't even aim. He just lobs shit in the air, says 'Inshallah,' and runs like a raped ape.

Can't triangulate 'im that way.

"Anyway, about me. Okay, I wanna see this team do some real shit."

Top put his pen to the notepad: "Gene. Dickhead." and drew four-leaf clovers around the words.

"Bernie, okay, Bernie was a slug. Well, you'll hear about... anyway... how do I... it's like, my favorite movie was *Tombstone*, you know. Like, *that's* what I wanted when I went SF— not bein' a drill sergeant in a foreign language... okay, well, my language is something I want to work on. S'pose t' be Spanish, but the words are all out o' order, and I can't hear it without losin' track. At least it ain't Arabic, cuz I really can't make those hajji hackin' noises like a strangled cat... so, anyway, I like that scene, you know, where Billy Bob Thornton has the shotgun and he's comin' after Wyatt Earp, and Doc Holliday, man, he just says, 'Where you goin' with that shotgun?' You know, and like, 'I'll be your huckleberry.' I love that shit. I wish we lived in those times, not hangin' out in this shithole just to go back to the fuckin' suburbs."

Gene Pollard reminded Dale of a bear. He had lots of dark black hair on his hands and chest, big brown beard, hair thinning up top and a beer belly, or just the beginnings of one. A very animated bear—the guy was waving his hands around, his little red eyes all alight... Dale's brain went Pink Floyd now... still sung by Chipmunks.

We don't need no defecation
We don't need no grassy knoll
No shark knee spasm in the classroom
Teachers leave them kids a clone
Hey! Teachers! Leave them kids a clone!

All in all it's just another dickhead's Bhopal.
All in all you're just another dick that's too small.

GENE EMERGED FROM the operations hooch with an expression of stunned wonder. Bobby wanted to interrogate him, but Bobby was next in the box. Gene took the rest of the guys away from the door and urgently lit a cigarette before he debriefed them. Chief had already taken his leave.

"He just wants you to talk, I think. Like, 'tell me about yourself,' then he sits back with this look like you're a weird bug he just noticed. Coupla times he like laughed a little, but I wasn't sayin' anything to be funny, man. Truthfully, that dude is off, man. Not like a different drummer. Homey's got his own marching band!"

"See what I tol' yous," Pedro said. "That ol' man is fuckin' weird, dude. They smokin' some funny shit over there 'cross the fence. It's like he somewhere else, man. Like fuckin' Star Trek *out* there!"mm

A YOUNG SYLVESTER Stallone. With a beard. An E-7 named Bobby. Grinning like an idiot.

"So Bobby, what can you tell me about yourself?"

Dale pegged him within half a minute: class clown. *This is the ops sergeant? The intel sergeant now?* Dale thought about Belize, about cold beer and music, about Farah moving to the music wearing a crinkly cotton dress with pink and blue flowers.

"About myself, huh? Okay, I had a few problems at first, right. Before SF. You prob'ly know. I was a private in the 82nd, and I pissed hot for weed once. So I quit the pot. Got a Top Secret clearance even with the pot thing. I just drink now.

I'm married after all. You married?"

Top noticed a silence, eventually, and realized that he was supposed to answer.

"Separated."

"Well, I married this Jap girl, but she has an American name, Carolina, like in North Carolina. I got a picture of her in my wallet. You wanna see?"

"No." Dale wrote on the notepad: *Bobby. Dickhead.*

"Whatcha writin', Top?"

"Nothing. Just keeping track of the interviews."

"So, anyway," Bobby went on, "I just finished Operations and Intelligence School before this deployment... man, that was tough, especially the intelligence parts... okay, some of the ops, too. I'm not book smart, but I'm in good shape. Good shot, too. You ever been with two chicks at once?"...*Nice Shot...*

I wish I could've bet you
now I can whittle bait.
what you could've bought me
I could've paved some space
they think that early bending
was your schlong
for the most part they're bright
but look how they all got donged
that's why I say hey man, nice snot
what a good snot man...

OUTSIDE, BOBBY WAS BRIGHT-EYED and smiling like a kid who had just watched someone levitate.

"He hums!"

"What?" begged Opie.

"He hums, homie! Like real low, but if you listen while you talk... he wants you to talk... must be some Delta Force mojo psych technique he knows... but while he's listening to you, he hums real quiet. And stares at your eyes without blinking. Captain Bob said this dude can speak Iranian better'n I'ma-did-a-job." Bobby giggled, "Our team sergeant might be some evil genius, fellas!"

"What's he want you to say?" Opie asked.

"Just ramble, man. I think he's tryin' to figure out how to use us on missions. Like some third-eye shit. Just talk like we talk at the tent. I told him sex stories, and the motherfucker never blinked. Just hummed like he was makin' his own background music."

FALL WAS DIPPING snuff and spitting into a Coca-Cola can.

"Tell you about myself? About myself, eh? Well, I know my weapons inside-out. If it's man-portable, then I know that weapon inside-out. But the thing is, I may not be in that much longer." Fall leaned forward like he was doing a sales pitch. "See, these guys over at XYY Security, well, my buddy, Ben Virden, he's one of the contractors... he's an old SF commo man... well, he says I can make a hundred and twenty K a year, all bankable, so it's like, why should I stay in on an E-7's pay, when I can pull that kinda money down."

"Fall. Dickhead." Dale drew circles with smaller and smaller circles inside them.

"But that don't mean I'll sham on ya, Top. I'm gonna work my ass off 'til I sign out. And Virden and them, you know, they make more money than all that... I mean, this place is a great big fuckin' ATM, except when you wear these." Fall plucked at his uniform blouse. "But 'til then, Top, you need anything on weapons, I gotcha back." *Yeah, Floyd again... Floyd in deep-voice.*

Bunny, yesterday
Get a good slob with PURÉE *and your O.K.*
Bunny, gives ya gas
Grab that ass with both hands and make a pass
New car, scimitar, crossbar daydream,
Think I'll buy me a French I-beam
Bunny, ipecac
I'm all right Jack, keep your glands off my-y-y-y crack.

"I SAW HIM write something when I told him I was thinking about going over to XYY," Fall told them.

"What's that mean, ya think?" asked Woof.

"Well, he kinda smiled when he wrote it, so it wasn't like it pissed him off."

"Was he humming?"

"I couldn't hear that, but yeah, he like tapped his foot and even bobbed his head, but those eyes, man... he puts a radar lock on ya."

"OPIE. DICKHEAD."

"I'm the team sniper. I shot twelve of these fuckin' savages already." Pursed lips. He had thick head of auburn hair that made him look boylike, even with the red turkey beard. Eyes like blue saucers kept gaping open unexpectedly. "Honestly, I wouldn't trade one American life for this whole fuckin' place. But 'til I get back to the world, I'm here to do the job." Opie winked at Top, twice in succession with the same eye. Top tilted his head at him, then realized Opie didn't know he was winking. He had an entire repertoire of unconscious involuntary facial tics. "I'm a professional. You ask me, though, best thing for this place is a neutron bomb. More of 'em I shoot, the better I like it." The eyes again, popping open like he was airing out his this irises... *Dylan...*

Now you don't gawk at clouds
Now you don't bean no shroud
About having to be loungin' for your next spiel.
Cow does it kneel
Cow does it kneel
To be without a bone
Like a drum beat tone
Like a bowling throne

"HE'S ALRIGHT," SAID Ope. "Just quiet."

"Quiet like Son of motherfuckin' Sam," said Gene. "I'm tellin' you, dude, he's crazy as a sack o' squirrels." Pedro gave seven or eight nods of affirmation.

THE NEXT DICKHEAD was Woof.

"They call me Woof, you know, cuz I raise dogs. I love dogs. My wife loves 'em, my kids, too. You got kids?"

Woof waited for an answer... and waited... *This one was a little heavy, too,* thought Dale. *They must feed them well here at the mess hall.* With a Georgia drawl. *Mess hall, Georgia drawl, mess hall, Georgia drawl...*

"One," it finally came. "I have one child. She's in college."

"I got two," Woof resumed his monologue. "Boy six, girl four, and they love dogs, too. I have a pointer, an Alsatian, and a Jack Russell. I like dogs better'n people, you know. You can tie 'em to a post and beat 'em, and they're still loyal, y'know?"

120

Don't they say people look like their dogs? This guy didn't look like any of those dogs. He looked like... *a dickhead.* Woof saw Dale laughing to himself and thought Dale was enjoying his remarks about tying a dog up and beating it. So he drove on, smiling back now.

"I'm the senior medic, but I let Baby Doc do sick call. Hector? He needs the practice, y'know. But watch for him, that one. He's a fuckin' Jesus freak or somethin'. Church twice a week if he can, fuckin' mackerel snapper... you're not Catholic are you?"... *Who was that guy? Billy something...*

Come out Magenta, don't let me mate.
You Catholic girls fart then rotate.
Aw, but moon a potato that thumbs-down the freight.
I might as well be that dumb.
Well, they towed you a thumbscrew, told you to weigh.
They bit you a dimple and clocked a driveway.
Aw, but that cheddar sold Golan Heights a toupée
for rings that your flight had fun.
Only the hood fry dung.
Only the hood fry dung.

WOOF WAS FROWNING when he reemerged.

"I tried to talk, like y'all said. Was like I wasn't there. Bobby, that shit you said is stupid. Your boy is fuckin' whacko. Cheese done slid off his cracker, man!"

"SIS," HE WROTE. *And I shall call him Loretta...*

"Top, I'll be honest. The boys say you just want us to talk about shit. So I'm gonna tell you about the shit I put up with on this detachment. I'm senior commo, but I do *most* of it. Guess I shouldn't talk out of school, but Top, since you're

121

comin' in fresh, I don't mind doin' the comms, but *all* of them? I mean, Pedro? Sergeant Correa? All that guy does is work out and take supplements and shit, and look at himself in the mirror at the MSA gym. Then he's too tired to work. I'm puttin' in, sometimes, eighteen hour days doin' *all* the fuckin' comms, and he just works out and watches porn."

Dickhead.

"Sorry, I guess I'm comin' off as some kinda pussy, a fuckin' whiner or somethin'. But you check, we always got comms, and Pedro's either watchin' Malibu Muffdivers or doin' flutterkicks."

"Sergeant Sisson. Sis?"

"Yeah, Top."

"How many more people are out there?"

"Two, Top.

"You ever hear this song?"

Sis looked at Top like he was a jumping spider.

"Hmm hmm hmm... We come off the scoop, Palm Beach... hmm hmm hmm... My grandfather had to pee... hmm hmm hmm..." Dale nodded silently for a moment, then, "There's a chorus about coming home."

"Top, I never..."

"Not important. Something you said about Malibu triggered a memory, that's all. Go on. You were saying that Pedro is your junior and he just works out and jacks off to porn, and you let him get away with it, then you have to do all the work."

"Well, I uh..."

"Have you ever thought of writing him up?"

"Well, Top, this team has done a lot of shit together..."

"You mean you guys all have shit on each other, right?"

"Top..."

"It's pretty common, you know. A-Detachments go down-range, they do shit they don't want their wives to know about, or they break laws together. Now Pedro has you by the short hairs?"

Sis was looking at his feet.

"It's alright, Sis. Give it some time. Let me be the heavy."

Sis looked up again, a flicker of hope smoldering beneath his confusion.

"Send in the next guy."

"HE'S FUCKING CRAZY, right?" Pedro said.

Sis looked at Pedro. Then he smiled.

"I kinda like the guy."

THEN CAME EDDY.

"I'm from San Antonio. I shoulda been a medic, then I coulda done Phase Two at home, but I don't mind explosives, and I tell you the truth, I hate putting' my hands in body parts... medics, man, they like feelin' guts. Don't like blood and guts, so I'm an engineer. My buddy, Hector? Baby Doc? He did San Antonio, but you know where he's from?" *Dickhead.* "Tecumseh, Michigan. What kinda Mexican comes from Tecumseh, Michigan? I love my *hermano*, but I don't get people who wanna study urine under a microscope and stick a thermometer up your ass. What was your MOS, Top?"

Top heard this one, and smiled.

"I was a medic."

Ay, ay, ay, ay
Canta y no llores

123

Porque cantando se alegran
Cielito lindo, los corazones

He knew those lyrics! He was back again. This was almost over.

THE LAST INTERVIEW was with the junior medic. Top knew by now that he was a "mackerel snapper" named Hector Fermin, a Staff Sergeant from Michigan. Baby Doc entered and shook hands before he removed his helmet and grounded his weapon.

"Master Sergeant," he said. He seemed quiet, almost submissive. Short, sturdy, good looking kid. Like Dale back in the day, before he started to get "stockier" around the waist.

"A.D," Top said. "Or Top. My real name is Abner Dale, but people tend to laugh when I say that." Top gave a bit of a laugh. "See what I mean?" He found himself wanting to cheer this melancholy kid up.

Baby Doc smiled dutifully, grounded his gear neatly alongside the table where he had propped his rifle and took a seat.

Before Top could ask him to talk about himself, he volunteered.

"Master Sergeant, I don't think I belong here."

For the first time today, someone at least had his attention.

"Why are you saying you think you shouldn't be here? Here... on the team? Here in Afghanistan?" *I don't know what the fuck I'm doing here either.*

"Both, I think. Maybe not even the Army. I don't wanna cause trouble, but I'm havin' issues with a lot of stuff I see here." *Join the club!*

Hector was the only member of the team who was clean shaven. Having very little facial hair, he had decided, apparently, not to look immature and unkempt all at the same time. He was small, like Dale, and wiry as only a twenty-four-year-old can be, reminding Dale of a soccer player. Dale had noticed long ago that the best grunts weren't put together like weightlifters, but like soccer players. Or swimmers. Baby Doc had a thick shock of straight black hair with chaotic cowlicks and the blackest eyes Dale had ever seen on a live person. Darker even than Farah's, whose eyes you had to study to differentiate the pupils from the iris.

"Stuff?"

"Stuff I think is illegal, stuff against my religion."

"Are you Catholic?"

Doc nodded.

"If you're looking at conscientious objection," began Dale, "I've worked with a coupla guys on CO's. I gotta tell ya, it's granted on religious grounds, and the Catholic Church doesn't have what they call 'a consistent position of pacifism'."

"Not that. Maybe that, but I mean stuff that's going on here in the FOB. Stuff the contractors are doing. Our guys are kind of doing it, too."

Dale thought for a long moment, then sighed.

"Hold on," he said, reaching for his pen.

Nanji

HIGH AT A CURVE on a mountain road, at a paved turnout, three militia men were lit by a tea fire. Bundled against the night chill, headscarves down around their necks, Kalashnikovs slung over their shoulders, they alternately gazed into the little fire and up at the lights of Kabul glittering far down behind them like a constellation splashed onto the stygian dark of the great valley.

Cheveaux-de-frise obstacles made of angle iron and painted international orange were lined up to force the nonexistent traffic off the main lanes and through the checkpoint on the turnout which was bounded by a surprisingly modern three-beam guardrail. Nightjars kroo-krooed here and there along the slope as they hunted moths. An owl caroled mournfully from above the checkpoint punctuating the steady chirrup of crickets. The men hunkered close to the column of smoke to ward off mosquitoes. The fire drew insects, and the insects drew bats that flashed in and out of the firelight, coming so close that the men could hear the huff of their wings. The men hardly looked up when, at least ten kilometers across the black valley, a sudden spray of light erupted—tracers—followed a few seconds later by the distant staccato of auto-

127

matic weapons fire that sounded like someone thumbing a pack of cards. No one remembered a time when gunfire was not part of the background noise, like the birds and the bugs.

The men heard a truck in the distance approaching from the high side of the checkpoint—away from Kabul—and peered into the darkness. One guard stayed by the little fire while the other two ambled to the middle of the paved apron. The truck grew gradually louder until the beams of the headlights glared and swept along the road cut, the light growing brighter, the engine's growl amplified. Then the yellow headlights hove into view, high-beams flashing twice by way of a signal as the truck slowed down and pulled onto the apron. It was a dingy-brown flat-faced Mitsubishi with a canvas-covered bed.

The militiamen stood aside. The brakes squealed as the truck slowed to a stop. The driver killed the lights and dismounted. He was dressed like a militiaman, in a gray *shalwar kamiz*, his head covered with a rose-colored *kufi* visible now only in flickering firelight. He wore a pistol belt with an American Colt 45 in a holster. Another man jumped down from the covered bed, Kalashnikov in hand. The men greeted one another with handshakes and air-kisses across each cheek. The driver produced a pack of cigarettes and passed them out to all but one, who refused. He lit them up, just as they all heard a second truck.

Grinding up the slope from the Kabul side of the highway, the American MRAP armored truck trundled around the turn in a glaring blast of halogen headlights that made the men squint and turn their faces toward the valley. The MRAP pulled in nose-to-nose with the Mitsubishi. Someone inside set the brake with a ratchet noise and cut the engine. The sudden silence was followed by a sudden darkness as the lights winked off, leaving everyone utterly night-blind.

The militiamen heard a door open, a boot hit the step, then the ground. Eyes strained to adjust to the darkness. A tall sturdy figure blotted out the stars. It was Virden, the American contractor. He had an HK416 assault rifle slung over his massive right shoulder: a big man with big muscles. The militiamen knew him well. This was an inside game. The American contractor was positioned to prevent any interference from ISAF authorities in their very lucrative little enterprise. The other door opened. Virden's confederate, a security contractor, another white man named Shedd, nicknamed "Peanut" for his oddly shaped head, joined the group, carrying a CAR-15.

A few words were exchanged using bastardizations from three languages, then Virden and Peanut were introduced to the Afghan driver of the Mitsubishi. He led them to the back of the truck, opened the flap and shouted "*Ayez piyadeh!*" Bumps and scrapes from inside. The tailgate gave a rusty squeak as he lowered it. Three disheveled and terrified teenage girls climbed down, gathering their dirty dresses around themselves as they dismounted. Peanut shined a flashlight in their faces, lighting up tear-streaked dust and red eyes.

"Nice," Peanut pronounced. "Nice young cooz." He and the Afghan driver herded them to the MRAP, which he and Virden had dubbed the "Batmobile." Then Virden handed money to the driver and the chief at the checkpoint.

IT WAS CALLED the Chinese Restaurant by the Americans who knew about it, even though the Chinese characters on the sign across the sign across the façade read "Import-Export." In downtown Kabul, one block off the Kolula Pustha

Road, Nanji's place was quiet during the day when surrounding shops bustled, appearing for all the world as a dull, quiet office. Nanji had a high steel security gate over the entrance to a semi-subterranean garage where up to six visiting vehicles could back in and park unobtrusively, manned with a perennial rotating guard armed with a rusty Kalashnikov. In 2005 there had been a crackdown on the brothels because foolish men had advertised them with signs such as "Paradise" and "Men's Room." The NGO staffers and the diplomats reveled inside and out as if they were touring Bangkok, outraging political Islamists. But Nanji had escaped notice. He had adopted a strategy of discretely catering to a vetted clientele interested in very young women—girls, really.

During the day this street bustled with hawkers, noisy traffic jams stank of diesel, men carried food on their heads. It was crisscrossed by hijab-clad women and fashionable young men wearing western clothes and gaudy watches.

Now, at 2:50 a.m., it was very quiet, a lone moth-besieged security light illuminating the black steel grille across the front door. The three upstairs windows were likewise caged, with pale green curtains concealing interior plywood window panels that provided around-the-clock separation between the outside world and what went on inside. The downstairs window was closed up with a dull green shutter. There were no streetlights nearby and the security lamp shined a lonesome pool of creamy light over the entrance. At this dreaming hour the air itself held as still as a hunted animal.

The quiet was shattered by the racket of an approaching large vehicle. The Batmobile glared down the length of the street like a klieg light. They pulled in front of the Chinese Restaurant and parked, engine running.

Virden dismounted from the passenger side and strode into the cone of light. He pounded on the steel cage door, and shouted "Nanji! It's me! Open up!" The door cracked open, letting escape a slender wedge of light. Peanut left the driver's door open and trotted to the back of the truck, opening the rear hatch. A small slight man in silk pajamas came out of the building to unlock the steel cage door.

"Kata sha!" shouted Peanut at the women, who hesitated.

"They're not Pashtun," Virden told him. "They dunno whatcha said."

"The fuck are they?"

"Iranian."

"Cool," Peanut chuckled.

Peanut motioned the girls down. They clambered off the back of the Batmobile, stiff from being packed into the cramped vehicle, big-eyed and sour-smelling with fear. Peanut pushed them past Virden and Nanji through the door and into the building.

NANJI'S OFFICE WAS two steps in, through the door on the left, just before the stairs that launched from the entrance. His office door was a stainless steel Grainger security door with a keypad. Nanji left the door hanging open behind him. Virden went in behind him while Peanut herded the three girls up the stairs, through the green wooden door at the top and into the "lounge"—a bunch of throw pillows on an Afghan rug around three massive circular Japanese tea tables. The girls were deposited in their new homes—cubicles around the upstairs perimeter furnished with tick mattresses covered by floor mats to sleep on and "work" and two light blankets apiece.

Virden admired his own arms in Nanji's office mirror while Nanji pushed the outside door closed. Virden had sleeve tats down both arms... nice guns for forty-five. Virden liked wearing just his chest rig and t-shirt, even in the chilly night, showing off his arms like a prairie chicken puffing out in a dominance display. Nanji stumbled in, still only half-awake from his interrupted sleep, his thinning hair matted from the pillow. People said he looked like a young Deng Xiaoping; but right now he didn't look all that young, with baggy eyes and a sleep-slackned face. Over his silk pajamas he wore a short-sleeved silver pullover with white florets and silver embroidery on the sleeve hems and the collar. Nanji flipped on the main lights, drowning out the night light on the wall. The office walls were painted mauve with saffron trim and expensive crown moulding. On the walls hung a Qiu Jing painting of a red flamingo, a Hua Tunan falcon in ink, and a circular mirror—before which Virden had been preening—framed in feather-pattern brass, hung next to the door that led to Nanji's bedroom. Nanji has nice shit, Virden thought, detaching his gaze from his own arms in the mirror and looking around the room, but it's still put together in a pimp's style. The floors deodar cedar, covered with a Karuqal rug—pale salmon and blue predominating in eight-pointed star fractals. The Hangzhou Ximu wall safe was concealed behind a Zhou Chunya print of two dogs whose lolling tongues picked up the mauve motif. Elaborately carved Indian rosewood office desk, surface curved into a great "J", with matching rosewood round-backed armchair; and yet more blond rosewood for the stocked minibar. On another wall, a cotton hanging, pale pink on the border fading to gold in the middle, of black silhouette figures copulating, the man standing, the woman wrapped around him with her arms and legs.

Hey, thought Virden, it's a whorehouse. Something with sex is appropriate. Virden recognized none of the décor for what it was, but he knew money when he saw it. His family back in Ohio would be blown away if they knew he was doing business now with a Chinese pimp in Kabul. Life was exotic, and he was armed, and free!

"Euro okay?" Nanji asked, reaching into his safe. "Don' have enough dollah."

"Euros are fine," said Virden.

MINUTES LATER, VIRDEN pushed up so he could accelerate his pelvic thrusts. He was about to cum. The girl gasped for air as she was relieved of his weight, sobbing and turning her face to the side. Virden had just broken her in. They were inside one of the cubes the girls were given to "work" and sleep. Hers was furnished only with a mattress, a flimsy end table, a pitcher and a washbasin, all lighted with a single dim orange bulb. Virden knew that in time, once she accepted her situation, she would begin to add her own little touches—postcards that caught her fancy, maybe a radio. Virden growled as he felt his orgasm wash over him, pushing up inside her as she winced in pain. Afterward, he could hear Peanut in another cubicle, breaking in one of the other girls, his grunting harmonizing with her whimpering. Virden pulled out, not looking at the sobbing girl, reached for the little towel that was provided with the pitcher and basin, and wiped a ring of slippery blood off his deflating dick.

Peanut's girl screamed at first, but after he was inside her, she seemed to almost disappear, her teary eyes going kind of vacant. He could hear Virden's girl in the next cubicle, whimpering in little gasps like a broken record... breath, breath, breath, gasp, breath, breath, breath, gasp... Breaking them in was part of their payment. Peanut heard Virden cum and took that as his cue to go for it and cum too. He pulled out at the last moment so he could get up on his knees and pump ejaculate onto her face and belly. That always turned him on in the porn clips. She flinched out of her trance when semen hit her in the eye and suddenly crab-scuttled back into the darkest corner of the cubicle. A few minutes later the two men headed back to Camp Virtue.

Hideous dream

Kenan Theater
University of North Carolina at Chapel Hill
July 1, 2010

THE KID WAS good, his baritone voice brimming with gravitas. The program listed him as Adam Baier. As Brutus, his face was visible over a cloaked shoulder as he addressed a dagger laying in his right hand as if it were a book. A bluish spotlight isolated him on the stage.

"Between the acting of a dreadful thing," he told the dagger, "and the first motion, all the interim is like a phantasma or a hideous dream." At that the young thespian raised his gaze to an imaginary point on the stage far in front of him. "The genius and the mortal instruments are then in council," he continued, "and the state of man, like to a little kingdom, suffers then the nature of an insurrection."

Lucius materialized from stage left, to tell Brutus that Cassius and his co-conspirators had arrived. Deangela stole a look at her dad. Dale, half-smiling, was captivated by the play. He was dressed in an ivory linen suit with a periwinkle shirt, silver cuff links, accented with matching bow tie and a pocket hanky—Carolina blue in honor of her school, accenting his blue-green eyes, with white polka dots. He was shaved clean with his thinning salt-and-pepper hair trimmed short.

They attracted plenty of furtive glances when they came into the lobby before the play. A very odd couple they were, he the fortyish, sturdy, short man (Dale was five feet eight inches when barefoot), dressed to the nines, and she, the copper-skinned biracial teen in her funky butch thrift store threads—old gray pleated men's slacks, a yellow, short-sleeved Polo shirt, her purple Crocs—and with that explosive, untamed head of hair. Both of them secretly enjoyed the way they made people scratch their heads trying to figure out their relationship; and Deangela was delightedly surprised when her dad showed up so nattily dressed.

This night at the theater was their last "date" before he would leave again, this time for eight to nine months, he said, after which he was going to file his retirement papers. He had fought the deployment, but his new qualification in Farsi caught the attention of the bean counters at the Pentagon, and they matched him up with an open slot in Afghanistan to run a detachment in 6th Special Forces. He fought the assignment all the way to Washington, D.C., lobbying for a teaching job at the Special Warfare Center, so that he could be close to Deangela and Farah in North Carolina. He was eligible to start collecting his pension in May 2012, and that's exactly what he intended to do. His language was not Pashto, he argued; but the branch representative told him that hardly anyone on any of the teams spoke Pashto anyway—they had all been trained in Arabic, Urdu, and Farsi. For that matter, the team that wanted him was Spanish-speaking, "as you are," the branch rep emphasized. The detachment was just getting their Afghanistan rotation. Combat is training is combat is training. Game over, Rover: he was going to Afghanistan.

The play was Deangela's idea. Dale drove up from Fayetteville that afternoon, and didn't have to report in for deployment processing until the 3rd. He could crash on the couch at her apartment tonight. She had cleared it with Sam. Dale had studied English literature before he met Deangela's mom in 1990, and was a Shakespeare fanatic. He had taught her some of the plays—King Lear and Macbeth were his favorites—when she was ten. When the two of them loitered in the lobby with the remainder of the post-performance audience, they raised their voices to hear each other over the buzz.

"So what were you grinning at when Brutus was talking to his knife?"

"The language. That language. That's exactly how you feel when you've decided to do something with scary consequences. 'Like a phantasma or hideous dream.'" A shadow passed over his face.

Deangela, looking away and not noticing, chimed in, "'The genius and the mortal instruments,' the reason and the flesh..."

"'Like to a little kingdom'," he merged back into the moment. "The microcosm and macrocosm..."

"The great chain of being..."

"You remember that?"

"Late medieval scholastic philosophy, Daddy. Two years ago."

"So it all comes together. You know that feeling they describe, when the die is cast... Well, maybe you don't."

"I get it, Daddy. The anxiety remains even after the decision is made. It's 'the nature of an insurrection,' a rebellion, in action and in the heart... it's the simultaneous dread and thrill one feels with the decision to engage in a transgressive act."

People around them had begun to eavesdrop while pretending they took no notice.

DEANGELA AND HER father strolled from Kenan Theater down Franklin Street back to the apartment past the darkened bookstores and boutiques. The apartment's lights burned brightly upstairs. Sam was home. Deangela dug a ring of keys out of her pocket and used one to open the outside door to the ground-floor hallway. They mounted the worn wooden stairs, Dale noticing that the banister was loose. Deangela worked the key into the apartment lock. Sam was coming out of the kitchen when they entered.

"Sam, this is my dad; Daddy, Sam."

Sam was drying her hands on a dish towel. She draped it over the oven handle and strode over to offer her hand to A.D.

"Pleased to meet you, Sam. I've heard a lot about you. People just call me A.D."

"A.D., a pleasure." She had a firm handshake, still damp.

"You wanna have a glass of wine with us?" asked Deangela.

"Not tonight, sweetie. Heading out as we speak. Filthy Birds are playin' the Cradle tonight. Law student decomp in progress." The clock on the wall said 11:10. "Deangela didn't tell me her pop was so swank. You're very elegant."

"Special occasion, you know. Shakespeare with my daughter."

"Keep the women off 'im, De," Sam said to Deangela. Dale blushed a little, making Deangela and Sam grin.

Sam had her hair twisted onto the crown of her head, secured with a red scrunchie. She wore a loose, sleeveless calico dress and her Brogues. She lifted a colorful Guatemalan bag over her shoulder and opened the door.

"I'll leave you two to hang out. I'll try not to wake you when I come in, A.D."

"No sweat," said A.D. "You won't bother me."

THEY OPTED FOR orange juice instead of wine and were splitting a big bag of pistachios that made a mounting heap of shells in the middle of the table.

"So," Deangela said, pushing broken shells around the table while chewing. "Why didn't you go to grad school?" She felt anxious now. This topic was always a tense one. Dale didn't like to discuss the past, at least not the personal details. But he was leaving for a year. And his recent, sudden, seemingly random cognitive departures were beginning to alarm her. A hazy sense of discomfort had grown in her about his orders for Afghanistan.

Dale took a deep breath, sighed, looked at the ceiling, the cupboards, the floor... and her. He took a sip of orange juice.

"*You* were born." Her face fell a little, and he added, "That's not to say it was your fault. I was into your mom. We were inseparable, and we were crazy-pleased when she got pregnant. But we had gone into debt some, and no one in the U.S. would recognize her Belizean nursing credentials. So we needed to send her all the way through nursing school again. That was the plan. I went to the recruiting office and found out that they would put me in the army at the grade of E-4 because of my degree. Full medical coverage, housing allowance, subsistence allowance, extra money if I jumped out of planes. A degree in English plus a dollar and a half will get you a cup of coffee, so it looked like a good deal."

"I ask Mama what split you up... or whatever it is you two are doing... Maintaining separate domiciles? She never tells me. You've never told me. Was it the Army?"

Mogadishu, Somalia
October 4, 1993

SPECIALIST FOUR ABNER Dale didn't know how a thirty-minute, stick-and-move raid was now in its third hour, turning into a complete catastrophic fiasco. When they got there, an old Special Forces medic from Regiment who had done the Grenada mission was complaining that this reliance on direct helicopter insertions was going to get them into trouble, and he turned out to be right.

This was supposed to be a simple snatch, with Delta boys in the middle, Rangers on the strong points, in broad daylight. But RPGs were exploding all over the place, and when the first birds went in the rotor wash threw up so much dust that the follow-on birds had to take another orbit. Some of them, it was unclear how many, then missed their planned insertion points. Then, when they received incoming rocket-propelled grenades, the chopper pilots started to dodge. Dale saw one Ranger on an adjacent bird peel off the fast-rope and burn in from more than fifty feet up when the bird jinked to dodge a rocket. Dale had hit the ground off his fast-rope and chased after his team leader, running between a two-story concrete house and a ten-foot concrete security wall. Small arms fire sprayed at them before they reached cover, and Sergeant Franks, his team leader, pulled in with a limp. He had been shot in the toe. There was a good deal of blood oozing from the ripped toe of his left boot and turning to a mud-clot with the dust.

"Fuck, fuck, fuck..." Franks kept repeating. Staff Sergeant Winfro, the squad leader, somewhere else, who the hell knew where in the confusion, was squawking on Franks' radio, asking for a position. Dale kneeled and pointed his A2 across the street, as did PFC Jacolette, his teammate.

"The fuck should I know!" shouted Franks, then keyed his mike and replied to Winfro, "Stand by, over." A burst of incoming chewed up the street right in front of them, and all of them drew back into the gap between the wall and the building. Dale dropped into the prone, shouldered his weapon left-handed, and inched back around the corner of the wall to see where the fire had come from. Jaconette was big-eyed and spacey—in the first stages of combat catatonia. Franks pressed himself to the wall and dug the laminated objective-sketch out of his cargo pocket to check his position, trying not to think about the blood and pain in his shattered toe. Another burst ripped past, and Dale caught the muzzle flash from less than a hundred meters out coming from what looked like a utility shed or a pump house. He aimed at the structure, and let go with ten or so rapid-fire single shots. Two figures appeared, then disappeared as they withdrew, and he chased them with four more rounds. His muzzle blast kicked up dust immediately in front of him, making it impossible for him to see whether he had hit anything.

Franks got back on the radio, the laminated sketch laying on the ground by his feet, A2 in his right hand, his left on the radio that was taped to his chest harness. "Foxtrot Three, this is Papa One, over."

"Papa One, go ahead," came the staticky reply. Another burst, from further away by the sound, ricocheted down the street, followed by a crashing boom as an RPG exploded no more than fifty feet off to their left. Now their ears were ringing.

"Fox Three, we are one block west of our planned insertion point, and we are taking heavy automatic weapons fire, over."

AN HOUR LATER they had almost managed to link up with the rest of the squad. They were moving from street to street, toward what they understood to be a downed chopper, when they saw the other team of Rangers leapfrogging the same direction. From downstairs in a two-story building someone let loose on the approaching team with two machine guns, forcing it into an alley, whereupon it returned fire with M-16s and apparently a SAW. The SAW went through at least a hundred rounds, a lot of them ripping past Franks' team and forcing *it* to take cover. If they fired at the Somalis who were firing at the other Rangers, then they would fire on those Rangers just as the other group had just fired on them. This was a fratricidal geometry, and they needed to move away—fast.

They could tell that Franks's foot was hurting badly. His limp was getting worse and he was going gray-faced. The bloody hole in his boot was full of filth.

"We gotta get one street over," Franks told Dale and Jaconette. Jaconette still looked a little shocked, but Dale did force him to fire back once, just to snap him out of his panic-daze, so at least he was still responding to orders. Franks looked like he was about to puke. He pointed to their rear, where there was another concrete wall, maybe eight feet high. "You guys hoist me over first. Dale, you get boosted by Jaconette, then snatch him over when you're on top."

Dale and Jaconette both nodded.

When Franks dropped to the ground on the other side of the wall, they heard him cry out because when his injured foot hit the ground. Jaconette bent a knee for Dale to step on. When Dale was astraddle the wall he reached down and offered a hand to Jaconette. Dale strained backward against Jaconette's weight until Jaconette had both of his arms on top of the wall. Dale dropped down on the other side by Franks and within seconds Jaconette dropped down too. They were in some kind of courtyard, with a big house—or what used to be one before this place turned into Thunderdome. The courtyard was between them and the street, adjacent to a concrete house that had neither windows nor doors—just gaping, empty apertures. Then they saw three "technicals"—the converted Toyota battle trucks used by Somali militias—drive past on the street beyond the house, and they all hit the dirt.

"Fuck me!" Franks went on. Then they saw the women, two of them. They appeared, almost like magic, in one of the empty doorways and stared at them wordlessly. The team stared back. Dale jumped when shots went off right next to him—bam bam bam bam bam bam. The two women wilted in the doorway, one twitching, the other still. Dale saw the heat plume floating over Franks' barrel.

"The fuck was that for?" Dale demanded.

"They're spotters," shouted Franks. "Don't you fuckin' question me, motherfucker! They are fucking FOs. Move up and check the bodies." Frank was off the rails with pain and fear, pinging, trigger-happy. Jaconette was standing now, wide-eyed again. Dale went forward and stopped short of entering the house. One woman, with an olive skirt, a green-and-white shirt and a head covering, was missing half her face. The other, who wore some tie-dyed thing from head to toe, had blood on her belly and chest, her right leg bent unnaturally and bleeding around the exposed femur. She was breathing, just barely, but her eyes were already fixed. Then he saw the baby. It was wrapped in a filthy gray blanket, propped in a corner on the dusty floor in the empty room, and had what looked like snot all over its face. The baby was too skinny for a baby, and it didn't even whimper. It just stared blankly back at Dale.

Farmers and fellatio

Intercontinental Hotel
Kabul, Afghanistan
July 10, 2010

ATTACKS IN YEARS PAST forced the Intercontinental to dig up the exterior vegetation for improved visibility, to install security booths and traffic spikes and to set up an electronic security gate for the underground parking garage. The hills above the hotel were dotted with security positions manned by president Hamid Karzai's new army, so that reporters, contractors and nongovernmental organization representatives could sleep, drink and sunbathe without having to brave small arms and rocket fire. The hotel itself, from the outside, was Stalinist in architecture: boxy, functional and soulless. Inside, the décor was a clumsy replica of Vegas in the fifties—shiny, smooth, replete with harsh, high-contrast straight lines and right angles.

The lounge was a twilight zone. Even at high noon on a sunny summer day, like now, the brown parquet floor, the nearly black stained wooden walls, the red table settings and the black Afghani macrame hanging from the dark ceiling beams maximized an impression of darkness, inevitably drawing the eye to one of two places: the bright light over the ranks of shiny liquor bottles behind the bar—arrayed on black shelves, of course—and a translucent view of the lobby and the exit to the swimming pool presented through the two layers of glass wall of the adjacent gift shop. That's where the reporters' eyes drifted when they weren't addressing each other across the table, to which they had to pull up a fifth chair so that they could all sit together.

Gaston Villeneuve of *Nouvel Observateur*, a Frenchman fluent in English, leaned back and studied the brown beer bottle in his hand—a cold, sweating Sim-Sim. He hadn't changed his starched blue short-sleeved button-down shirt since the press briefing and the sweat stains around the armpits had dried into matching wrinkle zones. The lager's label depicted a pretty, palmed oasis at sunrise undergirded by both Arabic and Cyrillic scripts. Rosemarie Kirby sat next to him with a glass of white wine, trying to ignore his dirty shirt and dusty socks—*he wore socks with sandals for Christ's sake*—her body turned away from him. Next to her sat Connie Mason, two empty glasses of Cabernet before her and another one almost finished. For a skinny woman, she always seemed to be able to hold her liquor. She had her legs crossed sideways to the table and twisted her shoulders to hover around her glass. Next to Connie Mason sat George Yowell, his gelled hair still appearing solid enough to ricochet a bullet, nursing a bottle of Amstel and looking a little cornered because a quarrel had erupted between Rosemarie and Gaston, who sniped at each other any time they came within range. Between George and Gaston sat Phillip Ferguson, an heir to some vague political fortune in Connecticut who aspired to being a stringer for TIME but mostly wrote filler for a variety of content mills and blogs. Phillip was thirty but his bantam frame, moonlike face and thick hawser of brown hair made him look eighteen. He came to Afghanistan on his own dime, as he had to other conflict zones over the last five years, trying to break into the business of journalism. No one doubted his initiative or even his bravery in facing certain risks, but his writing was atrocious: unfocused and sentimental. Phillip was pounding a second Budweiser to wash down *mantus—Afghani meat dumplings* he had bought from a cooking stall near Shahr-e Naw Park. He wasn't invited to the press briefings, so he trawled Kabul each day looking for fresh human interest stories with his constant companion—a sketchy, armed local, his bodyguard and interpreter—who demanded for his services the outrageous sum of fifty dollars a day.

"Major Carroll is just doing his job, Gaston," said Rosemarie. "You treat him like he's Colonel fucking Kurtz or something. You know what a PAO is."

"It stands for prevaricating his ass off," retorted Gaston. "Even the title, 'public affairs officer,' is cunning, don't you think? 'Public affairs'! It's an anesthetic. Oblique language to divert the *actual* public from his *actual* role of gaining the public's acquiescence to this adventure. Read Uwe Poerksen on plastic words."

"His *actual* role," said Rosemarie, "is public affairs."

"My God, can you really be that obtuse. His fucking job is to speak his lines, like a talking doll or an answering machine. His lines are an official story."

George couldn't resist intervening.

"Why does it have to be an official 'story,' why isn't it the official 'account.' You're editorializing when you frame it that way."

"'Framing!' You just can't help yourselves. You've all mastered this bridge-to-power speech until it's mastered you. No wonder your writing is shit. So you believe that combat vignette about the kid killing the 'terrorists'?" He made finger-quotes with one hand, gripping his bottle with the other. The locals are saying he destroyed a truck full of watermelons and killed a farmer."

"Gaston," Rosemarie was back in the game, peeved at George's attempt to rescue her. "The alleged fact that the truck had watermelons in it does not preclude that it was also carrying a rocket-propelled grenade."

"*I* am editorializing?" Gaston laughed, setting down his beer and fishing for his cigarettes in his breast pocket. At George: "You see, she is now his lawyer." Turning to Rosemarie, who was draining her glass: "Are you his attorney, Rosemarie? Or are you so blinded by your infatuation with him... oh," mocking her, "Good Morning, Will, will you please fill my cup with your knowledge and then allow me to fellate you?"

Connie gave a sardonic grin as Phillip and George both blurted out their objections at Villeneuve's casual sexism.

Rosemarie held her hands up, "That's okay, boys. I'm a big girl. Perhaps Gaston is jealous that anyone would fellate the good Major—he *is* a hotty—because Gaston hasn't been fellated himself ever since he stopped bathing." Connie snorted. Gaston smiled at the tablecloth as he tamped down the tobacco in his Gitane on it.

"Are you sure your Republican network would approve of your hormonal affinities for an African-derived officer?" He put the Gitane between his lips and pulled a Zippo out of his pocket to light it. Exhaling a stream of smoke away from the table in a show of mock-courtesy, he said, "You still haven't responded to my point about the dead farmer."

"She did..." Phillip started to say, but Rosemarie facepalmed him again.

"I said that these *farmers* may have had RPGs. They may moonlight as Taliban. You can't *not* know that."

"Precisely my point. Neither can you. So your default is to reproduce anything your boy-toy says from his perfidious podium. If it were a white American farmer, would the facts behind the 'official account' become the subject of further inquiries, or would you lockstep to your laptops and do your duty as the hotty's stenographer? Have you even..."

"I'd fuck him," Connie volunteered, now on her fourth glass of Cabernet. "I'd fuck his brains out. Doesn't mean I wouldn't call him on it if I caught him in a lie."

Phillip and George squirmed a bit in their seats. Gaston lifted one of Connie's empties across the table and tipped a half-inch of ash into it.

"To catch him in a lie," Gaston explained, "you have to abandon your default presumption that everything that passes his oh-so-sumptuous lips is absolute truth. It would mean actually leaving the fucking hotel to talk with some Afghanis who are not on the NATO payroll."

"Right," George interjected. "With our phalanxes of bodyguards and armored vehicles to prevent us becoming the Sunday evening news as a Taliban propaganda video. Do you know how much publicity they could get by kidnapping me?"

"Phillip doesn't mind touring the town," rebutted Gaston, almost making Phillip smile. "He has one bodyguard-interpreter." Turning to Phillip, "Where is your estimable English-speaking thug today, anyway?"

"Rastin is in the parking garage with the Suburban."

"Oh the life of flunkies!" Gaston turned to Rosemarie again, enveloping her in a smog of lager and tobacco. *I can even smell his socks*, she thought. "I put it to you again, dear

Rosemarie. Does this dead farmer merit any inquiries? Do you think he had a mother? A wife? Children?"

"I'm not listening to this commie bullshit anymore," said George abruptly, scratching his chair back over the parquet, tossing back the last of his Amstel and stalking through the door that led to the lobby, his gelled helmet of a hairdo still rated to withstand a shaped charge.

Connie waved at the bartender and said, "I love our little back-chats." Gaston snickered, pulled on his cigarette one last time and dropped the butt into a wineglass with a hiss.

"One of your *chevaliers* has quit the field, Rosemarie," quipped Gaston.

"What was that about communists? Have the Russians landed?" Connie laughed.

"Your paper is pretty left-wing, Gaston," said Phillip, emboldened by his second Budweiser and Gaston's acknowledgment of his physical courage.

"Phillip, my friend," replied Gaston, "in the United States, everything west of Richard Nixon is considered left-wing. You probably don't remember him, but he was a paranoid Cold War lunatic..."

"I know who Nixon was!"

Rosemarie fluffed the back of her hairdo with her hand, and said, "Gaston," finally dropping the posh French pronunciation now and pronouncing it as "Gas-Tun," "your paper is consistently anti-American, and we, as Americans, while we are not the stenographers of power you claim we are, happen to believe that our armed forces ought to be allowed a certain presumption of honesty, at least until evidence to the contrary is discovered. It's a thankless job they didn't ask for."

"First of all, you will find not a word against Americans *per se* in my employers' paper but criticisms of the policies and actions of their government. This does not make us anti-American. You are an American religionist... no, no wait a minute, you had your say, let me have mine. You worship *America* as a kind of golden calf that demands human sacrifice. Some of us do the same for *Mère France*. Secondly, the idea that the armed forces of the United States are doing anything thankless is ludicrous... wait, hold on... it is ludicrous, because your culture worships them. It worships the soldier. You refer to them reflexively as heroes—as 'our' heroes—even though the vast majority of them have done nothing that could be construed as heroic, meaning simultaneously daring and altruistic. English is my third language, Rosemarie, so I attend more closely to meanings and I am more sensitive to the ways in which a term such as 'hero' is pauperized as propaganda."

"Gaston..."

"You just told me that 'we'—meaning, I assume, the press—'owe' anyone who wears an American uniform the presumption of honesty. The basis for this claim is that their jobs are thankless... a *non sequitur*, by the way, so even if their jobs were thankless, which can be proven to be untrue... they are thanked profusely all the time by people who have no idea what they have or haven't done... this is not evidence of their inhering honesty."

"So you want to assume the opposite? That they are all liars?"

"I didn't say that. Major Carroll is not 'them.' Major Carroll's job is one in a thousand, and it is to manage perceptions. But as journalists, if we are to be worthy of the title, we ought to be worldly enough to recognize the ways in which power works. You and I both know, I hope, that official statements, in this age of simulation, are not designed to reflect realities, but to have a desired effect on the audience. Public Affairs Officers can only be interpreted through a hermeneutic of suspicion."

"Gaston, that's just a cynical pose, part of your *dramatis persona*. You are the one who wants to have a desired effect on the public."

"It's skepticism, not cynicism, my friend. And yes, we address our work to the anonymous mass, but that's not the point. The point is, what is our relation to power? Are we standing apart from it as critics, or are we colluding?"

"It's not that simple, Gaston," interjected Phillip.

"What is not..." Gaston started to ask, when Connie chimed in.

"You're a self-righteous prick, Gaston. But we love you anyhow. Anyone want to join me at the pool? I'm headed out there to watch tattooed contractors tan." She scooted her chair back, almost tipping it over.

Gaston watched her walk away. He turned to Phillip.

"We should spend more time together."

Frequency and consistency

THE SIDES WERE rolled up on the General Purpose Large tent that served as Detachment 649's billet but the mosquito nets were left down and tucked under the sandbag walls. A steep shaft of midday sunlight fell across the southern end, warming a stack of equipment boxes stacked under a dozen or more boxes of MREs that the men only ate when they couldn't get DFAC food, when the snack bar was closed or when they were patrolling. The rest of the tent was in the shadow. Cots lined the long axis walls, personal gear piled at the ends with a walkway down the center. Parachute cord was laced through the interior to hang damp or sweaty clothes. At the north end a wide-screen television was on, set atop a sandbagged camp table and connected by a hundred-foot power cord to a generator four tents down.

Pedro, looking bored and a little angry, was watching the television play his porn DVD. A woman with a lot of makeup and impossibly high heels was having sex with three men, one with his penis in her mouth as she knelt over another man on his back who thrust into her vagina, and the third man perched behind her with his legs astride the laying man as he thrust into her anus. Gene was lying on his cot, across from Pedro, gazing surreptitiously at the film. Pete was in the corner furthest from the television screen, trying to concentrate against the distraction as he typed on his laptop.

The phony moaning on the porno was temporarily drowned out by the earsplitting roar of a C-5 passing very low overhead on its landing approach. Baby Doc came into the tent and dropped his tactical medical pack on his cot midway along the tent—the medical pack he strapped onto his rucksack for operations. He sat down and began opening snaps and zippers to inventory the contents. Gene had alerted when Baby Doc entered the tent. Baby Doc sighed and pretended not to notice as Gene rocked up into a sitting position to get out of his cot. Gene was a hypochondriac, constantly hounding Baby Doc for exam opinions and medications.

"Got a minute?" said Gene, hovering over him. Baby Doc couldn't even muster the energy to feign surprise.

"Wha's goin' on, Gene? How was guard last night?"

"Is what it is, y'know. Need t' ask you 'bout somethin'."

"Shoot."

Gene sat down next to Doc on the cot. "Last few days," Gene explained, "I been havin' problems... when I shit."

What? fucking no! Doc drew a long, deep breath and suppressed the audibility of his sigh. "Problems how?"

"I don't go but every second or third day, and when I do, I shit these hard balls."

"So you're constipated." *A medic's job is always too much information.*

"I mean, yeah, but tha's not normal f' me, y' know? I'm wonderin'..."

"What?"

"Well, if it might mean I got colon cancer or somethin'."

"It doesn't mean you have colon cancer. You're only, what, twenty-six years old?"

"Yeah, but people in my family, they catch cancer quite a bit."

"You don't *catch* cancer, Gene; and a little bout of constipation doesn't mean cancer. If you're so worried about cancer, you need to give up your Marlboros."

"That's bullshit." This always provoked the stupid belligerence of the nicotine addict. "My granddad smoked until he was ninety before he died. But I'm tellin' ya, Doc, this is really not normal for me. My shit, it looks like rabbit turds, only bigger."

"Rabbit turds..."

"Yeah, and I gotta push so hard to get 'em out, I feel like I'll pass out."

"That's orthostatic hypotension. You bear down too hard, and you're dehydrated. Your blood pressure drops. Like when you stand up too fast and get really dizzy. That happen a lot?"

"Well, sometimes."

"You're not drinkin' enough water. That'll constipate you, too."

"This is more than dehydration," Gene pleaded. "I been dehydrated before and still shit turds that look like tubes, y'know, and they float." *No! Please!* "These hard turds I squeeze out every second or third day, they sink like rocks." There were few things Baby Doc cherished less than mental images of the frequency and consistency of the detachment members' excretions.

"Okay, so you're not drinkin' enough water, and you eat too much meat and dairy. Tried eatin' more fruits and vegetables?"

"I was hoping you might give me some stool softeners."

"Stool softeners..."

"Uh huh."

In the meantime, Pedro switched his DVD to something called *Gaggers*, where men shoved their dicks down women's throats, causing the apparently very young women to gag while the men called them "sweet little cum-sluts." Pedro the romantic...

"Stool softeners..." Baby Doc repeated mechanically. He opened yet another zipper on his tac-sack and pulled out a strip of plastic packets. He opened one of the packets and pulled out a little bottle of bisacodyl. He shook four into his palm and handed them to Gene. He didn't have any stool softeners, but he knew that these four stimulant laxatives would put Gene in the port-a-potty within hours... with a vengeance, and maybe deter his selective hypochondria.

"You're off today, right?"

"Yeah."

"Take two of these now, and two more in four hours. Stay close to the latrine. Don't take antacids or eat dairy products for four hours. And for constipation, drink more water, eat more vegetables and less meat and dairy."

Gene looked at him.

"You don't have colon cancer, but if you want, I can send you to the post MD and see if he'll recommend a colonoscopy."

"What's that?"

"They give you laxatives for two days, then knock you out, inflate your lower intestine like a balloon and run a fiber optic camera up your ass to look through your intestines."

"Lemme think about it," said Gene, rising to return to his surreptitious porn viewing. "Thanks, Doc."

ODA 649 Operations Hooch

THE OPS HOOCH didn't look like a hooch at all but like a modular classroom the size of a double-wide trailer (which is what it was). Inside, folding tables were lined up, with folding chairs behind them. A podium stood before three over-and-under sliding white dry-erase boards. Stashed in the corner there were two tripods with butcher's block tablets hanging from them. Featureless, shuttered windowless and with bright fluorescent overhead lights, pale beige walls and a scuff-resistant synthetic floor, the place could be a hospital room or the set for a Beckett drama. Dale and Captain Bob had pulled two chairs out of line to face each other. Dale sat with his legs crossed, knee over knee, his hands folded in his lap, the captain with his feet wide, elbows on his knees, leaning in expectantly. The air conditioner was shut down and the door left open, letting in the greasy tang of gasoline generators and the aroma of fried onions from the DFAS.

"So how were the interviews?" asked Bob.

"Interesting," Dale lied.

"Their edge is off," the captain said. "Bernie, their last team sergeant, was pretty uninspiring. Colonel Thomas wasn't keen on using them for anything except local reconnaissance."

"Recon is important," Dale replied. "Is it targeted, or just RIFs?" (Reconnaissance in force involved searching whole areas without having any particular targets in mind, once called "search and destroy.")

157

"RIFs. The Colonel doesn't trust his junior officers, and he really didn't trust Bernie. Bernie was kinda fat, and Thomas hates fat guys. It's an image thing. But Bernie just wasn't operationally sound either, and everyone, including the boys, knew it."

Dale didn't reply to that. He just looked vacantly into Captain Bob's eyes. Dunny straightened up a bit, crossed his legs to mirror his team sergeant, rubbed his hands together, shifted his eyes, and smirked.

"What do you know," Dale finally asked, "about a place called the Chinese Restaurant?" The smirk froze on Dunny's lips and died in his eyes. He held Dale's gaze for a moment longer, then looked down at his watch. He even turned the watch up and squinted at it before it felt silly, dropping his hands back to his lap and clearing his throat.

Displacement, thought Dale.

"Chinese Restaurant?" he laughed vacantly. "You sick of the chow hall already, Top?"

"I hear rumors," said Dale. "Rumors you can buy sex with young girls at a place called the Chinese Restaurant."

Dunny laughed again, returning Dale's gaze now, almost as an act of will. *Was he being solicited?* "Hey, Top, you know the Army. If you haven't heard a rumor by nine in the morning, you're required to start one. Haha!"

Dale returned a mirthless smile, said nothing?

"One of the boys tell you that?" asked Dunny.

"Just local scuttlebutt. Heard about it around the FOB."

"I'm married," said Dunny, regretting it the moment he had blurted it out. Dale said nothing. "The Chinese Restaurant you say they call it?" Dale nodded, his blue-green eyes still fixed on Bob's face. "Interesting. I dunno..." said Dunny, eyes flicking down and left.

Dale broke off his gaze and smiled broadly. "Hey, if you don't know, you don't know. Just curious. I need to go stow some gear, if it's alright, Sir." He rose. Dunny was silent as Dale headed to the door.

Dale turned in the portal.

"You know anything about a contractor named Virden?" he asked.

"Yeah, Virden," Dunny's eyes dropped again for a millisecond. "Yeah, ex-Group guy, communicator. Little on the macho side, but he seems alright. Some of the guys know him. The commo guys. I think Fall hangs with him sometimes. One of the boys tell you something about Virden?" Dunny cleared his throat.

"Fall seems to think Virden will get him on contract with XYY Security."

"Yeah." A skittish chuckle. "Yeah, it's hard to keep guys in nowadays. XYY, all these other contract security outfits, they pay. Boy, do they pay!" Again the twitchy little laugh. "You thinking of that after retirement?"

Top had already headed for the door as he replied, "I'd rather hit my testicles with a framing hammer... No, just curious. Trying to get the lay of the land, Sir."

SOME SUNSETS PROMISE, some threaten. Dale couldn't make out which this was. He was Top now; he would have to get used to this new name. He had been hanging out between the DFAC and the Base Exchange along Main Street, hoping to see what birds might make an appearance at dusk. The sun had slid down beyond a rail of clouds leaving a bright pink incision along the horizon.

Two Specialists, black women, went into the PX, one chunky, one not, both looking small in their helmets, both carrying antiquated M-16A1s. Neither spoke, but they stayed close, maintaining a little moving security perimeter of their own. Up along Main Street in the direction of the communications building, bristling with a Klee print of various antennae, a gaggle of smokers shared their vice and enough humor to evoke a few ripples of disheartened laughter. One of the port-a-potty doors thumped like a tub as a contractor left it and headed toward the construction and maintenance crew's billet.

Dale's eyes followed the contractor. Then he caught some movement behind the row of portable toilets, a gesticulation, hands talking. Peering more closely, sidling over a bit to see who it was, he spotted them a good thirty meters away. *Captain Bob and that Fall guy (yuckety-yuck).* The conversation appeared agitated, anxious with a blade of antagonism showing. But it wasn't Dunny who was on the offensive. Fall seemed to be threatening the captain, or at least dominating the exchange. *Dunny, Captain Bob, meek as a fucking mouse in front of a subordinate.* Shaking his head, Dale drew back into the shadows. These were the birds that interested him now.

Dunny held up his hands in a kind of surrender. Thrusting his face toward the ground like a busted teenager, he was talking a mile a minute. Then the power dynamic changed, and Fall dropped his face and raised his hands. Both stood for a moment, then talked it out. Dunny gave Fall a reassuring squeeze on the shoulder. Dunny said something more, and Fall nodded his assent. Dunny looked around him, then slipped off behind the phalanx of portable toilets toward the detachment's tent. *Like a married couple having a fight. This team is compromised, a leaderless clique.*

Dale held his position in the shadows. It was getting dark fast. Afghanistan was like that: a brief dusk, then pitch-black. The instantaneous darkness was accentuated by the fact that the base didn't burn external lights, and it was the policy to black out windows and apertures: no reason to give mortar men reference points by which to adjust fire. The garrison flag over the Base Headquarters suddenly snapped in a gust, sounding almost like a shot, and Dale started just a bit.

Fall pushed a chunk of Copenhagen into his lower lip, stepped into Main Street, spat once and headed in the opposite direction from Dunny. Dale watched Fall step through the door of the communications building.

The two women came out of the PX, heading directly toward Dale. When one noticed him standing there against a bunker, concealed in the night shadow, she squeaked and clutched at her partner.

"Sorry, sorry," he said, then the other one squealed. "Sorry, no problem, okay, no problem. Sorry, didn't mean to scare..."

The thin one made a hooting noise, then said, "You scared the shit outa me." He looked at her name tag. Specialist Clark.

"Oh my God!" was all her companion could very emphatically say. Specialist Jones.

"Really sorry," he said again, trying to sound as non-threatening as possible. Then they saw him well enough to make out the six-stripe chevrons on his collar.

"Master Sergeant," the thin one said. "We jus' din' see you." They were both busy trying to adjust their comportment to his rank.

"'It's okay," he told them again. "My fault. Really."

Both of them were holding one hand over their hearts like they were about to say the Pledge of Allegiance. Top saw the door opening again on the communications building down the street.

"I apologize, ladies. My bad. Y'all go on now, and get back to your billets."

"Yes, Master Sergeant," they said in unison, and whispered as they walked away.

Fall was coming back out, and a big guy behind him. Must be Virden, Dale figured. Tall, maybe six-three. Gym body... well, what some guys call a jail body, the upper musculature more overdeveloped than the legs. T-shirt to show all his ink. Shaved dome. Ample blond-brown goatee. Then the door swung shut, and the two figures disappeared from the interior light. Dale couldn't distinguish what they were saying, but he could differentiate Fall's breathless midwestern tenor from Virden's gravel baritone.

"Who?" Virden demanded, so loud that Dale could hear it almost a hundred meters away.

Then bits from Fall: "...don' know... Dunny... Dale..." Dale heard that. Word was spreading. Since his interview with Baby Doc, The Chinese Restaurant was starting to look like a blood trail.

WILL CARROLL WAS mounted up on Anita Barber doggy-style. They were in his office with the lights out. She was on the floor with her uniform trousers around her ankles, his hands shoved up into her uniform blouse holding on to her breasts while he thrust into her from behind. Only his trousers were down, just enough to do what he needed so pressingly to do, the front tails of his uniform blouse draping each of her buttocks like a surgical field.

"Yes," she released a whispered moan. "Yes, push it up in me, right there. Fuck up in me." He thrust again, echoing her urgent susurrations, "In you, mama. Right up in you, mama."

A THIN HAZE of cloud masked the stars, the moon still hidden. Dale stood outside the team tent whittling at a stick. The sounds of the night were drowned out by an incoming cargo plane doing a blackout landing, bearing another deposit of the steady inflow of goods from afar required to keep Camp Virtue watered, fed, busy, patched up and entertained.

Eagle scouts

BABY DOC COULDN'T sleep. Since he had told Dale about the Chinese Restaurant the guys had gone all cagey. The Captain had been staring at him, too. He knew Dunny whored with the boys. So did Bobby when he was the Team Sergeant. It was like a team event, at least for most of them. Sis didn't go, nor himself. They were the designated billet guards, because they weren't interested in fucking twelve-year-old girls. But the SF rule applied: what goes on downrange, stays downrange, especially when it's your command element. He wouldn't have said anything had he not heard Pedro and Woof talking about how young they were. Pedro laughed and nodded when Woof said, "She was so fuckin' small, man, I had a flashback to sixth grade."

Now that Baby Doc had told Top, that shot couldn't be unfired.

Baby Doc and Sis would be the rats because Top had said something to someone, Dunny most likely, and the atmosphere within the detachment crackled with suspicion. Baby Doc had many months left here, they all did, and a breakdown of trust like that... well, it can affect operations. He just didn't know what the right thing to do was. So now he lay

165

there on his cot, in the dark-dark, denned in with a little wall of gear stacked against his cot like a kid's blanket fort, listening to the wind make the tent pop.

That's when he heard whispers too faint to discern their meaning and sensed motion. Someone else was awake in the tent... more than one... two... Baby Doc held very still, not trying to rise because the cots squeaked, the nylon fabric stretched over them like drum skins. He heard a cot fame creak near the murmuring, then another. Someone was getting up, sneaking. The boys didn't whisper and slink around to use the latrine. They were leaving... they were up to something!

"GENE, YOU READY, dude?" Pedro whispered, clasping Gene's arm. Pedro was moving very slowly. His cot made noise when he rose.

"Yeah," Gene whispered back. "Lemme get my weapon." He was farting like a bull and surrounded by the stink, a poison cloud that followed him. He carefully lifted the M-4 that leaned on his cot, ensuring that it didn't bump into anything. "Couldn't sleep anyhow. Been to shit like ten times. Doc gimme some pills."

"Too much fuckin' information, man. I'll go first."

Gene heard him pussy-foot away in the darkness, watched his vague silhouette fill the door flap, then vanish. They had staged their chest rigs outside earlier, behind the generator, where its noise would cover them suiting up. Gene waited a beat, then followed Pedro.

FORD WAS ON the gate—a contractor. He used to be some kind of cop—a bent one, apparently, because Leonard Ford loved not just the big money he made as a rent-a-cop in Afghanistan, but also Afghani hashish. Contractors weren't being drug tested on Camp Virtue, and Lenny smoked it like the world was coming to an end. The grunts picked it up for him at the Chinese Restaurant to bribe him, along with the other gate guards.

Lenny loved Afghani hash, but Lenny was scared shitless of Afghanistan. He was a known and unapologetic "fobbit"— someone who never set foot off base (hence FOB). He was content to stay inside the razor wire 24/7 as long as he could ride that cannabinoid train through his own psychic Shangri-La for $342.47 a day plus meals and a bunk.

At night he could sit on the gate with his night vision goggles, beef jerky, salt and vinegar potato chips, Payday candy bars and Red Bulls, gawking at the stars, the lights of Kabul far down the valley and the foxes hunting field mice. During his nine months here he had gained more than twenty-five pounds. Fuck it, with that sweet blond *charas* (hashish) you didn't sweat the small stuff. It made him a little paranoid about rockets and mortars, which he imagined vividly when he was baked, but the three feet of reinforced concrete of the bunkered gate made him feel better.

He had just smoked a chunk using a Red Bull can for a pipe when he heard a Hummer approaching from inside the compound. Had to be Correa and Pollard from 649. They were resupplying him tonight, so the guard log would never reflect their departure. Lenny figured they were headed to the Chinese Restaurant, to get some of that not-even-barely-legal pussy. He couldn't figure it out; he always liked older women himself. These Group boys were always kind of profane and edgy, way further outside the lines than he was... But he thought, *Hey, it takes all kinds, no? Special operations means "spe-*

cial" men, and they ain't all gonna be Eagle Scouts.

The approaching Hummer was blacked out with just the infrareds on. Lenny opened the hatch on the back of the tower and clutched the handrail to descend the concrete steps. The rider's side door cracked. An arm extended. Lenny took his package, stepped back up inside the bunker, closed the door, and pushed the button that rolled the gate back and dropped the security spikes.

GENE DROVE WHILE Pedro navigated.

"Fuck, we're doin' this, man," Gene spat the words for emphasis. He was pumping himself up like a boxer.

"Yo dude, we goin' to a rare place, doin' what other men only fantasize about. You down?"

"Oh, I am *so* fuckin' down!" He inhaled a deep breath through his nose, banged the steering wheel with the heel of his hand. Then another cramp hit him in the belly, and he had to stop to shit on the ground. Pedro wanted to ride him for it, but he kept his mouth shut until they were moving again and near the village.

"Catch that left comin' up, look like a big goat trail." Gene downshifted, peered through his goggles, caught the track and slowly turned. The infra-reds, seen through the goggles, shined forward in phosphorus-green monochromatic beams that cut into the gloom. Pedro raised his goggles to check his GPS again. "You should hit a high spot for a minute, then it falls kinda steep for around a half-klick, long left, longer right, then up again."

"Got it." The track conformed exactly to Pedro's outline.

When they headed sharply back uphill, Pedro lifted his goggles again to check the GPS. Suddenly, the IR headlights showed they were surrounded by low ground. "Stop here," Pedro directed.

Gene killed the IR, killed the engine. "Let's jus' sit here a few minutes, make sure it's quiet. We go down there, lose a Hummer, we go to prison."

Pedro relaxed into the idea. *Sure, let's wait a bit.*

"Why does a dog lick its dick, dude?"

"Because he can," Gene answered. They muted their tension-breaking laughter in the interest of stealth.

The house was sun-brick and mud, green in night vision, its details alive like they could see the atoms vibrating. The roof timbers extended over the front like a great comb. One door led to what they assumed was a root cellar, the other to the main house with a tall, shuttered front window. Bedded down around the house were sleeping goats, with their heads turned and down like they were hiding their eyes, their forelegs curled beneath them. Insects and amphibians chirped in the low ground.

STORAI WAS DREAMING about muddy water when the village dogs started barking. Then one of the rams rose, stamped and snorted a challenge, the rest beginning to bleat. Storai sat up in the bed next to her mother, Bakhtawara. Storai pushed the blanket off her feet and pulled down her nightdress.

"*Mor,*" she whispered, shaking her mother alongside her. Her mother came awake just in time to hear gravel crunch outside the house, and sat bolt upright. The door snapped open with an explosive crack, and they both screamed in the darkness. Then the bright white light hit them in the eyes. Men were inside the house, speaking in ugly voices, saying things they didn't understand.

"Shut the fuck up, bitch!"

They were still screaming when one of the lights dropped the beam to the floor and hands took hold of Storai, one clamped over her mouth, suffocating her as her sinuses filled with terrified tears. Then the other light came close, and the other man—they sounded like Americans—hit Bakhtawara with something, and Bakhtawara went silent. Storai wriggled and kicked, but the man had strong hands, then he lay on top of her to restrain her.

"Quit fuckin' fightin' me, litta bitch!"

"Ol' bitch is out, man. I butt stroked that mufucker."

Storai was trying to scream, trying to get free, but the man was on top of her hard, mashing her face with his hand. He was wearing hard things that hurt her, hard things around his belly and chest. He rattled when he moved. His breath stank and she smelled blood.

"Take 'er outa here."

"Wherema gonna take 'er?"

"Then jus' do the bitch, man. Do 'er wi' ya knife, dude."

"I'll get fuckin' blood all over me, man."

"Stop fuckin' fightin' me, litta bit..." He grunted with the effort of holding her down. "Choke the mothafucka out, then, dude. I got biness w' litta bit... You jus' hol' still, litta hajji girl."

Storai felt herself drifting away.

BABY DOC LAY awake. Someone else had risen after Pedro and Gene. He knew who they were. Those two were probably headed to Nanji's place. But this last one? No one went any- where alone. He listened to the generators humming. A vehicle here and there moving people on and off guard points. Gusts of wind. Crickets. Geckos. Then, out in the depth of the night, a couple of miles away at least, he heard a shot. Then another.

Perfect legs

Camp Virtue, Afghanistan
July 12, 2010
0110 – Delta

LENNY DIDN'T KNOW this guy, but he knew taking a Hummer out at night alone was a pretty bad idea. It was a 649 Hummer, so he had something to do with that crew.

"Coupla my guys just left a while ago," said the passenger when Lenny came out to greet him. "I'm new on the team, and I'm s'pose t' meet 'em at the Chinese Restaurant."

"I'm Lenny," Lenny said, offering a hand. "Whatcher name?"

"Dale," he said, smelling a cloud of hash and beef jerky as he shook the hand.

"Yeah, you shouldn't go by y'self, man. Hajj is *out* there."

"I'm a big boy, Lenny. I just need directions to the Chinese Restaurant so I can meet the boys."

Chinese Restaurant
Kabul, Afghanistan
July 12, 2010
0220 – Delta

NANJI LOOKED OUT at a dark figure who was pounding on the security door. Dressed in street clothes and carrying an assault rifle, the figure claimed he was a friend of Virden's, saying so first in English, then Farsi. He said he had money—dollars.

0240 - Delta

NANJI CALLED HER Lolita but her name was Peyvand Tehrani. She was fourteen, she told Dale. They sat whispering in her cubicle. Dale had paid Nanji double—thirty dollars—for barging in like he did. When she took Dale inside, she was surprised to hear him speak Farsi to her. She was even more surprised when he explained that he didn't want to have sex—just talk, very quietly.

His name was *Avner*, he told her. What he was doing was very dangerous, and she had to keep their conversation a secret. He asked a lot of questions. He would be back, he told her, but he wasn't sure when. He told her to be patient, and that made her cry. He held her hand for a little while, then left.

Camp Virtue Dining Facility
July 12, 2010
0700 - Delta

THE ENTIRE DETACHMENT was at breakfast. Dunny and Dale were at a separate table on the other side of the chow hall. Pedro and Gene were uncharacteristically quiet. They looked a little hunted as they picked at their food, even as they exchanged red-eyed smirks. Baby Doc was silent too. He stared into his plate like he was searching for something in his eggs, flipping glances up to look at Gene and Pedro. Something happened last night, he knew, and he was uneasy not knowing what it was. *Something bad*, he thought.

Sis was going on about the oil spill in the Gulf of Mexico and how it would destroy his uncle, a Galveston shrimper. Opie commiserated with Sis, expressing concern about how difficult it seemed to cap the spill. Eddy remarked that BP should be "burned," that some guys ought to go to prison for this.

"We *are* those guys," interjected Opie. "This shit is about oil."

"What shit?" demanded Fall.

"This, Afghanistan, the war."

"Bullshit!" Fall reacted. "Ain' no oil in Afghanistan, man."

Opie came back at him. "Bases, dude. It's about bases. Putting the Air Force fast movers within range of the oil. Ever hear of China, man? Right there on your map, buddy. Right there, 300 miles from where you and me eatin' grits and eggs, Hondo."

"China don't have that much oil, man. We ain't after China. Close China, and we'd have to close every store in the States. Fuck, we'd have to close the PX!"

"Not the point, dude," Opie ready again with the rebuttal. "The man wants to make sure his hand is on the tap. No, Afghanistan don't have oil..."

"Just heroin!" Bobby said, grinning, trolling for humor to divert the conversation into a safer direction. "Hey, you know why women got pussies?"

"So men will talk to 'em," answered Eddy. "You need new material, Bobby."

Fall picked up the thread. "You know why women got legs?" The boys were smiling now. The political talk had passed. "So they don't leave slug tracks on the floor." Everyone laughed except Baby Doc, but Gene's and Pedro's smiles resembled rictus. They were wearing masks and Baby Doc watched them.

Opie decided to do his part to allay the tension of political speculation. "You know why you can't trust women?" Pause. "You can't trust anything that bleeds five days a month and don't die."

Baby Doc spoke before he realized he was about to: "That's your mothers and your wives, your sisters and your daughters you're talkin' about."

The tension was back with an embarrassed silence. Opie broke it.

"Lighten up, Baby Doc. We're jus' fuckin' around. Hey, my wife has perfect legs." Another pause. "Feet on one end, pussy on the other." The table cracked up, almost stridently. Baby Doc's face grew dark. Pedro and Gene still wore smiles that didn't reach their bloodshot eyes.

The black female Staff Sergeant entered the DFAC. She picked up a tray and headed to the chow line.

Bobby used his little girl voice: "Chlamydia." The table hooted.

DUNNY AND DALE huddled together across a table. Red-eyed from his late-night foray, Dale held onto a mug of black coffee with two hands. Dunny couldn't seem to shut up, as if talking could make that big question mark about the Chinese Restaurant go away.

"...not tryin' to turn 'em into Delta operators, but they could use some tips and training on straight DA operations..." Dale listened distractedly, then drifted back to thinking about Green Ramp at Fort Bragg.

Green Ramp

Fort Bragg Army Airfield, North Carolina

July 3, 2010

THE PARKING LOT was on a rise above the airfield, the asphalt baking in the sun which glared off the glass of the cars. The sparse, dry grass around it was riddled with fire ant hills. The wind blew as hot as a blast furnace. Deangela helped her father unload his luggage and gear from her beater car. Daddy was in his utility uniform, shaved clean, hair trimmed. Sweat trickled out of the short hair at the temples and was beginning to wet his collar. She hadn't seen him like that for years —shorn and in uniform. Deangela wore baggy shorts that exposed the unshaven calves of her muscular legs, flip-flops and a t-shirt with a picture of Nietzsche that read: *"Nietzsche is dead." —God.* Philosophy humor.

"I hate this," she said, blinking tears back.

"Me, too." He wiped his eyes. "Can I ask you a question? About philosophy?"

Deangela mocked suspicion, saying, "O-kaaay..."

"How do you know when something is evil?"

"That might be a theological question," she said, the hot wind tossing her hair. He flashed on Farah's Catholic family in Belize, their little parish, the warm damp air flowing through the doors and the open, louvered windows, birds in the rafters and dogs roaming in and out. Farah's whole extended family—mother, three brothers, aunts, cousins—trooping in each Sunday at 8 AM, like a well-scrubbed occupying army. "Something called *mysterium iniquitatis*, the mystery of evil. Why are you asking, Daddy? What's going on? You worry me, you know."

The bags were on the ground. He enfolded her in his arms. "Sorry, hon. I know I've been off lately. This is the last deployment. I'm just gonna run a team. No idea what we have to do. I'll retire after this one."

"Last time?" She looked up at his face.

"Cross my heart. Clearing papers in a year."

"Can you hide out? Lay low?"

That made him laugh. "I wish. Tried. Failed."

"What you do..." She was sobbing again, her head pressed into his chest.

"Last one, I promise." Tears made bands on his cheeks.

She looked up. "My mother loves you, you know. We both do."

Sharing cigarettes

Intercontinental Hotel – Kabul
July 12, 2010
0843 – Delta

GASTON AND EMAL, his interpreter, met young Juma on the street across from the parking garage exit. Juma was very agitated. Gaston could hear the terms "*amrekayan*" and "*topakuna*"—Americans, guns. Emal asked a question in Pashto. Juma's agitation increased, and Emal held two hands up signaling Juma to wait. Emal turned to Gaston.

"In Zama, he say *amrekayan* soldiers, umm, rape a girl and keel her. Mother, too."

Gaston offered Juma a cigarette, which Juma took, then gave one to Emal and took one for himself. He pulled out a plastic lighter and lit Juma's, Emal's, then his. Juma had tears of rage welling up in his eyes.

"Do you believe him?" asked Gaston.

"I believe. He want you go see."

"See? You mean go with him?"

"Yes. Go with him. He show you girl, show you mother."

"The bodies? The dead bodies? There are still there?"

"Bodies there now. You go see."

"Where is Zama?"

"Not far."

"Why me?"

"He trust not *amrekayan*."

179

DRIVING TO THE LITTLE house in a Kia Borrego, Emal expertly dodged the potholes while Gaston focused on the crowd of men who huddled in expectation in front of them. As soon as the Borrego pulled up and Emal put on the handbrake, Juma and Gaston dismounted. Emal had to catch up to them, and when he did a surprisingly small old man, even by Afghani standards, stood before them, front and center. He was *numberdar*, the headman, dressed in a traditional *khet partug*—a tattered blue North Face pullover jacket—even in the already rising heat, and a white *kufi* tilted on his head. He had a magnificently thick gray beard and a Kalashnikov slung across his back, muzzle facing skyward. Two of the other men carried Kalashnikovs too. Emal had left his Uzi in the car and asked Juma to go back and look after it. Emal introduced the headman to Gaston as "Rahnamah Lal," and reminded Gaston to call the headman *Rahnamah*, or Leader.

Rahnamah Lal turned and the gaggle of men parted. Lal led Gaston and Emal to the house, which was perched on the edge of a small drop-off with a sandstone foundation and three steps leading to the door. The door hung precariously on a single twisted hinge and had obviously been broken into. Gaston smelled congealed blood and heard the flies before he even mounted the steps. He heard a woman weeping in a small brick house about thirty meters away, and he noticed soft crying and sniffling from among the armed men who stood behind him.

Gaston's shadow broke a column of sunlight that fell into the room from the door. Dust particles surged through the slanting rays. His gaze was drawn toward two white bundles stacked against one another next to the far wall. The girl and her mother lay wrapped in sheets. The blood had seeped through them and turned them brown. Then he saw the bloody streaks across the floor: someone had dragged the two bodies before they were wrapped. Gaston started when Elam touched his shoulder, indicating he should go on in, and took a step forward, breathing deeply now to wrestle down his nausea. Both Emal and the headman came in behind him.

The headman was talking softly to Emal. Emal grunted from time to time, indicating either assent or acknowledgement.

"You can look," Emal told Gaston. "Give respect, but look. Mother name Bakhtawara. Husband dead long time. Daughter name Storai. Daughter have blood..." Emal indicated his crotch, "...here. Virgin. Rape."

Gaston handed out cigarettes—to the headman, who had tears in his eyes, to Emal, and to himself. He lit their cigarettes, then moved deliberately and slowly toward the corpses, being careful not to step on the blood that was streaked across the stone floor. A rolled-up rug stood like a column against a wall. There were also broken pots, he now noticed, an upturned chair and blood splattered on the walls as well as the floor. In the small sleeping quarters lay two tick mattresses, one of them drenched in dark, dried blood.

He squatted next to the longer bundle, holding his cigarette away from it in his left hand, and folded back the sheet with his right. The flies rose briefly with the interruption, then dove back down to feast. This must be Bakhtawara, he realized. There was a huge gash across the left side of her forehead. He suspected that her skull was fractured because her head was vaguely distorted. Blood had pooled and dried in her left eye, drawing the flies in droves; the right eye was barely open and cast downward. He saw bruises around her throat: she had been strangled, and not gently. He opened the sheet further, looking for other signs of violence, but there didn't appear to be any. Gently, he folded the sheet back over Bakhtawara.

He pulled deeply on his cigarette, then stood up and set it on a little wooden table with the ember hanging off the edge. He almost passed out from rising too quickly and placed one hand on the cob wall to steady himself. Then he knelt down next to Bakhtawara, reaching over her to open Storai's shroud. Storai's eyes were wide open and dulled with dust and lifelessness. He could see that she had been a pretty girl, now bloodlessly gray. She was naked. There were two gunshot entry wounds right between her tiny breasts, and they were stippled with powder burns: she had been shot at point blank range. He couldn't bring himself to open the shroud to examine her lower body. He was willing to take their word about the broken hymen. He folded the sheet back over her, swallowed hard against the bile rising in his throat, then stood, more slowly this time, and retrieved his burning cigarette. That was when he saw it.

It glistened in a ray of sunlight that made it past Emal and Lal and hit the seam between the stone floor and the cob wall. A coin of some kind had rolled into the crack, with just its edge showing.

Gaston stuck the cigarette between his lips and knelt to tease the coin out. It wouldn't budge. Finally, he took a little pen knife out of his trousers, pried it out, grasped it gingerly, like it might bite, and inspected both sides of it.

"Emal."

"Yes, Sah."

"Would you get my camera equipment please, and ask these gentlemen to stay outside for a few minutes?" Emal pivoted. "And ask if anyone has found the used ammunition."

The colonel

United States Military Academy at West Point, New York
October 16, 1987

"MISTER THOMAS!" CALLED Captain March.

"Here, Sir," Cadet Thomas answered, then double-timed it over to Sergeant First Class Fogg to have his rucksack weighed. He rolled the rucksack off his shoulder and passed it to Fogg, who looped one of the shoulder straps over the hook on a hanging scale.

"Forty-seven," Fogg called out, and Captain March wrote it down in his notebook. Sergeant Fogg removed the rucksack and handed it back to Cadet Thomas.

Thomas was a "cow," a junior, and this year the flamboyant head of the Department of Military Instruction, Colonel Richard "Cowboy" Collins, had implemented a program that would select a dozen of the cows to attend the Army Ranger School in Fort Benning during their summer break. Sergeant Fogg had just been assigned to the Department as an enlisted Military Science instructor after a stint as a platoon sergeant with 2nd Ranger Battalion. Colonel Collins was all things macho, and all things Ranger, and he saw the assignment of Fogg as an opportunity to once again start sending hard-assed cadets to Ranger School—a practice that had been suspended several years earlier because of high failure rate and one cadet fatality. Fogg had to have an Officer in Charge and

Captain March was chosen to be that OIC because he was also Ranger-qualified and had just finished a tour with the 82nd Airborne Division as a company commander.

Fogg was given a free hand in the development of the course. His notion was that you don't take smart kids and try to make them into soldiers; instead, you identify future soldiers then try to make them into smart kids. He wanted a selection course to identify the students who had the mental toughness to get through the demanding training program, insisting that they could train them in the basics once they were selected for their character.

This was Day One of the selection program, and there were forty-one cadets who showed up. They had been told to appear in field uniform, with web gear and a packed rucksack that weighed at least forty-five pounds before they added any water. They had assembled in front of Thayer Monument on the north end of the parade grounds. Their task for that day was to travel over a marked, manned and circuitous route that headed up Washington Road, then up past Lusk Reservoir, out to Sacred Heart Cemetery via Stony Lonesome Road, and then back—a total of seven miles. Seven very hilly miles, and the catch was that you were to go "as fast as you can." In other words, you were racing forty other candidates for seven miles over steep hills with forty-five pounds of rucksack and another eight pounds or so of web gear, wearing boots. Water was extra but every cadet was required to have at least four quarts of water—another eight pounds that diminished as it was consumed. Cadet Boyd Thomas had no idea whether he would make the cut, but he had a ruthlessly demanding father in his head to spur him through the course, just as he had been spurred through West Point thus far.

Camp Virtue, Afghanistan
July 12, 2010

COLONEL THOMAS SAT at his desk, thinking back on that day. He came in first out of the whole group of forty-two. The gymnastics and the boxing had paid off. Colonel "Cowboy" Collins was there to meet him at the finish, with his trademark cigar clenched between his teeth. Collins never forgot him either; thereafter, every time he saw Thomas, he gave him one of those hail-fellow-well-met handshakes, making the other cadets envious. When at the end of the next summer Thomas, along with eleven of twelve other cadets, successfully completed Ranger School, they all became legends: seniors with the coveted black and gold Ranger tab on their shoulders. "Cowboy" Collins took personal credit for their extremely high graduation rate and SFC Fogg, who had prepared both the selection and training prior to Ranger School, could do no wrong at West Point from then on. Those were the glory days!

When Boyd Thomas graduated the Academy in late May 1989 his academic standing wasn't close enough to the top of the class to be choosen for the 82nd Airborne Division—paratroops, the choice assignment for Infantry officers—and he had to settle for the 24th Mechanized Infantry Division—tank jockeys—in Fort Stewart, Georgia, outside the GI town of Hinesville. By the time Thomas finished the Infantry Basic Officer Course and Airborne School it was December 1989. A month after he signed in to the 24th the 1st Ranger Battalion from nearby Savannah and all his classmates who had joined the 82nd Airborne Division invaded Panama. Many of them received the coveted gold star on their parachutist wings for the combat jump onto Torrijos Airfield. Thomas seethed at having missed this operation, and at the thought that any of his classmates officially became combat veterans before he could.

He was ecstatic when the following year preparations began for the invasion of Iraq, which involved months of intensive mechanized infantry training exercises at the National Training Center outside of Barstow, California. In July, his unit was deployed to Kuwait, where they were staged to jump off on the invasion in August. They did, but the Iraqis gave very little resistance, and aside from a couple of pot shots along the way his platoon of mechanized infantry saw no real combat during the entire operation. When they were redeployed in February 1991, he had his combat infantryman's badge, but his only award—aside from a campaign ribbon—was a Meritorious Service Medal, exactly like the ones that every other platoon leader received provided he hadn't gone AWOL or been caught drinking on the job. His CIB would hold some weight when he went elsewhere—it showed that he had been deployed to a combat zone—but in the platoon no one spoke of them because everyone knew they meant only that they had deployed, not that they had ever been tested in battle.

He was promoted to First Lieutenant in March that year, whereupon he requested—and was granted—reassignment to 1st Ranger Battalion, up the road at Hunter Army Airfield in Savannah. When he arrived, the CIB he wore over his left breast pocket at least hinted that he might have been in combat; and that, along with his still excellent physical condition, stood him in good stead with the young Rangers, who typically distrusted Lieutenants. He ran a platoon in Charley Company for just over a year and got married to a local student from the Savannah College of Art and Design, April Burrus. Then he was moved over to the Executive Officer slot. By the time he was promoted to Captain in January 1993, 1st Ranger Battalion had done no combat missions anywhere.

He requested reassignment to the 82nd Airborne Division—now that his combat tour and his time with the Rangers had given him some juice—and was able to pick up a Company Command in the 1st Battalion, 325th Infantry. They had been on alert in 1993 to render humanitarian assistance in Rwanda, but that order was rescinded. Several of his classmates were deployed to Somalia that year, but his unit stayed in Fort Bragg. One of his classmates was even involved in the day-long Mogadishu firefight about which a movie would be made; but Boyd Thomas missed that one, too.

In September 1994 they deployed to Haiti. That was originally a combat mission, but last minute diplomacy had transformed the mission into three solid months of guard duty for his troops around a giant baseball factory in Port-au-Prince. For that he received another Meritorious Service Medal.

After the deployment to Haiti, he and April went to see a doctor about why she wasn't getting pregnant. The physician at the clinic determined that he had some kind of antibody in his system that attacked his sperm and made it incapable of binding to eggs. He was relieved, because he wasn't sure if he wanted children anyway.

He applied for the Special Forces Qualification Course and was admitted in February 1995. By June of the following year, after the Q-Course and six months of training in Turkish, he was assigned to 5th Special Forces Group. But when he arrived he wasn't given an A-Detachment—a Special Forces operational team—but a staff job with the 3nd Battalion as an air operations coordination officer, or "S-3 Air." He excelled at this job, though inwardly bitter, and was promoted to Major in May 1999. His chance to run an A-Detachment was now gone and he was laterally promoted to the position of Battalion Executive Officer—nominally the second in command, who was in fact never in command. When the Battalion was deployed to Afghanistan in November 2001, barely two months after the World Trade Center/Pentagon attacks, he was stuck at a forward operating base near Kandahar and never saw combat except for one night when someone lobbed two wild mortar rounds into the perimeter and blew up a portable toilet.

He kept his mouth shut and soldiered on, and in January 2003 he was promoted to Lieutenant Colonel. Unlike many of his peers, who had accumulated substantial combat experience, he did not get a Special Forces Battalion but was assigned to the Special Warfare Command in Fort Bragg—the school's command for Special Forces—where his operations experience and his experience as an Executive Officer were invaluable in making sure that the right vehicles and aircraft got to the right place at the right time to support the students in the Special Forces Qualification Course and the Survival-Evasion-Resistance-Escape School.

In May 2003 his wife April filed for divorce and thirteen days after the divorce was final she married a Puerto Rican Sergeant First Class from 7th Special Forces Group. She was two months pregnant at the time of the wedding.

At that time, between 2003 and March 2005, virtually everyone in every service was involved in real combat operations in Iraq and Afghanistan. Medals were being passed out like Halloween sweets and promotions with them. Reputations were being made. Special Forces was receiving missions one on top of another. And he was stuck at SWC!

Then they assigned him a new First Lieutenant to run one of the motor sections. Her name was Gina Ong. Her family came from Singapore when she was two. The first time she was alone with him, soon after they were formally introduced, she asked him how old he was. Lieutenants never ask Lieutenant Colonels how old they are. But he looked at her smooth Chinese features and her lean, hard body, and instead of putting her in her place, he answered: "I'm thirty-eight." To which she responded: "Men peak at thirty-eight" and went back to work. And with that he found himself a new mission.

Sitting at his desk in Camp Virtue five and a half years later, he couldn't remember what he was feeling then, but he did remember that is was like madness, like demonic possession. The first time she showed up at the Fayetteville Inn, she came in without saying a word, pushed him down on the bed, stripped off her panties, hiked up her skirt, then positioned herself with her knees on each side of his face. She was already wet, and she came within a minute. Later, when they were both naked, she went down on him, then flipped him over and performed analingus while she stroked him with her hand. They climbed through each other like mountains and caves. He couldn't stop remembering that—and physically responding—every time he thought of her, even after everything else that happened.

Four weeks into the affair she told him she was seeing two other people: an Air Force sergeant and a topless dancer. She believed in polyamory, she told him. He boiled over, called her a sex fiend and a round-heeled bitch and told her that she had to stop seeing them. The idea that she was doing with other people what she did with him made him feel used and devalued and made him want to grab her by the throat.

He tried to erase her from his mind, but there she was every day at the motor pool. He started to avoid the Motor Pool, he found himself watching her from afar, seeing who she spoke to, and how. Then the calls started. He didn't want to call her, but he did, again and again. One day, after she stopped answering or responding to his messages, which alternated between begging and threatening, he had left her sixteen messages. That was when she complained to Thomas's commanding officer, Colonel Haywood. They were both consenting, single adults, she said, but Lieutenant Colonel Thomas was beginning to frighten her.

It was all handled quietly. She was reassigned out of Special Warfare Center and over to 18th Airborne Corps. Thomas received orders to report as the new Military Attaché at the U.S. Embassy in Ankara. And there he stayed, for almost five years, liaising with puffed-up Turkish officers, attending Country Team meetings at which he seldom paid any attention and frequenting the legal brothels to avoid any romantic entanglements. To his great surprise in March 2010 he was promoted to full Colonel.

There was a Task Force Commander position open that involved working closely with military contractors in Afghanistan, at a new base near Kabul. And there he was, Commander of Task Force Bird. Less than four months in he began to see how this was going to be his last assignment. He had reached his twenty years of service the year before and was now eligible to retire. The last promotion was a way of quietly encouraging him to do just that. The war was all on the Pakistani border then. Task Force Bird was a do-nothing money magnet for XYY Security, whose main mission was to transport incoming supplies to forward operating bases around Kabul. Their knuckle-dragging contractors accompanied the supply convoys. Thomas's main mission was to ensure the convoys left on time and to manage the base. In addition to just under 400 support troops, they kept one SF Detachment, a rotating platoon of Rangers and a section of Special Ops helicopters as a rapid reaction force that hadn't been needed thus far.

He soon decided that he had nothing to lose. He had pushed his one A-Detachment out again and again to gather local intelligence only to discover that they were shit birds. Their captain was bumping dickheads with the rest of the team at some whorehouse. Their team sergeant was a doofus and a wannabe comedian. Their wild-eyed sniper, with his crazy tics, was a goddamn loon who shot farmers from the camp's observation posts, claiming that they were planting mines—on walking trails that only they used. They had only killed two actual bad guys, and that was when their recon was compromised. It was a dysfunctional team, cliquey, the infighting and the fraternizing having eaten away any discipline they might have originally had. Then he found out about Dale.

His old classmate, Dicky Baker, a newly minted General now over at Joint Special Operations Command, had done him a solid favor. "Got a guy," Dicky told him, "one of my operators." Just finishing a Farsi course out at Defense Language Institute, and I can get him sent to you. You find decent targets, this guy will unfuck your team. Give him the ball, and he'll get it to the end zone."

Well, Dale was here now; and he had taken the team. Already there was one complaint about him from that pretty boy motherfucker, Major Carroll. Dale apparently dropped in for a coffee during one of Carrol's weekly lie-athons with the press, then went off on some tangent about fucking birds. *I like that*, thought Thomas. *Fucking Viking spirit. Carroll is a fucking mulatto tool.*

It was precisely at the moment when Thomas was thinking these thoughts that there was a knock on his door. Later that day, he would come to believe that the god of war had finally intervened.

"Enter," he said. It was his Executive Officer, Lieutenant Colonel Bermudy, a man whose bland features and shapeless face reminded him of an oyster. Bermudy just eased his featureless face past the edge of the door, with an expression—as much as that shellfish-face could express anything—like a kid on Christmas.

"You're receiving a warning order, Sir!" Thomas sat up straight. "High value target!"

THE SECURE COMPARTMENTED Information Facility, or SCIF, was small and well lit, with a high-security door and no windows. Three of the four walls, from corner to corner and floor to ceiling, were lined with shelves holding arrays of communications equipment. The files were kept in three large safes. Captain Palumbo, Thomas's Intelligence Officer, an olive-skinned, chubby man with bushy eyebrows and a shaved head, whose thick eyeglasses magnified his eyes, leaned smugly on one of the safes with his arms crossed while Bermudy and Thomas studied the four-page printout from the in-line network decrypter. Thomas read one page, then the next, passing the one he had just finished to Bermudy. When Bermudy was finished with the fourth and last page, he handed the whole sheaf back to Thomas, who looked at it again. They all stood still like a tableau for what seemed like a long time. Then the low buzz of the communications gear was interrupted by a little noise from Thomas—a squeak followed by a long sigh. Thomas looked up at Bermudy, smiling, then over to Palumbo, and smacked the pages triumphantly against his palm.

Camp Virtue, Afghanistan
July 12, 2010

THE TEAM OPERATIONS hooch was where work happened, such as it was. That morning they left the security door open to let in light and air through the bug screen. It was still cool and the air conditioner was off, leaving the room quiet except for the hum of the generator three buildings away. Each specialty—command, intelligence, engineer, weapons, communications and medical—had a field desk. Each had a tan three-drawer file safe. Beige metal folding chairs were scattered throughout the room. The walls were paneled with plywood to conceal the structure, which consisted of welded steel beams, reinforced concrete and sandbags. The room was encircled with overhead shelves on which the team's unused equipment and tools were stored.

Captain Bob was at his desk, clearing off paperwork. Bobby rocked back on a folding chair thumbing through the day's intelligence summaries. Sis was at the radio panel in the corner decrypting communications traffic. Pedro was sitting near Sis doing one-armed dumbbell curls with a forty pound weight and making an annoying snorting sound with each heave which stopped when there was a knock at the door.

Command Sergeant Major Eaves stood outside, trying to see past the morning glare on the bug screen. A short, muscular black man, getting thicker around the middle with age, clean-shaven, with a tight haircut under his MICH helmet.

His battle rattle and weapon were worn as if he were heading to the parade ground—clean, symmetrical, at shoulder arms.

"Six-four-nine," he called through the screen, his voice gravelly.

"Come on in, Sergeant Major," said Captain Bob already headed to the door.

"Mornin', Sir," said Eaves, removing his MICH as he passed through the doorway, reaching inside an olive-drab, cotton-duck shoulder bag slung diagonally across his trunk. Dunny had his hand out, and Eaves shook it, then stuck his hand back in the satchel and headed to Captain Bob's desk. The rest of the boys were standing at some vague semblance of parade rest: upright, feet apart, hands clasped behind the back.

"Sit down, gentlemen," said the Sergeant Major. "You're gonna need the rest." He dropped a sheaf of four pages on Dunny's desk. Dunny circled him to retrieve the papers.

"What's this?"

"Warnin' order, Sir," said Eaves. "Colonel Thomas wants to see you and your Team Sergeant ASAP."

"Five minutes, Sergeant Major. And thank you."

"Roger, Sir," and Eaves turned to leave.

When Eaves was just out of earshot, Bobby spoke.

"What's your name, little girl?... Chlamydia."

"Knock it off, Bobby, and go get Top. He's in the tent. Tell him we have two minutes to be in the Colonel's office."

The headman of Zama

CURTIS FISHER'S TIME was short: ten more days and he would be boarding a plane that would take him to Frankfurt, then the next one to New York. From New York, he connected to Baltimore. That's where Kayla would pick him up and they would drive back to Pikesville. They would pay off the house. He would apply to the Police Department, or the Fire Department, depending on which one was hiring, and they would start trying to have a baby. Two years in this shithole had been lucrative, and Kayla had her LPN now, but the separation has hurt him. His shift was from eight to sixteen-thirty, and it was just after ten now. He was thinking about Kayla, about her big brown eyes and her ample hips, when he saw the dust trail headed toward the main gate.

"Hotel nine, this is main gate, over," he spoke into the radio's mike.

"Gate, this is nine, go, over."

"Nine, gate, we got a vehicle inbound, over."

"Gate, nine, india delta? Over." (ID.)

"Nine, gate, stand by, over."

Curtis picked up the binoculars, aimed them at the vehicle, and rolled the focus ring until the vehicle came into focus. KIA Borrego, looked like three passengers, with a big black on white sign in the windshield that shouted PRESS.

"Hotel nine, this is main gate, over."

"Gate, this is nine, go ahead, over."

"Nine, gate, looks like press, over."

"Gate, nine, roger. Log it. Ring back when you find out what they want, over."

"Nine, gate, wilco, out."

THE SMELL OF DUST returned as the late morning sun drove the last of the dew from the ground. It had smelled like impending rain even under a cyan-blue sky, spotless from horizon to horizon. Major Carroll saw the Borrego parked in the visitors section inside the gate and three figures, two robust and one quite small, standing with the contract guard. Carroll was accompanied by his interpreter, Benham, who was wearing a uniform as well, hatless and looking like a priest or an academic with gentle eyes, a well-trimmed beard and a slightly stooped, strangely shapeless six foot stature.

Gaston and Carroll shook hands, neither of them looking each other in the eye.

"Major, this is Emal Zazai, my interpreter," he gestured to Emal, who offered a tentative hand to Major Carroll, "and this is Rahnamah Lal, the headman of Zama." Carroll made a slight bow to Lal, and Lal reciprocated without offering his hand.

"And this is my interpreter," said Carroll, indicating Benham, "Benham Marwat."

Benham exchanged *Salam-Alaikums* with the two other Pashtuns, accompanied by light handshakes and buses on their cheeks. When he greeted the old man, Benham gave a bow with the handshake and after the kiss placed his hand on his heart. Lal touched his heart in return.

"What can we do for you, Mr. Villenueve?" asked Carroll.

"Is there someplace we can talk?"

Carroll tried not to roll his eyes, unsure whether he succeeded.

THEY HAD PULLED UP five chairs in the press-briefing hooch, now cavernously empty except for the five of them. The podium and chafing trays were gone, the chairs stacked away and the floor open and buffed to a shine that made it feel even bigger. All five sat stiffly in a circle, and Carroll knitted his brows and steepled his hands in front of his face, tapping himself on the chin with his joined index fingers.

"Benham, ask him again what time this happened?"

"*Daa kaar kum whakht wasoo?*" Benham asked Lal.

"*Hagha wakht che spozmey ra khatala,*" said the old man. "When the moon began rising."

Benham turned to Carroll and said, "They have no clocks, but about twelve o'clock. Moonrise."

"Tell him we had no patrols out last night." Carroll kept his eyes on Lal as he spoke to Benham. "Ask him why he thinks they were Americans?"

"*Paroon shpa doi gazma na durloda. Tsa feker kawey, amrekayan wa?*"

Lal became very agitated at the question, and responded directly to Benham.

"*Da larey la kabala,*" he said leaning forward and holding up two fists. "*Khalqo da larey awaz warweida,*" he said, touching one ear now. "*Amrekayee larey wa,*" finger jabbing downward for emphasis. "*Bya topakuna,*" he continued, shouldering an imaginary rifle. "*Dwa fira,*" his voice rose, and he held up a thumb and forefinger. "*Amrekayee topakuna,*" he finished, thrusting his finger toward the ground again. There were tears of anger pooling in his eyes and his head had begun to quiver as if it weren't firmly attached to his neck. He breathed in deeply, then sat back, stroked his beard with a trembling hand, and fixed his eyes on Carroll.

Benham translated: "They heard a truck, an American truck. Then they heard shots, two shots, from American guns. Not Kalashnikovs."

"The Taliban have trucks," argued Carroll. "This may have been Taliban."

Lal understood and stood to his full five feet and glared stones into Carroll's eyes.

"*Taleban larey laree. Dda ba taleban wa.*"

There was a beat of silence before Carroll broke their gaze and turned to Benham. "What did he just say?"

Benham kept his eyes on Lal as he translated to Carroll. "This has nothing to do with Taliban. They were not Taliban..."

"*Doi taleban na wha,*" the old man was shouting now, chopping at the air with both hands. "*Da talebanoo sara heetch arra na larey. Haga wali wayee taleban wa? Ngelei sara pa zore zena shaway dah. Hagey sara zena shaway dah aw weshtal shawey dah. More bandi tak shawey dei. Talebano nada weshtaley. Hagha amrekayan wa!*" He held still for a moment, as the tears broke from their pools and ran down his face. Then he sniffled and wiped at his face, looking around, slowly sitting again as if he were embarrassed by his outburst.

"Why do you keep saying Taliban? This was no Taliban. They were killed. The girl was raped and shot. It was not Taliban. It was Americans."

"Who says Taliban are incapable of rape?" asked Carroll, then rescinded. "Don't translate that. Tell him we'll begin a full investigation."

Gaston spoke.

"Is this true? Is that your intent, or are you patronizing this man?" As he asked, Carroll cast his eyes downward, and Benham threw a furtive and questioning glance toward Gaston. Gaston gave the merest whiff of a nod, and they broke contact as Carroll looked back up.

"Mr. Villeneuve," said Carroll, now completely ignoring the Afghans. "I can assure you we will look into this. I can also assure you of our personnel's accountability." Then as an afterthought: "And if Taliban can chop off people's heads, they can certainly rape."

"It's not the same thing, Major, and you fucking well know it."

"And there are militias, too. These militias are not always disciplined not to rape."

"Well, Major," Villeneuve said as he rose to his feet. "It seems you've already arrived at your conclusions."

Carroll rose. "Sir, one of my NCOs will escort you back to the front gate. I have a meeting that started ten minutes ago." He looked at his watch and turned. When he did, Gaston moved alongside Benham and pressed a card into Benham's hand. Benham did not look at anyone as he followed Major Carroll out.

"WHAT'S GOING ON?" asked Dale. Dunny looked like he was about to piss his pants.

"We've got two minutes to be at Colonel Thomas's office. Let's go, Top."

Thomas's office was less than three hundred meters away, but Captain Bob broke into a dead run the minute they got out the door. *God save me from this shit*, thought Dale, as he reluctantly took up Dunny's eager pace.

They were still panting by the time Dunny knocked on Thomas's door.

Thomas was already circling his desk when they obeyed the command to enter, and they didn't even have time to come to the position of attention before Thomas was pumping their hands, Dunny's first and briefly, then Dale's for what seemed a full minute.

"Bob," he threw at Dunny by way of greeting, "and this is Top Dale. Dicky told me a lot about you. He was my classmate at the Academy." At least half a foot taller than Dale, Thomas squeezed in so close to shake hands that Dale had to tilt his head back to look him in the face. Dale could see the hair in Thomas's nostrils. The Colonel's once blond hair, cut close now, was fading to gray. Thomas was grinning now, unnaturally, because years of maintaining a fierce expression had permanently creased the skin around his bulging blue eyes. His teeth had little gaps between them and made Dale think of alligators. "I can't tell you how glad I am you're here, Top. Fuckin' providence is what it is, a gift from the Big Ranger. Dicky says you're a bad motherfucker, and we got a bad motherfuckin' mission." He released Dale's hand, Dale having said not a word yet. "Sit down, gentlemen," he aimed a flat hand at the two wooden chairs across from his desk, and headed back to his own swivel chair. As he sat he asked Dale how his in-processing had gone.

"Fine, sir. I'm just getting to know the team now."

"Well, get to know 'em fast, Hoss, 'cause you two have a mission, and it's not one of those horseshit RIF's or hajji-trainin' gigs either." Dale kept his face and body very still at the mention of 'hajjis.' "We got a snatch." He let that sink in. Dale shifted in his seat. Dunny looked like a possum in someone's headlights.

When Dale finally spoke, he was tentative, tactful. "Sir, you want 649 to conduct... a snatch?"

"649 *will* conduct a snatch, Master Sergeant," he said, still with the alligator grin, and placed both hands on his desktop. "You're gonna catch me a high-value target and tie a bow on that motherfucker."

"Sir..."

"Sir, hell," he plowed on. "We've got Usman Jahangiri in a village south of Charikar. He's a Sarbani intel chief, and he works between here and Balochistan across the border. He's a big-time sonofabitch and I want you to catch his ass alive. Our source has him at his location for at least three days. I need you there tomorrow night."

Captain Bob came out of his trance and answered, "Sir, 649 is ready." Dale tried not to react, but he discovered his mouth was hanging open before he pulled it together and re-arranged it to an expressionless visage. *These fucking nimrods couldn't snatch a purse.*

"Is this team daddy ready, Captain?" asked Thomas, pointing to Dale. What the fuck is anyone supposed to say to that, Dale wondered.

"Absolutely, Sir," replied Dunny, his eyes popped open to mirror Thomas's manic expression. Dale had been cut out of the conversation. "What assets do we have?"

Dale composed himself but started to hear dyslexic lyrics again. That *Police* song.

A coup d'etat and my mom is lost in space
A gleam of fright fries the holy seed in place
A book astounds but it's a moon band aid air base

I am so old my head needs a brand new face
Chicken's fryin' baby, baby please

"If I have it, it's yours, Captain. Let Dale here choreograph actions on the objective. He's forgotten more than we know about surgical ops. Bring me this fuckin' bad guy. This is a mission that'll make careers, Bob. Pull it off, and both of us will get slow hand jobs from the Generals and the journalists." Dale was looking through Thomas. Dunny was still exchanging the goggle-eye with his boss.

"Don't sit there starin'! Go issue a fuckin' warning order to your boys." Thomas squinted. He heard a noise. Was Dale humming? "Top?"

Dale pulled his focus down to Thomas. "Yes, Sir."

"Get the fuck outa here. Catch me this raghead cocksucker so I can run eight inches up in his guts."

TOP INSTRUCTED Dunny to announce the warning order in an hour. Then he headed to the zero range (he had never made it there the day prior) to align his M-4's sights. Dale was mounting a shallow rise that ended at a row of portable toilets along Main Street. He stopped when he saw Virden, unmistakably Virden, push out of the big communications building with its forest of antennas. The contractor was in his t-shirt and wearing a hip holster low, like a cowboy. Virden swung open a portable crapper door with a hollow squawk. Dale paused his humming to hear the latch slap into place.

Dale did it as quickly as the thought came into his head. He placed a shoulder against the back of the desert tan plastic shell and heaved with his legs. The Porta Potty flipped forward with surprising ease, and the noise from inside was part-scream part-roar. By the time the cabin crashed to the

ground Dale had already slipped into another shell three toilets down and casually locked himself in.

SPECIALISTS CLARK AND Jones were headed down Main Street to-
ward supply with a list for the North Aid Station where they
worked as medics. Clark was pissed. She had heard Captain
Pease, their supervising physician, talking with Staff
Sergeant Brock, the head medic, about his SOAP notes, and
Pease told Brock that "all women are pregnant until proven
otherwise, and all women are liars until proven otherwise."
"What kinda shit is that?" Jones cried out.

When Clark looked up from the ground, they both saw a
portable toilet crash into the ground fifty meters or so to
their front. Running to see what had happened, they could
already hear a stream of loud cursing from inside, and
brownish-blue fluid was running in every direction from under the toppled shell.

"Oh fuck," said Jones as they pulled up short. As they
danced around trying to avoid the blue liquid flowing and
trying to figure out how they could roll the shell, more people appeared. One civilian, a middle-aged man wearing jeans
and a blue denim shirt and two lieutenants—one male, one
female—wearing Ordnance branch insignia. The male, a stout
white man whose name tag read Webber, tiptoed into the
spreading blue pool and gave the side a push. When the shell
only rocked, and the cursing from inside grew more enraged
and frantic, Lieutenant Webber shook his head once, then
went ahead and planted his feet firmly in the blue shit-water,
dropped into an earnest squat, and rolled the toilet onto one
side, stepping back as the door dropped open before him.

"Oh. My. God!" Clark said, her hand on Jones' shoulder.
Rising out of the open door, as if the tan plastic shell were

giving birth to a monstrosity, was a drenched blue behemoth, a spitting, gagging, cursing hulk.

"Die, motherfucker!" the blue hulk roared at everyone, looking here and there. He advanced on the two lieutenants, who both held up their hands in surrender.

"Who did this?" he demanded.

"We didn't see," said the female lieutenant. Her voice was childlike.

Virden turned and faced the entrance to the communications building across Main Street. There were two black Spec-4's standing between him and the door with their mouths wide open. They jumped out of the way as he lunged toward them and the door. The chubby one let out a short scream.

"Outa my way, nigger bitch," the blue man growled as he went inside, leaving a blue-brown trail. Clark and Pease stood there stunned.

Dale emerged cautiously ten minutes later and chuckled all the way to the range, where he finally zeroed his M-4.

Monologue

Chapel Hill, North Carolina
July 1, 2010
Deangela Dale's apartment

"WHEN YOU WERE born," A.D. told Deangela, "I joined the Army. It seemed like a good idea at the time. There weren't any wars going on. The Iraq thing was over. The benefits were great: housing allowance, health care. Decent pay. And your mom needed to retrain as a nurse... no one here accepted her Belizean credentials. My own testimonials? Forget it! We were only married just over a year. And the recruiter told me that interracial marriages were pretty common in the Army. That may not seem important, and your mom always played it off like it was no big deal, but in Raleigh, North Carolina, no matter how cosmopolitan they like to think they are, we still got 'the look' everywhere we went. Complicated, this race shit. Even in Belize your mom was put down by lighter-skinned people. And she had to listen to congratulatory crap from other black people about how I was gonna 'put cream in her coffee' and make pretty kids. You *are* pretty... *I* think... but you see my meaning. Over here, in the South, there was this race and sex thing... white guys terminally freaked out by white women being with black guys, and yet a white guy with a black woman was something these same white guys would keep score with. Ugly, like 'you da man!' congratulatory stuff. Give a point to the white guy, which brings up a bunch of degrading shit about black women, and on and on. Same kind of stuff you were telling me 'bout men at school.

"You've heard all this... one way or another. But Farah and I, I think we fell in love in about ten seconds. It wasn't 'jungle fever' or any of that shit... I saw your mom, she saw me, and something hit us all at once, the same way, that said, 'mine.' Your mom says that's God, 'cause that's how she rolls, you know. Maybe she's right. But God and me, we can't seem to get on speaking terms.

"That was another thing, you know. We heard all the self-help advice about interracial 'relationships'." Dale made finger-quotes. "I don't think either of us ever thought we had something, like this thing, called a relationship... and we heard about cross-cultural 'relationships'." Finger-quotes again. "All the shit... different cultural values, different concepts of family, in-laws, blah-blah, blah-blah-blah-blah. But we didn't care. We belonged to each other... sorry, give me a minute, babe... we still do...

"Her folks were crazy about me, you know they still are... that's why we keep this separation away from 'em... break their hearts... me, I had my mom and my granddad... he got the hell beat out of him on the Freedom Rides on the Georgia-Alabama border... I come from a family that didn't harbor a suspicion of black people... took their licks for it, too... so we never had an in-law problem, and your mom told me if I let her bring you up in the church, we could negotiate everything else about that. I saw your Belizean family in church down there... altogether a good thing, the way they... I don't know, the way they showed up *en masse*, the way the big kids took care of the little kids and the little kids took care of the babies, and there were cousins and sisters fooling with each other's hair... that's why your mom brought you up in the church, even when I never really got it. And *that* was okay.

"So I joined the Army, and I had a college degree... okay, it was in literature, but the Army doesn't give a damn—a degree is a degree—and they made me an E-4. That's two years of rank for a diploma, and a nice starting salary, and I always liked challenges, physical and mental challenges, so I signed up for the Rangers, and then it was like a whirlwind. I caught on to the game quick enough... they haze you, you give the right responses... a little macho game, and if you don't go all jello on 'em, stay alert and don't go to pieces, then you get through. The only real attribute you need aside from bullheadedness is a little mental endurance. You're not a superhero; you're a glorified jock. I've been a jock, from twelve through college, a competition swimmer, even a little above average for a college swimmer. What the hell, I say, this is just a kind of adventure in deep education or something. I went to Infantry training, then jump school, then right to Fort Benning to a Ranger Battalion where they did another three weeks of hazing, and within a couple of months, because I was a sharp soldier, they hazed me again for three weeks, to get me ready for Ranger School, then I was hazed for eight more weeks at Ranger School. But like I said, it was a challenge, so in a way I kinda enjoyed it, because it turned out that I had this weird aptitude for ignoring the hazing and just... performing.

"But there was another thing, and here is where I fucked up royally... hindsight and all that. There are a lot of Rangers that really hate black people." His heart clutched when he saw her change of expression. "I know, I haven't told you this part, have I? A lot. Including in the chain of command. There's this goddamn Soldier of Fortune Klan shit subculture there that stays just below the radar... please don't look at me like that, you wanted to know how your mom and I got separated... it's on me. I caused it, but hear me out. I want you to understand this. I hated it, I hated that I saw it, and that I didn't know how to confront it... it was never overt, and once people realized that I was married to your mom, that part of the whole thing would sink down out of sight when I was around. But here is the worst part, God forgive me. I was really good at what they did. I was really a good Ranger, and people knew it, and I was recognized for it, and I found ways not to think about the other... and your mom knew. She spotted that shit a mile away, the first time she went to a company picnic. There was not one single black man in my line company. That's unheard of in the Army, but the norm in the Ranger Battalions.

"And she saw me liking being a good Ranger in spite of this thing going on there, and she saw my cowardice in averting my eyes from it, just to get through it, and she saw my weakness at getting away with it. And I saw her disappointment. Something came up between us then, something that had never been there before... and we loved each other, we still do, I love her more than... sorry... just... sorry, hon.

"I was overlooking something I hated in my unit; and your mom was forced to try to overlook something she hated in me... and there we were, two different kinds of coward... maybe coward is the wrong word. We stuck it out, nonetheless, got over the rough spots, loved you together... we made love... maybe this isn't... well, you asked. It was different... not just less frequent. Having a small child... well, you know. But it was different. Part of our connection was in reminiscing, if that's the right ... we tried to remember what it was like before, while we were... but it never was... the same... never would be... and I think we both grieved alone.

210

"At any rate, in 1993, there was this thing... I've told you a little about it... they made a movie about it that was nothing like what happened... well, we were sent to Somalia. We were all these white guys... there was one black guy in the whole company... and we were surrounded by Somalis. All the time... but we stirred things up and... well, there were some mistakes, predictable yet unavoidable mistakes... and, well, these militias, they always had the advantage... anyway, the whole mission went sideways one day, and some helicopters were shot down and, long story short, we were trapped fighting street to street for a long time... like ten hours long... seemed like two lifetimes. But this place, Mogadishu, it's a city, a ruined city, like something post-apocalyptic, you know, and there are people everywhere, and all the shooting, and we were little clusters of white guys, getting shot at by black guys, hundreds of them, and we couldn't always tell... well, it's kind of always that way... but we spent ten hours shooting at black people. And we... I'm sorry, sweetie... give me a minute... a lot of people were hurt and killed. Hundreds. There were mothers... and babies. Kids. This was the worst day of my life... worse even than when my granddad died.

"Anyway, I came home, but every time I saw you and your mother after that, I thought about this one baby we left... her mother was dead. And we just left her, half-starved in the middle of a firefight. How did we do that? We did that!

"So that was 1993. I left the Battalion as soon as I got my Sergeant's stripes and went to the Special Forces course. I wanted nothing more to do with the Rangers. I thought I could get out and leave all of that behind... and it kind of worked for a while. Special Forces wasn't as bad with that race thing as the Rangers, but there was still a lot of animosity toward black people. Not brown people, strangely enough, but black folks. By the time I figured this out, I had already changed the branch... and my job title. I was stuck there. When I was in training, I was studying to be a medic, and your mom and I, we got along really well, because she knew all this medical stuff, like an MD knows medical stuff, she can talk microbiology, and anyway... she helped me study, and for a while it was almost like... that barrier, it was there, but we found it easier to ignore. We had you, and you were suddenly doing these remarkable things, and we had a sense that things could change for us, and we'd like hit the reset button, you know. But then I was assigned to my unit, and I started to be gone all the time—you remember that—oh God, I hated to see you cry. I hated seeing your mom cry.

"But I had this ego, too... truth, God... and I just had to do the next big thing, and I went to that unit, to Delta... and during the first six months there, I was in training... and it was another outfit with absolutely zero black operators... and that thing came back between us, and it only got better once I was done with training and started doing missions... because I was gone... even more than I had been while in the Group.

Then one night—it was right after I had gotten home from a mission down south... this was five years ago—we had, uh... we made love, then went to sleep. And then I was back in Mogadishu, somehow... and when I woke up I had your mom pinned to the floor with my hand over her mouth... somewhere between asleep and awake, that wall between the separate rooms I live in inside my head disappeared. This has been happening a lot lately...

"I moved out the next day. That's why I kept a place close to you two in Fayetteville. Your mom was working at the hospital. You were with a great tutor... I didn't want... why do you want to know all this?"

Shrimp day

Camp Virtue, Afghanistan
July 12, 2010

BOBBY, FALL, OPEY, Woof, Eddy, and Sis sat around the 649 table, chowing down. It was shrimp day and they had their trays loaded with deep-fried prawns, cole slaw, hush puppies and corn bread. Iced tea was sweating in their plastic glasses. Shrimp tails were piled on their plates alongside smears of cocktail sauce.

"Where's the rest o' the boys?" Bobby queried.

"Pedro and Gene asleep in the tent," Sis said. "I saw Doc over at the aid station. Pete's comin' I think. Fuckin' with a computer or somethin'."

"Big surprise. They're missin' shrimp day, man."

Fall spoke with his mouth full. "Y'all hear about Ben Virden?" The whole table cracked up. Of course they had. A story this good spread like pinworms in a kindergarten.

"I heard that boy had to wash off in the leg showers," laughed Opey, winking with delight. "His own boys wouldn't let him in the batmobile 'til he got the shit off 'im."

"He finds out who did it, gonna be hell to pay," said Fall.

"Fuck you, Fall," said Woof. "Get yer fuckin' lips off his beaver-basher. That shit was funny, man. He's a pimp, dude. Fuckin' pimp."

"Yeah, ya know what'll be funny? When he catches the motherfucker..."

Woof interrupted Fall with a mock lat-spread and a growl. The table hooted, and Fall went dark in the face.

"Yeah, well ya know what else?" Fall said. "See if this one cracks you up. Top already knows about the Chinese Restaurant." That bit of news dropped onto the table like a subpoena, silencing everyone.

"Yeah," said Fall, feeling vindicated, "He asked Captain Bob about it yesterday."

Eddy asked, "How d' ya know, man?"

Sis said, "There go our downtown 'security patrols'."

Bobby, as always, put a positive spin on things. "How'd ya know? Maybe Top likes to get his pipes cleaned, too. Ol' dude like that, maybe one of those tight little teens be like a Vitamin B-52 shot."

"He seem like a friendly guy to you?" Eddy asked. The table grew quiet again. "He seem like someone who wants to fraternize with the young bucks?"

"No," opined Woof. "Ask me, that hummin', spaced-out motherfucker's unzipped. Fuckin' demento." Woof saw Captain Bob approaching, nodded in that direction. The boys all turned their heads. Captain Bob looked full of intent.

"Eat up, gentlemen," he commanded, "and be in the Ops hooch in fifteen minutes. Warning order. And not a word to anyone."

MAJOR CARROLL SAT on a black mesh office chair—the ergonomic kind with a pneumatic height adjuster. He was rocking nervously alongside Colonel Thomas's desk, a modular V of shiny blond pressboard resting on black steel file cabinets, which was now covered with satellite imagery, maps and co-ordination forms. Thomas was rocking too, in an identical office chair, not from nerves but from impatience.

"Sir, these contractors come and go as they please, and our guys have been strap-hanging with 'em for months. This place is loose, Sir." Carroll was leaning forward toward Thomas's elbow, and Thomas kept glancing down at one of the satellite images on his desk. "It may be nothing, but that French shark smells blood in the water and he's stirring up the natives."

"You're mixin' metaphors, Will..."

"Sir!"

"I get it, okay, Will? But looky here, we have the first decent mission we've had in months... a superlative mission, Will, and I can't be inconvenienced by this shit right now."

"Sir, it's probably bullshit, but like I say, we need to be ready to answer questions."

"These fuckers are lookin' for restitution checks, okay... but you're right. I trust you, Will." *You fuckin' half-breed twat!* "This is what you get paid for." Thomas turned toward Carroll, aiming a look at him intended to convey sincerity. "You handle this, okay, and keep everything off me for the next two days. Then we'll have a helluva press conference and no one will care that two camel rags got shot. It's Afghanistan, for Christ's sake!"

"... and raped."

"Huh?"

"One of them was raped, Sir. She was fourteen. The village headman had a meltdown right in front of me."

"They did a forensic rape kit on 'er? CSI show up? C'mon, Will. Keep this French faggot off me for two days." Carroll's face dropped. He sighed. Thomas placed a hand on his shoulder, and Carroll looked up again. Thomas's smile reminded Carroll of an alligator with rigor mortis. "Then we'll have a story that'll bulldoze this shit."

"Yes, Sir."

DALE WATCHED FROM in front of the ops hooch as a black Chinook helicopter chugged lazily toward the airfield tracing a line over the shipping containers that were stacked across the end of Main Street. Under the sun-bleached sky a curling line of dust blew past him in advance of a backhoe that was crawling toward him. He was armed with a notebook, to check off the names of the teammates as they trudged in, wearing battle-rattle over their t-shirts, weapons slung, MICH helmets hanging off of canteens. Pedro, then Woof, then Fall... check, check, check... Dale heard the truck coming up Main Street, but didn't raise his face to look at it until he heard it decelerate and stop, idling directly in front of the ops hooch. Fall stopped in the door, holding up the rest of the team, who started to grumble.

It was an MRAP, driver's side facing Dale. The driver's door creaked open. Virden stepped down from the vehicle, dressed in fresh clothes, his holster and belt still shining from wash water. He stood and stared directly at Dale. Fall dropped his eyes and went into the hooch. Bobby was giggling about something and headed in behind Fall oblivious to the developing vignette. Opie saw it though and elbowed Sis. Eddy and Doc walked around them without looking up. Gene picked it up and froze.

They all knew that Dale knew about the Chinese Restaurant, but they didn't know if Virden knew that Dale knew. This was on all their minds at that precise moment. The contractors were a law unto themselves, and here was one fronting Top off in plain sight of his own men. The only one not reacting was Dale himself, who cast a passing glance at Virden standing there with his shaved head, his tattoos, his war vest, and his wet pistol rig, his HK416 assault rifle clamped to the dash. Dale could have been looking at a housefly, for all the concern he showed.

"I got y'all," Dale said, a way of telling the boys to snap out of it and get inside. They broke contact with Virden's threat display and crowded through the door. Dale waited until they were all inside, then slowly turned and pretended to be pulling his skivvies out of the crack of his ass as he went inside. He heard the vehicle door slam, the engine rev, and the MRAP catching first gear as it clawed through the greasy dust of Main Street.

Inside, the boys were scooching around on their chairs. Opie stood, spitting snuff into a Coke can. Captain Bob was sitting in front, his knees together to hold a notebook he was scribbling in, with Pete looking over his shoulder. Bobby was sitting next to Eddy, smiling and whispering as he tugged at his dick. Weapons were laid on a long white plastic folding table inside the door. Gene and Pedro sat together silently with blank expressions. Eddy and Sis sat together, eyes on Captain Bob, while Eddy wormed a pinky up his nose. Doc hung his war vest over one chair and positioned another chair for himself to sit on at the table next to Fall.

Captain Bob cleared his throat, then told them, "Okay, settle. This is our warning order." The twitching subsided and pens hovered over pocket notebooks. "Colonel Thomas has issued a warning order for ODA 649 to infiltrate northeast of Charikar at twenty-thirty hours ZULU, July 13—that's zero-zero-three-zero LOCAL, July 14, to capture or kill Taliban intelligence chief Usman Jahangiri—that is," he spoke more loudly and emphatically here, "with a strong preference for capture..." A couple of the boys groaned, but Dale silenced them with a look. "...in order to return Jahangiri for interrogation..."

Bobby let out a mock squeal and the boys started laughing.

"At ease!" Dale roared. They had never heard his voice raised before and went all silent and contrite. "This is your warning order, not the fuckin' Comedy Zone." Well, there was an old-school NCO hiding inside that Sybil motherfucker after all. "Go ahead, Sir."

ODA 649 WAS on an eighteen-hour planning cycle. Dunny deferred to Dale on the tactics and concentrated his own efforts on coordinations, especially with the supporting aircraft. Dale organized a layout inspection of everyone's combat gear, making sure that the gear was all serviceable and that their electronics had fresh batteries. Bobby organized a test fire at the range for all the weapons from which Dale was excused, having zeroed and test-fired that very day. Sis and Pedro set up communications, coordinating with the tactical operations center and securing their one-time pads, testing and re-testing every radio. Doc and Woof inventoried and repacked their operational aid bags and Woof got on a secure line to have flunetrazepam and ketamine delivered. Dale, the ex-medic, told them that they were going to inject their prisoner with this "roofie cocktail" as soon as they secured him, to hedge against resistance. Gene and Eddy secured rations and prepped hinge charges in case they had to blow doors open. Pete worked as the liaison between the ops hooch and the TOC. Opie and Fall picked up ammunition and grenades—

frags, CS, three colors of smoke and two white phosphorus.

Dale was hovering over two 1:50,000 topographical maps with his protractor and a mechanical pencil when Bobby came into the ops hooch with a packet. Bobby had been conducting his intelligence coordination and picked up satellite images of their target.

"Top?" Dale looked up. "Top, I'm sorry about that fuckin' around in the warning order. Won't happen again."

Dale looked at him for several seconds, as if he didn't hear. Then, suddenly, he replied.

"Okay."

"We're not used to doin' missions like this. Not used to a team daddy who knows what he's doin'. I'm a fuck-up sometimes, Top. But I'm operationally sound... promise."

"That's good," said Dale. "Because I'm not going past the ORP. You'll be the senior enlisted man on the target."

"What? Why?"

The ORP was the "objective rally point," a point secured by part of a unit near but not on the objective. From there the rest of the unit launches into its actions on the objective and returns there after those actions to make preparations for exfiltration or extraction.

"That's our extraction point. It's not sexy, but it's critical. You wanna carry this guy back to Camp Virtue?" Bobby shook his head. "I've had all the action I can stand in one career, Bobby. You guys can handle the wet work on this one. Now, let's see what these sat photos look like." He pulled the photos out of the envelope and tossed the envelope into the trash can marked "BURN."

"Bobby, have you ever considered how fortunate we are to have deodorants that don't cake up or stain?"

TOP HAD ORDERED them to maintain silence during meals. In the dining facility the other troops—accustomed now to 649's boisterousness—took note of this atypical silence. There was an operation afoot and not the usual.

The ops hooch accumulated paper, then that paper made its way to the burn barrel. The tables also filled with disposable coffee cups and soda cans which eventually filled the trash barrel. The pilots came in with Dunny, going over routes and checkpoints. Dale pushed Dunny to prepare his operations order within six hours of the warning order. His rule was to leave two-thirds of the prep time for code memorization, rehearsals and rest. Outside, the sky was the color of lead as the sun set like a burning fuse behind the ridgeline of Mount Ser Devaza west of Kabul.

The order was scheduled for 1900 Local, after the boys had supper. Then they would rehearse after dark at least twice and bed down after breakfast. Dale told Dunny he was stepping out for some air.

Dale's fingertips tingled and his head felt like it was wrapped in a fluffy bandage. He planned for himself to be off the actual objective—they needed to separate the two leaders and the two medics, and that seemed reasonable to him—but he still had the sense that he wasn't really there and that he was planning a mission that was not really going to happen. And he couldn't get Farah and Deangela out of his head. For years, the way he operated was to leave home at home and work at work. *A well-policed boundary is the key to happiness. Good fences, good neighbors. Something like that.*

He strolled down Main Street toward the airfield, past the zone of synthetic-lavender stench he had created with the tipped toilet. He smiled to himself, not thinking of Virden covered in blue shit but because he had made up his mind to kill Virden the first chance he got, thinking of it as a chore or an errand that needed doing.

There were six russet sparrows lined up on the commo hooch's roof. Sand martens were swooping and diving through the dusk like the barn swallows back home. *It was the birds*, he caught himself thinking. Birds were breaking down the borders between work and home, home and work. *Damned birds don't respect gates, walls, boundaries, borders...* What were the sparrows eating? Shouldn't there be some kind of seed? The darkening sky was gunmetal gray, under-scoring a drowning blaze of apricot where the sun had tucked behind the ridge. The songs with the wrong lyrics started playing in his head again... The Temps:

I've shot so much money the knees canopy.
I've shot a shitty bong and the birds eat the fleas.
Well, high bless your day, Snot pan takes my breath away,
Uncurl (uncurl, uncurl) Clockin' out to u-u-un-curl (Uncurl!).

He walked past other soldiers kitted up with vests and helmets, taking no note as they stared at him because he was wearing plain fatigues with nothing but a sidearm. He passed the Base Exchange, the "Hajji shop" where a local peddled knock-off shades and Afghan "lickies and chewies" and the Burger King trailer where a dozen or so troops were lined up for a familiar dose of monoculture. He advanced into the gloaming as he approached the end of Main Street, sur-rounded with stacks of cargo containers and thick concrete pillars to deflect shrapnel. In one of the aviators' bunkers near the airfield apron a dog yipped—one of the few pets on the base.

He had joined the Army to care for his daughter, who would be his only child because Farah had suffered complications during delivery that rendered her infertile. He thought about the people in the Air Force who remotely piloted drones. They showered in their apartments in places like Nevada and New Mexico, dressed, came in to work, shot up crowds and houses thousands of miles distant, then picked up their kids after school or soccer practice on the way home. *How the fuck did they do that?* At least he, before he would be allowed to kill, was forced to go through several gates—the good-byes, the drive to the base, the processing, getting on a plane, getting off somewhere else... like a ship moving through locks. Sure, there was that thing when you were home, that inability to totally reconcile the two realities. Here, your kid was playing a game as she sat in the casement window while the smell of frying garlic wafted in from the kitchen and someone was mowing grass outside. There—where you had been a hundred hours ago or a month ago or six months ago—was this other thing, this thing with armed men and lots of poor people and blood and corpses every-where. Death and disfigurement lurked in every shadow. But at least that boundary, that gate, was there. There was Farah and Cinema 15 and streetlights and bookstores and Deangela with her binoculars tagging nuthatches. And then there was Ojo de Agua or Mogadishu or Virden making six figures by doing nothing while selling kidnapped girls to a Chinese pimp.

PTSD my ass, he thought, channeling an imaginary tough guy. *Trauma is not the issue. The issue*, he thought, *is with keeping these two realities properly separated.*

Here, he was a super-soldier preparing to kidnap a Taliban intelligence chief—at least that's how that bombastic nitwit Thomas saw it—*Does Thomas have any clue how fabulously fucked up this team is?...* but Dale couldn't focus. He didn't think he had slept at all, but he had been able to doze a bit. And when he did, Deangela was roaming around unprotected in the commo bunker with Virden and his buds. And then Virden was with Farah, stalking her through the wards at Cape Fear Hospital. And these damned songs with the lyrics wrong made him want to push daggers into his ears! And then he would be awake, again.

The sky was like dark slate now, throwing off desiccated heat. He would kill Virden soon. He had no choice. *It is,* he realized with a jolt, *the most important thing.* He knew how to do it: gain proximity; act; leave. His plan was simplicity itself. He was a *good* assassin.

Deangela thought he was a Shakespeare buff, a birdwatcher, a good dad; but her dad also killed on command; or he just killed on a whim. He was a killer when he was with his daughter, and a good dad when he was a killer. He was a good killer-husband who tried to kill his wife because her black face looked to him like a threat in their Mogadishu, North Carolina bedroom.

Rehearsal

July 13, 2010
Camp Virtue

PLANNING SAPS ENERGY. By midnight everyone was a zombie. The bitter coffee wasn't overcoming fatigue so much as turning people from tired to tired and jumpy. But that's when the order was scheduled, so there were fresh steaming cups next to pens and notebooks as the boys sat lined up at desks casting bloodshot eyes up at the array of dry erase boards covered in sketches, corkboards with maps and satellite photos. Clear plastic overlays covered the maps and images with variously colored lines and letters indicating critical points, references, control measures and routes.

Pinned up on one corkboard was a blown-up mug shot of Usman Janghiri from a Pakistani catch-and-release arrest made two years previously. Janghiri had an unusually round face and a very thick beard that appeared reddish without any help from the henna favored by older men. His eyes were light; not quite blue or green or even brown, but something in between—almost colorless—giving him a slightly crazed appearance with the camera lights directly on him. There were three prominent moles lined up in a row, extending from below Janghiri's right eye to the edge of his beard—like black tears running down his face.

Dunny, as pie-eyed from fatigue as the rest of them, had droned through the order's first two paragraphs—Situation and Mission—and gone through Execution until he reached the Actions on the Objective sub-paragraph.

"For Actions on the Objective, I'm turning the order over to Master Sergeant Dale," he said, and flopped into a chair flanking the display boards.

A topographical map was projected onto a pull-down screen. The satellite images were posted with plastic overlays indicating routes, control measures, and the target.

Dale's bowels rumbled in synch with a C-5 taking off out on the airfield, drowning the hum of the generator and the buzz of the fluorescent lighting. The roar of the jet faded and Dale heard Opie spitting snuff juice into a can, strangely amplified, and caught a whiff of wet tobacco and stale saliva. Pedro sniffled and scratched his calf. A fly walked along the rim of Pete's polystyrene coffee cup sucking at the flecks of wet sugar. Eddy took a long draw on a Mountain Dew, his thick mustache and jug ears looking suddenly enormous, like a cartoon character. Baby Doc rubbed his eyes and Dale thought he could hear them squeak. Fall, Woof, and Gene were all getting fat, their midriffs rolling over their belt lines as they sat. Fattening men with tattoos: Fall's tribals on both arms; Woof's wolf on his right shoulder, peeking out from his t-shirt; Gene's Aces and Eights on his thick forearm. Gene's thinning dark hair gave the appearance of a pale mushroom extending from his forehead to his crown surrounded on the sides by darkness. Woof was digging around in his ear with a pencil eraser. Sis was bent over his notebook, baby-face down, looking as if he were about to nod off. Pete, with his tinted transition-glasses, still looked like a bookie—maybe a Greek bookie, with that thick black beard. Baby Doc was squared in his seat now, his *pelo indio* sticking out like an electrocuted straw man. Dale was seized with the sudden urge to blurt out, "Richer, longer lashes will transform your life," but he suppressed the urge, along with the guffaw that almost came out instead. "Do you all want whiter teeth and fresher breath?" *Did I just say that?*

"Top?" Dunny called out. Everyone grew still and looked up at him. He imagined pulling a string out of his back, and he began talking, even as he imagined that he was in Weymouth Woods with Deangela. He saw her raise her binoculars.

"...The trick on a warbler... on a snatch is to create a nonlethal zone within a lethal permeter around the target. The only guy you have to recognize is him." He points to the photo of Jahangiri. "Anyone else in the building, you eliminate without hesitation. This guy, you look at his hands. If he doesn't have a weapon in those hands, Fall and Pedro will call out 'WOO-dray-gah!' and 'Target, Clear.' That's your cue, Doc and Bobby, to move in, keeping clear of Pedro and Fall's line of sight with the target, and lay on hands. This building's smaller than you imagine. You'll rub up on each other in there. Keep to your sector, even if it's three feet of wall space, or you'll commit fratricide. Single shot only. Bobby, you'll restrain and cuff. Baby Doc, the second his hands are in the flex cuffs, you inject him in the thigh with the roofie cocktail. It'll take a few minutes, and it shouldn't be enough to make him a dishrag. If we can walk him, that's a big plus. We don't wanna carry him if we don't have to. The extraction LZ is still three and a half clicks. Cap'n Dunny will give three short tweets on the whistle. That tells Gene and Pete you're coming out the door. Gene and Pete will pull off the back of the building, fall in behind the inside team, and cross the street. When Opie and Eddy count out the last man, roll up the file, and make a beeline to the ORP. At this point, speed is your best security. Haul ass and to hell with the racket. Just don't shout. Sis will call Woof and me in the ORP on the FM hand-held. If that fails, he'll send up a pin flare..."

He broke off momentarily, and stared at the back of the room.

"Top!" said Dunny. "Top?..."

THEY REHEARSED ON the airfield three times that night: landing zone assembly, ORP sequence and actions on the objective. When they were done less than an hour remained before dawn. There was no moon. It set at dusk the day before. Visibility was nil except for starlight and spotty bits of backlight escaping across the base. That was a good thing, because that was exactly what they could expect during the mission scheduled for the coming night. Within minutes of heading back the first hint of twilight appeared in the east.

The DFAC was getting ready to serve breakfast by the time they dropped their gear in the ops hooch. After breakfast they would all bag out for a few hours. There was an eruption of what-the-fuck-this-is-fucking-bullshit-man discontent when Dunny walked in and announced that they were about to receive a briefing from the public affairs officer. They were all hungry, tired and cross. *What the fuck did public affairs have to do with this operation now? They hadn't even launched yet. Were they expecting Anderson fucking Cooper on the target?* Captain Dunny, eyes sandy and bloodshot, was cross, too, and he gave it right back to them.

"It's not a fuckin' request, goddammit." He threw his vest into a corner, dropped his M-4 onto the heap. "In your fuckin' seats, ten minutes."

SLEEPY, IRRITABLE MEN FILED in and took seats in the folding chairs. Major Carroll stood front and center, ready to give his briefing. When the last man, Pedro, was seated, Dale nodded to Dunny.

"All present, Sir," Dunny said, taking his own seat.

Carroll stood at ease, feet shoulder-width apart, hands clasped behind his back. He turned on a benevolent half-smile as he looked from one man to another.

"Thanks, Captain Dunny," he said, then cleared his throat. "Gentlemen, I apologize for getting you up. I know you're resting in anticipation of a very difficult mission, but something has come up. There is a reporter, a French reporter, who's making suggestions about a crime that happened two nights ago near Dahst-e-Barchi."

Gene and Pedro held their eyes unblinkingly forward. Doc, who had been chewing on a fingernail, looked up. Dale narrowed his eyes and began biting absentmindedly on the pad of his right thumb.

"Apparently, a young girl and her mother were killed," Carroll explained, "and the villagers claim that the young girl was raped. Could have been Taliban or militia, or could be an attempt to get compensation from ISAF. But some of the villagers insist it was Americans." His voice said this was obviously bullshit, but American officers had to perform their due diligence. "We expect to conclude that investigation fairly quickly. Until further notice, no one is to say anything to any member of the press. We are to have no contact with the press. We are neither to confirm nor to deny any story to the press or your friends or your family."

"Where would we meet any press?" Bobby blurted. Dale and Dunny gave him a look.

"I won't take questions," Carroll said. "Say nothing to anyone. Full stop. Return to your bunks." Then he stepped off on his left foot and headed out the door. Dunny called them to attention, and they all rose.

Carroll stopped and turned, one hand already on the door.

"And, gentlemen, this may be the most important mission of your lives. A lot is riding on you. Good luck, and godspeed."

Pedro and Gene didn't sleep at all that day. Neither did Baby Doc.

Snake

BY NOON, DISRUPTION of their sleep rhythms and suppressed anxiety about the mission were keeping most of them awake in spite of their fatigue. Men in this situation half-sleep, fake-sleep, or give in to restlessness and accept that they will do the mission on raw endurance. A few men have the gift of no imagination, and they sleep. Eddy was like that, and he was snoring like a pug.

Baby Doc was leafing half-absently through the team's medical records. His head was not in the mission. Instead, he was thinking about the Public Affairs briefing on the rape and the murders. He could feel a paralyzing vigilance radiating from Pedro and Gene. Baby Doc had heard the shots, the time of the shots, and the whispered departure that preceded them. There were always distant shots in Afghanistan, but he knew what these were. Each successive confirmation unbalanced him more, the unwelcome knowledge unfurling in his belly like a poisonous flower.

A SOAP note in Pedro's record. What was this? *S - PT complains of painful genital sore, l/d shaft of penis. O - open lesion w clear discharge, vesicles. A - genital herpes. P - acyclovir, 400mg oral TID x 10 days.*

Hector gazed at the note, then he gazed through it. He looked across his shoulder to where Pedro and Gene were lying still on their cots, both with their faces turned toward the waist-high wall of sandbags around the outside of the tent. Gene's cot was only a body-length from Hector's field table.

231

Hector stacked the medical records neatly, squaring the edges, then placed Pedro's record on the top, open to the page with the SOAP note showing Pedro had genital herpes.

PEDRO TIRED OF attempting sleep, so he was watching a porn film on his television with the sound turned off. A blonde woman in black stockings and shiny black spiked heels was straddled across a white man whose face was hidden, topping him, while another man, this one black, had penetrated her anally from behind. The black guy looked a little bored, and the woman's buttocks rippled every time he thrust into her. It was hard to tell whether her grimace was meant to represent pain or pleasure. Pedro looked bored, too.

Gene was fidgeting, pacing through and around the tent, repeatedly making adjustments to his equipment and his rucksack. Hollow-eyed from lack of sleep, his expression seemed hunted. He had pulled the detonator assemblies out of the rucksack for the third time, re-rolled the waterproofing and the protective sheet of bubble wrap and was pushing it back in through the Velcro mouth of the flap when his eyes fell on the stack of medical records. Doc wasn't anywhere in sight, and no one in the tent was looking... Pedro was listless, glued to the silent sex scene.

NINE PAIRS OF boots were aligned outside the door of the inter-preters' prayer room. The contractors had built a wooden day-billet for them, with bunk beds for overnight stays and naps, a ping-pong room with two tables for cards and dominoes and a prayer room with a high window that faced to the West. Benham was inside, alongside Jahid, Rafik, Omar, Hamdast, Rabi, Razi, Payam, and Maalik. Each knelt and bowed on his own prayer rug. Upon completing their prayers they rolled up their rugs and retrieved their boots outside the door. They sat down on chairs and cots to tuck their uniform trousers into the boots. The camp commander insisted that the Afghan Militia Forces, including the interpreters, maintain uniform standards identical to those of his own subordinates.

The interpreters stuck together, in part because the other AMFs—those whose English was poor to nonexistent—were both envious and contemptuous of them, seeing them as suck-ups and collaborators, even while all AMFs were seen as collaborators by many Afghans. This dynamic placed additional pressure on all the AMFs, but especially the interpreters, to assert their identity as Afghans, more so, as Pashtuns, when they were apart from the *amrekayan*.

When the nine interpreters sat down at their table in the dining facility, in their room, which was adjacent to the larger one used by the *amrekayan*, Benham had the floor. He spoke quietly to them all. At first they ate as they listened, but as he continued they placed their flatware on their plates, fixing their attention on Benham. A wave of agitation arose as Benham went on, and wrath darkened their faces. In a sudden explosion of angry chatter, they went from still and receptive to animated, gesticulating angrily.

The hubbub attracted looks from some of the Americans through the open portal that separated the AMF facility from the American one. Benham warned them to calm down, slanting his eyes and pushing his lips out at the stern faces of the armed Americans peering through the portal. The noise dropped but the boiling fury remained.

THE WIND OVER Camp Virtue generally blew out of the north, seldom hard but often steady, with occasional gusts that twirled the orange dust into dancing columns. For that reason trash was burned on the South side of the base near a deep fissure that ran up the side of the plateau. The dining facility's garbage was dumped in the fissure while burnt combustibles formed a ragged heap of ash out of which stuck indistinguishable scraps of charred, black metal. Three privates from the support detachment—Ames, Rozin, and Long, in full battle kit—unloaded fractured wooden pallets from the back of an open deuce-and-a-half truck.

Ames was a black kid no more than five and a half feet tall with silver braces on his teeth that seemed to sparkle when he talked, which he did incessantly. Ames was light-skinned while Long was dark—"almost like those African dudes"—with several thick keloid scars on his neck where he had been mauled by a dog when he was eight. Long lifted weights and was big on top, even as his calves were skinny. Rozin was pale and blond, flat-faced with high Slavic cheekbones that were perpetually sunburned and peeling and white eyelashes that made him look sick, although he couldn't remember ever being sick a day in his life. Rozin and Long took turns responding to Ames's monologue, courteously sharing the mild burden of Ames's geeky chatter.

Ames was on the truck bed, passing the forklift pallets down to Long, who passed them to Rozin, who stacked them in a heap on the pile of ash and rubble.

"...Penn was good in *Milk*, don't get me wrong," Ames held forth, "but Mickey Rourke is a genius, man. And he gets passed over again. *The Wrestler* was better than *Slumdog*, yo, but that's beside the point. My point is that Best Actor shoulda gone to Mickey Rourke... not just because he's brilliant, man, but as a lifetime achievement kinda thing, you know? Who else coulda played the range of characters

Rourke has? Look at the parts. There's *Diner*, there's *Barfly*, *Rumble Fish*... even in his small parts, like *Rainmaker*, the guy is the ultimate method actor. He gets inside the skin of his characters..."

The last pallet hit the heap and Rozin abandoned Long to Ames and the 2009 Oscars so he could get the pile of newspapers out of the cab. When he retrieved them and stepped back out of the cab, Ames was still energized, not even pausing as he handed the gas can down to Rozin, while Long stood there at the back of the truck blowing little puffs of air out one after the other that sounded like corks softly popping.

"... in *Spun*... hey, just one of the most under-recognized films of the decade, man, his character—the meth cook—man, it was inspired, fucking hallucinogenic, man. That speech on pussy? 'You gotta speak to that pussy, son, make a vow to it.' That was inspired..."

Rozin was stuffing newspaper all through the heap of pallets. Long did his duty, responding to Ames:

"What? What movie was that?" Sure, he was egging him on, but Ames was going to talk no matter what.

"*Spun*, yo..."

Rozin soaked the pile with a half-gallon of gas. "Fire in the hole," he called out, lighting an MRE match, then using it to light the whole book. He threw the burning book of matches at the heap, running back, and the gas went up with a whump. The papers caught fire, launching glittering bits of ash into the air. Then the wind shifted, now coming from the south and into their faces. The gas flames almost singed their eyebrows. As they retreated, Ames jumped off the back. The smoke chased them until they sidled around toward the big crack in the ground where the DFAC garbage was dumped.

The garbage drew rats, and some of the guys had pellet pistols they would bring out to shoot at them. Ames, Long, and Rozin alternated between watching the fire and scoping out the garbage for rats. Ames had just transitioned into a so-liloquy about the meth epidemic when Rozin suddenly squealed and tottered backwards. Less than ten feet from where he was standing, emerging from under the burnt brush along the edge of the burn site, was a thick Levant viper: a conspicuously fat orange-and-white snake with a head the size of a pig's heart and saddle-shaped like a bad comb-over. The reptile was almost five feet long and being driven into the open by the heat. Ames fell silent, and all they could hear was the crackling of the fire. They stood still at a distance and looked at the viper. It lay motionless and looked back. The fire grew hotter as all three of the Privates wordlessly watched the snake. Undulating slowly, its thick body heaving like a wave, the snake slithered back into a cooler section of debris in the garbage trench.

The coin

HEARING A BEEP, Major Carroll looked up at the Motorola hand-held sitting in the charger on a corner table in his office. Staff Sergeant Anita Barber was taking notes, and her pen froze above her notebook as she looked up too. The red light on the unit was blinking. It beeped again. Carroll rose to get it.

"Papa Alpha," (Public Affairs) he said when he hit the button. "Go ahead, over."

Barber watched. A moment passed. Carroll scowled.

"Can you tell him to come back tomorrow?" Another pause, then he put the radio down on the desk, muttered "Fuck me with a Twinkie!" and picked it back up. Barber set her notebook and pen down and got up out of her chair.

"TELL HIM THAT if he doesn't see me," Gaston told the gate guard, a tattooed Samoan with his radio held before him like a book he was reading, "I'll be calling my editor tonight with a very scandalous story."

The guard pulled the radio close again with two hands and looked skyward as spoke: "He says if you don't let him in, he's gonna write about a scandal or something."

The guard smiled wearily at Gaston while they waited for a reply. Five seconds, ten, fifteen.

"Tell him someone's coming to escort him."

The guard was still doing his muscular Samoan Mona Lisa smile. "Someone finally went through their books huh? You find out how much they charge the government for paper plates?"

GASTON FACED MAJOR Carroll across the desk. They exchanged a pro forma handshake.

"What can we do for you, Mr. Villeneuve? Please, have a seat." Carroll sat back without waiting. Villeneuve remained standing. Carrol could smell onions, tobacco and aftershave. The reporter had cleaned up and had even put on an ironed, button-down, sky-blue shirt for the visit.

"Major, could you help me understand a military custom I have observed?"

"What would that be, Mr. Villeneuve?"

"Gaston, please. Major, you are familiar with the military custom called... what is it? Ah yes, the 'coin check'."

"Of course. Everyone in Special Operations is."

"If I present you with a coin, correct me if I am wrong... and if you do not have your coin, then you have to do pushups or buy me beer or jack me off or something... and if you have the coin, once I have challenged you, then I have to do the pushups or buy the beer. Is that how it works?"

"Yes. It's a fraternal thing. Not familiar with the masturbation tradition; perhaps that's the Foreign Legion you're thinking of."

Smiling briefly and reaching into his pocket, Villeneuve asked, "Is this the kind of coin you use?" He held out a large and tarnished nickel-plated coin on the palm of his right hand. It bore an image of the globe with a great 6 over it and a scroll over the top that said "6th SPECIAL FORCES GROUP

(AIRBORNE) and a scroll along the bottom that said, "DE OP-
PRESSO LIBER."

Carroll glanced down at the coin without otherwise moving, then back up at Villeneuve. "Surely, Mr. Villeneuve, you
didn't make threatening noises to gain entry into this installation so you could coin-check me. If I do my pushups, will
you go away? I certainly won't touch your penis." He put his
hands out to feign assuming the pushup position.

"But what about the Foreign Legion? Ah, well... It's not
that simple, Major. I found this coin. I thought that perhaps
someone here had lost it..."

"Forgive me for being short... Gaston, but you are rapidly
closing the distance between here and what we refer to in
America as 'my last fucking nerve'."

"... in a crack in the floor of the house where Bakhtawara
and Storai Yusafzai lived until they were murdered two
nights ago. It even had blood on it, which I have collected for
testing. The two NATO 5.56 spent ammunition cartridges that
were handled by the villagers probably won't yield useful fin-
gerprints now." Carroll blanched, his face going copper to
gray and back. "But the other sample I'll have tested is feces.
Human feces. It was left on the ground, far from any commu-
nal latrine, precisely where the villagers showed me the
truck tracks. One of the perpetrators needed to defecate either before or after the deed. It may contain DNA, we'll see.
Storai was fourteen, if you'll recall. She was also raped before
she was killed." He put the coin back into his pocket. "The
surname is more a tribal identification, not like Carroll or
Villeneuve. Bakhtawara means good luck, or something like
that. Ironic, no? Storai means star. These details will human-
ize these women, though fourteen-year-old Storai will hardly
be seen as an adult in the minds of my readers..."

"Mr. Villeneuve, let me stop you."

"Gaston, please."

"I told you the last time you were here, we are investigating. We can't draw any conclusions about this incident until that investigation is complete. *Nor should you!*"

"Major, I have not drawn any conclusions either. I have witnesses who say what they say. I have the photographs of the scene... they are horrendous, Major. I have this little coin. And I have your doublespeak about you-plural conducting an investigation of yourselves. I have DNA samples collected from the young girl's body," he lied unconvincingly. (Doing so would have outraged the armed men of the village who would have viewed it as a desecration of the corpse.) "If I could be convinced that there is a serious investigation, then I might also be convinced to withhold my story until it had a bit more... context."

Carroll was up now, stalking off to Villeneuve's left. "Mr. Villeneuve... Gaston, if you will hold your story for two days, I will give you details of how the investigation will proceed, and I will promise now to keep you abreast of every development in that investigation. Anyone might pick up a coin that could have fallen anywhere at any time. Surely, journalistic ethics demands that you not trade in innuendo."

"Thank you, Major." Villeneuve offered Carroll his hand. Carroll took it. "If you would send your escort in, I am prepared to return to my hotel. I'll be expecting a call from you by day after tomorrow. Here is my card with my number. *Au revoir, monsieur.*"

COLONEL THOMAS NO longer seemed distracted. He stood looking at Carroll, and Carrol stood there looking back at

Thomas. Thomas dismissed Carroll and called his communications chief on the landline with instructions to bring the programmable inline encryption device for an urgent message.

JSOC Headquarters (Forward)
Near Jalalabad, Afghanistan
July 13, 2010

GENERAL "DICKIE" BAKER was no longer "Boss." He had three layers of commanders under him now, even here—especially here. The old intimacies of that tight little unit at the Chalet were a memory, and the operational tempo here was brutal. He had less than three hours of sleep when the message came in from his old colleague who had apparently gotten himself into another fine mess even while being shelved away at Camp Virtue.

Dickie picked up his landline and dialed.

"Send me your three in person," he told someone on the other end of the line.

Camp Virtue
July 13, 2010

PEDRO HAD MUTED his porn flick so the other guys could rest. Then he nodded off. He saw a great penis coming through a basement window and there was blood on a chilled bottle of wine...

Gene smacked him awake with a none-to-gentle backhand to the shoulder.

"*Carajo!*"

241

Gene was standing over him, and someone snored in the background. Gene was quiet but his eyes burned with wrath.

"We need to talk."

Pedro tried to roll over. "Chill the fuck out, dude!"

Gene slapped the back of Pedro's head then, and Pedro leaped to his feet ready to fight.

"Outside," Gene said. "Now."

Pedro tried to regain his composure, then squinted, leaning into Gene quietly but menacingly. "Dude, chill the fuck out. Just stay cool, man. It's just a couple of hajji bitches. We do this thing, we stay alive a few months, have our fuckin' adventure and we go back to the motherfuckin' real world. Ain't like we gotta stay in a war zone for life, man. We had our cake. We'll eat it, too."

"Outside."

"THEY GOT NOTHIN', man, unless you act like..."

"You have herpes, man?"

"What?"

"Herpes. Genital herpes."

"Dude, whatchoo trippin' 'bout?"

"I saw your medical records, Pedro. It says you have genital herpes."

"Are you outa you fuckin' mind, *huele bicho*!?"

"I'm married, motherfucker!"

"Dude, what the fuck!"

Gene got within an inch of Pedro's face, his eyes flicking, and whispered urgently, "I fucked her after you did, Pedro. I can't take herpes home to my wife, goddamnit."

"That whatchoo trippin' 'bout?" Pedro backed away from Gene's tobacco breath and grimaced. "Dude, I was cured of that shit three years ago."

"You can't cure herpes, Pedro."

"Says who, man? I got an osteopath, this dude cures it all the time, man."

"Pedro, this is bullshit. This is just some fucked up bullshit!"

"No shit, Gene! No shit! This dude, he had me eat this shit looked like packin' plastic every day for a month. I ain't had a outbreak since. He cured me, 'mano."

"Fuckin' bullshit!"

Pete woke up to their rising voices.

"Hey! Tryin' to sleep here. Damn, guys!"

Gene whispered again, "I need to get some antivirals, man. This is *so* not good, *so* not good."

Gene stalked away and Pedro muttered to himself, "*¡Me cago en la crica de tu madre!*"

Baby Doc watched them through the equipment piles in the tent feeling like he was standing in the wind at the edge of a high, high cliff.

Dogpatch disappears

Camp Virtue Airfield
July 13, 2010

SOME CALL IT the "already-not-yet," that pre-mission ready-to-launch atmospheric. The sun had slipped behind the mountains. The day was no longer light but not yet dark. They had committed but the pieces were just being lined up. But already it is done. How it will turn out we don't know—not yet. But we Will. Do. Something. This is an in-betweenness, a state of abstraction magnifying the reality.

The Detachment sat on their rucksacks as the airfield grew dark, noticing everything as if the volume had been turned up. Now the maintenance crew was tinkering with that helicopter. Now one of them coughed. Now a wrench fell. Now the sky started to look painted. Now the birds were startled as a cargo jet roared to a landing in the background. Now a bat took off from a nearby building. Now they smelled the smoldering trash. What might death be like? Which "now" will bring it on? Is death the smell of burnt trash, the flicker of a bat, a handful of gravel or a hospital room with fluorescent lights and a television showing an ad for cheaper hotel rates? So many forks in the road, all of them leading to a dead end. The world will slip and slide along just the same, with or without you.

Outside the airfield, amid the high rocks, a golden jackal was startled by something no one else could hear.

THE DARK TRENDED toward absolute. Still they waited on the apron of the airfield, each member of 649 closed in tightly with his own thoughts. By 2300 hours the choppers were cranked and blasting, rotors thwacking with sparkling trails of phosphorescent light outlining the rotor spans. The MH-47 had two rotors, the joke being that the Chinook was the only chopper that could have a blade strike with itself. The two AH-6 "little bird" gunships sounded like giant wasps alongside the guttural howl of the MH-47. The night was cool and starry, the airfield blacked out and there was a half-moon that seemed to rest between two silhouetted peaks.

Someone somewhere broke the inertia and Dunny passed the command: "Saddle up."

THE AIRFIELD MARSHAL switched on his two infrared flashlights and watched as a dozen equipment-laden black silhouettes stood up and lumbered into a queue at the bottom of the 47's tail ramp. Battle rattle, rucksacks, weapons and helmets outlined distorted masses perched atop twelve sets of impossibly thin legs. The marshal flipped down his goggles and the team lit up in grainy green monochrome, their eyes aglow like animals on a highway at night. The crew chief leaned out and gave a whistle loud enough to punch through the engine noise; and the team began filing up the ramp.

Mountains near Charikar, Afghanistan
Midnight, July 14, 2010

THE PARTIAL MOON had set, solidifying the darkness around a flat depression amid treeless mountains. Out of the breezeless silence came a falsetto *bhoo'-hoe*: a Eurasian eagle owl, sensing a far off sound before hearing it, sounding an alarm, then taking flight.

Barely audible, a hum, slowly growing in intensity to a buzz, then a growl. If a human had been present to observe this ad hoc landing zone, the growl would have been accompanied by approaching black holes in the sky: a big chopper, blocking the stars. The little bird gunships ripped past in the blackness, sounding like sewing machines and flying like hornets, called "killer eggs" because of their egg-shaped fuselage; one with rocket pods, the other with twinned miniguns. The hornets started to orbit around the LZ as the MH-47 sank into the shallow depression, the pilots watching the edges of the rotors through their goggles for possible blade strikes. The clamshell in the back was already open and the front wheel stayed off the ground as the detachment ran toward it, top-heavy, lumbering Sasquatch-like off the back. They stumbled right and left to establish a hasty perimeter. The big chopper levitated, rocked for a moment, tilted forward, executed a 180º pivot and roared away. The little birds buzzed twice more through their right-turn orbits, then tagged along behind the MH-47. Their noise swiftly faded, as if sucked into a black hole. Each member of the team could now hear himself breathe.

The starlight was too faint to make a difference and everything on the dark ground was a stumbling block. It was full of hard, hidden things—obstacles pregnant with hazard, hazards behind hazards. The eagle owl had flown half a mile but the team could still hear it. *Bhoo'-hoe.*

HUMPING IS WALKING, but not like everyday walking—giving the dog a stroll or going to the corner store to buy a lottery ticket. When a grunt humps, even if he is a highly trained, slightly self-important, specialist grunt like everyone with a Special Forces tab, he walks in the dark with almost a hundred pounds over body weight, and his feet slip, scuff, stumble, and strain over black, invisible ground. If he slips just so far the wrong way in the wrong phase of his step, he will totter and topple with all the weight. The threat of falling is always there. When grunts hump, someone always falls. Over the course of a good hump—not that it feels good—pretty much every grunt will fall at least once. Maybe that's how they came to be called grunts—falling foot soldiers who say "Oof!" as they hit the ground.

It's nighttime and the grunt is walking on a compass bearing over unfamiliar rough terrain. There are small stones that bruise his feet, big ones that twist his ankles and erosion channels that can swallow an entire leg. There are thorns, switches and broken branches to lacerate his face and hands, and even the skin under his pant legs and sleeves. There are rocks to bark his shins. There are sudden drops and rises. He is ninety-five percent feeling his way through, the rest coming from his meager night vision. You can walk with those goggles for a while, but then the headaches start, escalating to vertigo and nausea for some. So the grunt night-humps blind, saving the goggles for when they are on or near the target. Creatures observing the proceedings from behind a rocky outcrop that night would have seen twelve laden men walking single file at a fixed distance from one another, their outlines barely visible in the starlight.

They rested for a few moments, then they got up again, scuffing and bumping along in the dark.

Dale walked last, as rear security and to ensure that there were no breaks in contact. He thought back to all the manuals on tactics and techniques, all the bullshit doctrines that suggested that ground soldiers could assume some formal, pre-fighting formation—the tactical wedge, or whatever. How easy that shit looked in a manual and how utterly idiotic it was to try it on the ground, especially at night. Soldiers who are patrolling at night walk single file, period, and even doing that can get complicated if one part of the file, blinded by darkness, walks off and leaves the rest. He reiterated his standing rule to them during the order: "You are responsible for the man behind you in the file. Lose him and you will answer to me." That made them look back. A lot.

Twelve men is a convenient number, divisible by two, three, four and six. His feet fell and his mind drifted. Five and seven inside of twelve, two plus three and three plus four. Plus a dead Virden. He suppressed his laughter.

Crunch. Grunt. He heard one of the men fall.

FALL, THE MAN, was on the point. He held up a hand, signaling a halt. Dale gave a double-kiss noise to backstop the hand signal in the dark. The rustling and scraping of their progress faded as the team complied. Then Dunny shuffled past the file to join Fall, who was looking between two boulders at a few weak lights in the valley ahead. Another person shuffled to the front. Dale dug his GPS receiver out of his chest rig. He unfolded the night-blind, put it to his face, pressed a button and a seam of green light surrounded his face. Then it was gone. Dale tucked the GPS back into his chest rig.

Dale whispered to Fall and Dunny, "I'll take point. 200 meters to the ORP. Pass it back." Each man in the file leaned back to the man behind him, whispering, "200 meters. ORP."

THE OBJECTIVE RALLY Point (ORP) is a place near the target that is not the target. It is a place to shift gears between overland movement and actions on the objective: a control measure to reset the detachment in the face of all those unpredictables. This ORP was on a high plateau shaped like a lopsided pancake covered with a little dry grass and spiny dwarf shrubs. The team formed a small perimeter and waited for ten minutes until the site quieted down and they could listen for other activity. Once they were cleared Woof and Dale stood watch while the rest dug around in their rucksacks and prepared gear for the mission.

One at a time, each man finished his prep for the objective, brought his rucksack to the center and stood in a gaggle. Then Bobby lined them all up. Charikar was visible below, about 800 meters distant, its few dim lights twinkling in the valley. The village was quiet and dark. Pete was breathing hard, wide-eyed in the darkness, almost hyperventilating. Baby Doc quietly crossed himself. Eddy saw him do it and crossed himself too. Stripped now to chest rigs, backpack radios, weapons, body armor and helmets, the detachment filed quietly out of the ORP, leaving Woof and Dale to secure it for their eventual return.

Dale whispered to Woof as the last of the rest of the team filed out, sending him to stand between a big boulder and a little one and to listen and watch in the direction from which they had arrived. Dale posted himself on the opposite end of the ORP, facing the target, less than fifteen meters from Woof. Dale found a shallow depression and dropped down on both knees.

For a while, they could hear the rest of the team's foot-falls crunching over the stony downhill slope. Once the noise was gone Woof settled in and checked his radio.

Very quietly, Dale began taking off his helmet and body armor.

Pope Army Airfield
May, 2004

AT A CHILDREN'S PLAYGROUND just past the end of the runway of Pope Field, Farah and A.D. looked at each other and waited for a C5 to finish its takeoff. A.D. studied Farah's hair, a boy-short afro lit by the sun and circling her head in a tight halo. Once the roar of the plane subsided they could again hear the background noise of children playing raucously. It was a warm, sunny day, the wind dancing against their faces.

"I know ya good man, an' ya trapped in a hard man's body." She was telling him. "I love da good man. Ya baby she loves 'im, too. But ya live by a sword, ya gonna die by a sword. Now ya walk around wid all dem dead Africans in ya head. Ya mind fulla dead bodies, lovah. Ya canno' sleep wid me, nay live even in da same house. Ya tink I don' see a white man in you? That ah don' stroogle across dis rivah between us? Ya not choosin to live apart f' me. Ya choosin' dat uni-fahm. Ain't bein a white man ya problem. Bein a man ya problem. Work as a street cleanah, ya become a street cleanah. Work as a nurse, become a nurse. Ya workin' as a gunfightah. Dat watcha wanna be? Watcha wancha baby's papa t' be? I got t' go, lovah. I'm not a priest o' psychiatrist."

Mountains near Charikar, Afghanistan
July 14, 2010, 0148 Local

THE DETACHMENT HALTED eighty meters from and twenty meters above Charikar. The steep side was less likely to be under any effective observation at night. Dunny and Bobby pushed their faces into the goggles to seal the green light. Dunny's FM broke squelch in his earpiece, and he heard a vague whisper. He pulled at the radio attached to his sour smelling chest harness, mashed the key, and said, "Last calling station, say again, over."

It was Woof, from the ORP.

"Bear, this is Nasty, over." "Bear" was Dunny's code name, "Nasty" was Woof's.

"Nasty, Bear, go ahead, over."

"Bear, Nasty. Dogpatch is mike india alpha, over." (Radio alphabet for "missing in action".)

Bobby twitched. "Huh?" he said.

Dunny leaned into Bobby, pulling the earpiece out and putting it between their heads. "Did he say Dale is missing?" Without waiting for a response, he whispered back into the mike, "Nasty, Bear, did you just say that Dogpatch is mike india alpha?"

"Holy shit," Bobby muttered a bit too loud. This set the rest of the team scuffling around in their positions. Pete was suddenly on them.

"What happened?"

"Top is no longer in the ORP," Bobby whispered, while Dunny muttered, "Fuck, fuck, fuck, fuck me, fuck!"

Pete gave out three consecutive sighs, then gripped Dunny by the arm, almost causing Dunny to drop his weapon.

"We have to abort this mission," he hissed.

IN THE ORP, Woof sat squashed down between three boulders. Sweat was pouring over his whole body. Suddenly, he abandoned radio discipline:

"I am freaking the fuck out here, y'all. I said he is gone. That certifiable motherfucker is gone! I am here all by my goddamn self! Fucking need guidance, over!"

THE SOUND OF Woof's urgent whisper washed over the team and their restlessness increased.

"Keep it down!" Bobby commanded them in a stage whisper. "Fuckin' target is right over there." He turned, and lowered his voice, "Whatcha gonna do now, Captain?"

Dunny spoke into the FM: "Do not move, Nasty. I say again, do not move. Stand fast, and wait one, over."

"Bad sign," Pete suddenly said out loud. Dunny grabbed Pete by the neck so hard it sounded like a slap: "Shut. The fuck. Up." Then, to himself, whispering: "How in the hell can someone just disappear?"

There was a sudden repetitive whimper, like a rodent calling out in three syllable bursts: "Oh my God. Oh my God. Oh my God..." It was Pete, slouching toward catatonia.

There was a long pause. Then Captain Bob took a long breath and tried to remember some yoga breathing exercise his wife had told him about: exhaling longer than inhaling. Finally he spoke: "We continue the mission."

Pete seemed to be praying now; the same murmured prayer again and again: "No, no, no, no, no..."

"Shut the fuck up, Pete!" Bobby hissed at him. "Get the fucking sand outa yer clit and shut the fuck up!"

"Nasty, this is Bear, over."

"Go ahead, over."

"We're gonna charlie mike, how copy, over?" (Continue mission.)

Another long pause—an anguished one.

"Roger," Woof answered. "I copy. Charlie mike. Out.

COLONEL THOMAS PACED like a caged tiger inside the Task Force Operations Center. He did a sudden about face when his signal officer called him, a red-headed Captain named Elijah Bond.

Thomas strode through the staff, people and equipment like Moses parting the waters until he was hovering over Bond, who was seated in front of a communications array.

"What've you got, Captain?"

"Sir, the team has lost a man." Bond kept still in his seat, facing forward at the technical array.

"Lost him?" roared Thomas, looking around the room like the answer to his question was an escaped hamster. "KIA? Are they in contact?"

"He's missing in action, Sir. Code name Dogpatch."

"That's fuckin' Dale!" he shouted again. His entire staff was now crowded behind around. "That's fuckin' Dale! How in the holy fuck do you lose a fuckin' Team Sergeant? I'm puttin' Bob Dunny's balls in a cider press!"

Actions on the objective

Charikar, Afghanistan
July 14, 2010 – 0212 Local

THE LAST CONTROL point near the target turned out to be a public latrine of sorts— a patchwork of piles of human excrement spread over an indistinct region of darkness. This field of shit hadn't been indicated on the map during planning. Sis was the first to step in it, and when he did the smell burst forth like a poisonous puffball and suffused them all. Somewhere up the mountain behind them, where they had left Hillman and Dale, a spring fed the trickle of water. They could hear it down here. It was probably where locals rinsed their hands after taking a dump. Eddy dropped down to one knee to feel for it, then realized that he too had just mashed out a pile with his kneepad. He cursed out loud. Bobby whispered:

"Shut the fuck up, yo! We're like a hundred meters out, goddamnit."

"This is a fuckin' shitter," Eddy whispered in protest.

"Shower in Lysol when we get back. Right now we're in fuckin' Apache country!"

Dunny grabbed Bobby by the elbow.

"That's the house, over there," Dunny whispered. "It looks exactly like the satellite image."

He's getting ahead, thought Bobby.

"Sir, satellite images are deceptive. The building is over there!" He pointed to a smaller structure buried among other stone buildings. "They all look like the satellite image! Inkblots and dirty diapers look like satellite imagery!"

"We need to abort this mission!" It was Pete. He had come out of nowhere.

"Shut the fuck up!" Bobby and Dunny said it in unison.

"Get back there," Dunny whispered, "and get your shit together, Mr. Townall. We're not aborting a fuckin' thing." Pete sighed, then sighed again, stomping off.

Bobby turned back to Dunny. "Your call, Sir. You're in charge. But I remember the sat image, and there were, like, houses on three sides. I really think I remember three, Sir. That one only has two."

"It's on the backside maybe. I'm goin' with my gut. We hit *that* one."

THEY SHUFFLED INTO position. Bobby cringed at every noise they made, every sound now amplified during their approach. A dog started yipping a football field away. Captain Bob was bathed in sweat. Eddy couldn't figure out whether he wanted to go down on his right knee—the one covered in shit—or his left knee as he took up a position on left flank security in the rocky street, so he stood even though it increased his silhouette. The thought occurred to him that he might die with some strange Afghani's shit on him. Opie was on right flank security, his heart fluttering as he knelt there, and he couldn't figure out whether it was anticipation or the Red Bull he had chugged at the release point. He had a thick dip of Copenhagen in his lower lip, but he wasn't able to generate enough saliva to moisten it, and his stomach was burning. Sis was on rear security, across the street—if you could call it that, all ten rocky feet of it—facing the release point.

He keyed his mike, and sent the Forward Operating Base the Schedule Code for arriving at the breaching point: "Hotel-six, this is Lima-niner. Petunia. I say again, petunia, over." In his earpiece, he received the reply. "Niner, six. Roger. I copy, petunia, out." Pete was on the other side of the house, on forward security, as it were, trying to control his hands which were shaking violently. He gripped his weapon hard and locked the muscles across his shoulders, chest, back, and arms, willing himself into a fixed pose, like a statue. Then he stood there bargaining with an unfamiliar God that he would never this or always that if only he would get back to Camp Virtue safely. Gene stood against one corner of the house next to a window that was closed tight with wooden shutters. He was watching the immediate backs of Pedro, Fall, Bobby, Baby Doc, and Captain Bob. They were lined up, in that order, to go through the front door, their weapons at low-port, pressed nut-to-butt into each other to get as many as possible through the door as rapidly as possible. Each of them was lit up inside with that tingling disquiet that preceded a parachute jump or a deliberate attack. Gene would stay outside after the breach.

Dunny reached up with his left hand and squeezed Baby Doc's left shoulder. Baby Doc passed the signal to Bobby in front of him, and Bobby passed it to Fall. Pedro, as first in the door, was nearly aquiver with anticipation when Fall squeezed. Pedro keyed the light on his 12-gauge shotgun, aimed the light at the top hinge and fired. The blast seemed to tear the whole night apart. Down, he aimed the light at the lower hinge. There was a scream from inside. He fired the second round, and the door settled a-kilter in the frame. Pedro kicked it once, then again, and it toppled to the right and inside. The entry team's white Mag-lights were on now, their goggles flipped up.

Pedro went left to the corner, not six feet away. Fall's corner on the right was less than four. Bobby and Baby Doc went down the middle toward an interior door. That was where the screaming came from. Suddenly the door opened.

Pedro hit the old man who came out with a shotgun blast. The old man, wearing striped pajamas, seemed to tilt sideways, then he flopped straight down on the rug beneath him, blood flooding from under him like someone opened a faucet. The screaming old woman came out behind him. As she dropped to her knees to grasp her dead husband Fall let loose with a three-round burst from the M-4 that tore off the back of her head.

Outside, Gene had knelt below the window, facing outward to reduce his vulnerability. His head was just above the bottom of the window. Two of Fall's three rounds had passed through the parietal and occipital bones of the old woman's head, spalling and hitting the stone and cob wall behind her. One of the rounds passed mere millimeters from her head and hit a slightly concave stone embedded in the wall behind her that happened to be apatite—a hard crystal. The bullet, weighing 55 grains before it hit the stone, split in two with the impact. One of the two fragments, weighing 21 grains, flattened into a sharp disk by the impact, ricocheted between Pedro and Bobby, caught the corner of a bit of granite embedded in the other wall, turned downward, pierced the wooden shutters of the window slowing down to 307 feet per second and entered Gene's neck from behind neatly severing his cervical spinal cord between sixth and seventh cervical vertebrae. When the bullet came to rest Gene was already some kind of dead—not the coming back from the dead kind of dead. Gene toppled backward into the wall, where he came to rest with his head on the ground and his knees still tucked clumsily beneath him. No one saw this happen. Nor did he have time to realize what happened. Some would consider that a perfect death.

"Go! Go! Go! Go! Go!" shouted Dunny to Bobby and Baby Doc, who were staring at the piled couple. They hesitated, then plunged through the door from behind which the old couple had come. They waved their flashlight beams across everything—the cob walls, a threadbare rug, a rickety chair, rumpled bedclothes, an old trunk. Then they both stood very still for several seconds.

"Whatcha got?" demanded Dunny from the other room.

"Clear," Bobby called back.

The team suddenly fell into a stunned silence and stood frozen in their own spots. Fall broke the silence.

"Uh-oh," he said. Then the silence resumed. That's when they heard voices from around the village shocked awake by the gunfire. Bobby and Baby Doc returned to the main room and waved their flashlights around.

"Oh no," was all that Baby Doc could say. One by one, the lights were extinguished until the room was black again. Then Fall had a coughing fit. The men tipped their goggles back down while Fall struggled to suppress his coughing. Their eyes became pale green figments hovering in the dark. A gurgle escaped from the body of the old woman.

"Sir, we need to get out of here," said Bobby. Another moment of silence, another bubbling noise from the bodies... "Sir! We need to go!" Urgent voices were approaching and there were sounds of shuffling feet closing in on them down the unpaved street. Captain Dunny was frozen in the dark. Bobby took the initiative and headed out the door. The other men followed, weapons back at high port. Dunny suddenly unfroze and blew three piercing blasts on his whistle to signal withdrawal. The unseen group on the street went silent. Two groups of men stood silent and motionless within earshot of one another in the moonless dark.

As the detachment stepped outside, Pete wheeled around the corner of the structure toward them.

"We ready?" he whispered tensely. "We ready to go? Hajjis are coming."

"Where's Gene?" Bobby demanded. Pedro responded by taking off around the house to look.

"Oh, fuck!" they heard.

"What?" Bobby stage whispered.

Pedro appeared again, saying, "Gene's gone, man. He's hit. He's dead."

"Hit?" said Bobby aloud. Catching himself, he reverted to a whisper. "How was he hit?" No one had fired but them.

An involuntary cry erupted from Pete, as Baby Doc ran back to Gene's position. Then they heard Baby Doc's voice, a quiet voice. "Christ, have mercy!"

Bobby had taken over. "Baby Doc, Pedro, carry 'im. Quick! Goddammit! We're in Apache country! Captain Bob, you okay?"

Another beat passed before Dunny responded: "Yeah, yeah. Yeah, okay. Okay, let's go." Then it was as if Dunny had suddenly found his legs. "Let's go!" Dunny commanded. "Everyone across the street!"

Eddy was across the street, listening to both the approach of the Afghanis and the commotion at the house. He couldn't tell through his goggles who was who or who was doing what, but when they crossed the street, they were clustered around something—a body it appeared—that they dragged, heaved, dropped, then dragged again, their efforts accompanied by whispered curses. It was one of them, he could tell from the gear.

"Oh no! Wha' happened?"

The crackle of automatic weapons fire ripped up the street in front of them. The muzzle flashes were less than a hundred meters away. The team hit the ground in unison and squirmed helter-skelter in the dark, each man feeling ahead of him for some kind of cover.

Opie took the first action. He reached into his chest rig and tugged loose a pale-green, beer can-sized, heavy-as-lead white phosphorus grenade. He pulled the pin. The pin flew off with a "tink," followed by the muffled pop of the fuse.

"Fire in the hole," he shouted, slinging the heavy grenade down the street toward their now charging aggressors. The grenade thumped onto the street... one thousand, two thousand, three...

When the "Willy Pete" exploded, more of a loud "whump" than a bang, the whole street lit up in a blinding white fountain of fire—ten million candlepower—and white smoke snaked through the blazing streamers. Opie had thrown it just over the assailant's heads. The phosphorous fire backlit three fighters coming down the street, now around twenty meters away. The Afghani fighters didn't even take cover. Two just opened up on full automatic as they advanced, while one had begun rolling on the ground, his back and legs alight with the phosphorous. Their fire was high, directed down the street across the front of the team, and ineffective.

Eddy aligned his M-249 light machine gun and released a burst of fifty rounds that sounded like an amplified chain saw. The two remaining Taliban fighters wilted in their tracks. A child started screaming in one of the nearby dwellings. They heard no one else now, just the crackle of burning phosphorus.

Captain Dunny shouted, "Let's go!"

"Wait, sir! Wait!" said Bobby. They were talking aloud now; there was no point in stealth anymore. Baby Doc and Pedro were trying to lift Gene by his arms and legs, but they kept slipping on gravel and falling. Everything was easier now with the glaring white light from the WP.

"We can't wait," Dunny said.

"It's him," Bobby said, pointing to the dead face of one of the lit-up Afghani corpses. "I think it's him!"

"Him who?"

"The target, Sir! Goose-Man-John-Geary. The guy! Our target!" Bobby was already reaching into his chest-rig, pulling out the digital camera. "Wait here, Sir."

Pedro and Baby Doc had enlisted Eddy and Sis to try and carry Gene. Baby Doc had pulled a poleless stretcher out of his bag, and they were rolling Gene's body onto it. Pete was aiming his weapon back and forth along the street, looking as if he were about to panic and run away. Fall ran out behind Bobby, watching up the street while Bobby leaned over the corpse of one of the Afghanis. Bobby took one hand and straightened the dead man's face a bit, then began shooting pictures with a flash, even though the dead Afghan fighter's face was still lit by the now dimming phosphorus fires that burned all over the street. There were tree moles all in a row on that now familiar face. One of the corpses—the one that went down with the WP grenade—was still burning, emitting strangely green smoke.

Bobby finished taking pictures and ran back to the Captain with Fall in tow.

"Capture or kill, Sir. That was the mission. It's him. Mission accomplished."

Dunny showed a flicker of a smile. "Oh..."

"Let's book!" said Bobby.

The withdrawal to the ORP was clumsy, with men taking turns at the corner of the soft litter that bore Eugene Pollard's remains. Gene was a heavy motherfucker.

WOOF HEARD LOUD scuffing and scrabbling that made his heart race. Terror rippled through his body like a wave. The radio squelched.

"Nasty, this is Bear, over." Woof blew out a long sigh of relief.

PULLED INTO A tight perimeter, the detachment waited for the extraction bird. The corpse was still on the soft litter, now with a poncho wrapped over it and secured with two bungee cords. As they waited, each man again withdrew into himself as the outcome of the mission sank in. One dead. One missing. An old couple laying in their own blood in their own house. It was 0435 local. Clouds had obscured the stars and the darkness was nearly complete. In the distance, they suddenly heard the extraction chopper approaching, an MH-47E with two Little Bird gunships as escort.

THE CLEARING BARRELS looked like twin red cannons—like the short, pot-bellied cannons of the Civil War. They were made from 55-gallon drums with an eight-inch hole in the end and were propped up at a forty-five degree angle on an angle iron frame and surrounded by plump sandbags,. Like the bags, the barrels were filled with sand to safely absorb the bullet from an accidental discharge should some luckless, sleep-deprived troop improperly clear his rifle. Each member of the team dropped his magazine, charged his weapon to eject the chambered round, poked the muzzle through the barrel hole, and clicked the hammer onto an empty chamber. The barrels were positioned outside the Task Force operations building where the Detachment was going for their mission debriefing. The cloud cover was thin and the new sunrise suffused the camp in light the color of lead, queerly backlighting the candy-red barrels. The team took its time because they sensed that the debriefing was going to be a real hotwash. Gene's body had been intercepted by medics at the airfield but Baby Doc was still carrying Gene's rifle along with his own.

Major Dean, a plump, balding, humorless man with the face of an otter, was the Task Force G-3. He met them inside and directed them to a meeting room behind him. The room was small for a whole detachment plus the debriefing officers, with most of the space taken up by a long, plain, tawny-surfaced table. The walls were blond panel-board, unadorned, and the fluorescent lights threw a greenish hue over everything. A quiet window air conditioner was perched high on the wall next to the door. The place smelled like furniture polish and burnt coffee. A fifty-cup percolator was set up on one end of the table, with a tube of polystyrene cups, to keep the men awake. No creamer; no sugar; no chairs. This was no "Welcome home, boys!" It was an interrogation and the interrogators weren't happy.

The men had barely enough room to stand, so Bobby— who was closest to the coffee pot—just started filling cups and passing them down like doses of bad medicine. Major Dean, in a freshly pressed uniform and wafting a cloud of aftershave, stood just inside the door, his face blank and un-welcoming. The boys didn't even try to ground their equipment. In the time it took for everyone to quit shuffling about the room started to stink of sour sweat. Their camouflage face paint was rubbed off and streaked and they didn't look fierce now—just grimy. Several had dried, brown blood on their hands and clothes. Captain Dunny had the thousand-yard stare of a man facing execution.

Colonel Thomas burst through the door shouting, "On your feet!" even though they were all standing, and they all snapped to some approximation of the position of attention, made difficult by all the gear hanging off them. Thomas did not issue an "at ease," and instead launched into a spitting tirade.

"Gentlemen, let me be the first to say I am sorry for the loss of Sergeant Pollard. That said, let me ask... where the fuck is your Team Sergeant, Detachment 649?" No one answered, so he continued. "It's a rhetorical question, I guess, because no one seems to have an answer. I'm gonna leave you to the Task Force G-2 in just a fucking minute, oh ye saddened gentlemen of six four fucking nine, for your mission debrief. But let me say this right now. From everything I know, this so-called mission was a world class, blue ribbon goat fuck! Be glad right now that the Army has outlawed summary executions! The only thing that prevents this being an *unmitigated* goat fuck is that you have—to my understanding—a photograph of Usman Jahangiri's dead fucking head in your possession. And it fucking well better be unassailably authentically *that* fucking hajji cunt's head!"

He stopped and fixed each of them in turn with his shiny red eyes.

"You all and I will generate a 52-card pack of lies for the public about whatever the fuck happened there, just because we can't let them know that the elite, quiet professionals of Special Forces are a bunch of monkeys gang-raping a football. But I warn you now. Right fucking now. Do not fucking lie to my G-2, gentlemen. I want to know exactly what in the motherfucking hell happened out there. And I will find out, or JC never hung on a motherfucking cross!"

He paused again for a beat. "That is all," he said almost matter-of-factly. He pivoted, stomped out and slammed the door behind himself so hard that the whole room shook.

"At ease," Major Dean said when Colonel Thomas was gone. "Stack your shit the best you can. I'm sorry about Dale and Pollard."

THAT MORNING, TWO waiters were trying to keep up with orders at the Intercontinental Hotel's dining room. Virden and Peanut were shoveling in bread, fruit, and eggs near the pool. Connie was just joining George and Rosemarie at a table for four, all of the reporters looking freshly showered, though last night's martinis had popped some blood vessels in Connie's eyes. They all glanced over at Gaston from time to time, who was dunking a baguette in sweet coffee and talking to two men, European by the looks of it, who sat with him. Gaston's phone, in his front trouser pocket, went off with a rooster crow ringtone and he broke off his conversation to answer it.

SERGEANT BARBER LEANED deceptively chastely over Major Carroll's shoulder. His office door was open as he alternated between scowling at his laptop monitor and furious typing. The afternoon press briefing injected a sense of urgency into the entire staff.

"Not 'three Taliban,'" she suggested. "Sounds too minimal. Try 'several Taliban'... no, 'the entire formation of Taliban was killed during the engagement.'"

"What if they ask how many?" he quizzed her.

"No more than a dozen, our detachment was forced to break contact, so the exact number is still unclear. We are still reviewing the mission."

His fingers danced over the keyboard.

"That's good," he said, risking a brief but affectionate glance, then resumed his typing.

"WHEN DID YOU realize he was... how did you say it? Gone?" Major Dean had released the rest of the team, but he was still interrogating Woof in the little debriefing room. Dean had brought in two chairs, and they sat across the table from one another, Woof ragged with exhaustion, his eyes hollow and sticky.

"I keep tellin' ya, Sir, I'm not sure. I mean, he tol' me to cover our approach into the ORP. He went to twelve o'clock... or so I assumed. After a few minutes, it got really quiet."

"How long? How long before you discovered he was missing?"

"I dunno, Sir. When I called Captain Bob... Dunny. Maybe an hour, maybe less."

"No other noises? No suspicious noises?"

"Sir, he was just fuckin' gone. I never seen any shit like this, Sir."

"Do you think he was captured?"

"How the fuck... Sorry, Sir. I have no idea. I was with someone, then I was alone. Out there!" He pointed toward a low sky. "I was all alone in the middle of fucking Afghanistan. At night! Scariest three hours of my life, Sir."

Rot in hell

Mountains near Kabul, Afghanistan
July 14, 2010

THE WIND STIRRED AS THE sun warmed the air along the thin gully snaking between boulders, the morning light throwing off brilliant contrasts. An alligator lizard with alternating fawn and mahogany bands from nose to tail perched atop a red slab of sandstone soaking up the first rays. It cocked its head at the movement below, where Dale was picking his way through the trench, taking advantage of its concealment. His body armor and MICH were gone, left in a heap below the Objective Rally Point. Stripped down to chest rig, side arm and rifle, his face smudged with camo paint, he was sweating like a horse even in the cool morning air. He stopped to catch his breath. Resting on one of the stones for a few moments, he felt his age and his utter lack of sleep. He had less than a quart of water left in the canteen attached to the chest rig. He dug his last protein bar out of one of the pockets. Search and rescue birds with gunship escorts were popping up in the distance, near Charikar, looking for him.

Polypeptides, he thought. *Poly, many. Polymorphous. Polyamory. Polysaccharide. Polly Molly.* Higher along the ridge, three Afghanis, *Taliban*, armed with Kalashnikovs, whispered tensely. The *amrekayan* was out of range, perhaps 500 meters distant, and they debated how best to get closer to him for an attack.

GASTON AND EMAL looked up the street before they entered the parking garage. The rising sun lit the mountain behind the hotel, leaving the narrow street leading into the garage in a cool shadow. A breeze agitated the pines. Some idiot had left his Volvo beater parked near the entrance. Gaston cursed under his breath, seeing that there was barely enough space to get out.

Emal opened the front passenger door on the Borrego, propping his folding Kalashnikov inside, then climbed in. Gaston opened the back left door, tossed in his battered briefcase, slammed the door and climbed into the driver's seat, sucking his teeth. He offered Emal a cigarette, then took one for himself, pushed in the panel lighter and started the engine. As he backed out, Emal grabbed the lighter as it popped up, lit his own cigarette and held the lighter up for Gaston, who leaned into it after shifting into Drive.

Gaston angled the Borrego wide to the left as he approached the exit, angling to squeeze past the rusty gray Volvo, muttering *"Merde!"* again. There were hardly six inches on either side as he crawled through, and he was about to curse again when the Volvo exploded.

THE AFGHAN PATROLMEN, wearing olive green de Gaulle caps, were hanging around aimlessly with their hands in their pockets. Three militiamen had shown up, apparently to run things, and they were talking to the two Afghan medics who wrestled the shredded bodies out of the Borrego.

270

Journalists stood in the parking garage in a gaggle with several hotel employees at some distance from the scene of the explosion. Connie Mason was dabbing at her eyes. George Yowell had his arm around her. A collective gasp escaped from the cluster of onlookers when the first body was pulled through the shattered windshield, missing the head and the left arm.

Joint Special Operations Command Forward Operating Base
Khost, Afghanistan
July 14, 2010

THE PRICK-150 radio lit up, and Brigadier General "Dickie" Baker waited and listened.

"Plaster quest," came the disembodied voice. This was the operational schedule code for "mission complete."

"Roger, out," Baker replied.

A perfect tactical communication. In and out.

Mountains near Kabul, Afghanistan
July 14, 2010

MEHTAR, SHAMAL AND Syal crouched in the gully, weapons hanging over their shoulders on improvised slings, hands on the pistol grips, fingers on the triggers. Mehtar had spotted the enemy soldier minutes earlier: a bareheaded *amrekayan*, alone, with a rifle, picking his way through the *khowarh* for cover. They would climb out of this erosion ditch, inch over the short stretch of high ground toward the American's ravine, and shoot him from above. Mehtar motioned Shamal to go first. Without hesitation, Shamal clambered over the lip of the furrow, then squatted on top, waiting for the others. Syal climbed out, then Mehtar. Bent forward at their waists, they crept toward the edge of the ravine.

They all flinched when a covey of quail exploded from a screen of *olinoq* shrubs on their right. Syal, the jumpiest of the three, almost fired at the birds, and Mehtar was rebuking him when the first two shots—pop-pop, in rapid succession—hit Syal in the chest, collapsing him like his strings were cut. The second set of two shots killed Mehtar as he looked for the origin of the shots. Shamal stood erect, looking puzzled, when the final two shots went through his heart and thoracic spine. It was over in less than four seconds, and Dale climbed out of the ditch where he had circled behind them. He thumbed the M-4's selector switch to "safe." Then he stopped and stared at the bodies. Blood pooled quickly under each of them. Center-of-mass chest shots with open wound tracts. The flies arrived in less than a minute, numbers growing quickly. He wondered who would mourn these men.

"Sorry," he whispered, taking bits of their clothing.

Camp Virtue

THE FILTHY AND exhausted ODA 649 filed out of the Task Force Operations complex, heading back toward their billet tent. No one spoke as they tramped heavily down Main Street, their gear seeming heavier after they re-shouldered it. Gene's death and a ponderous sense of failure weighed heavily on them all.

Baby Doc was freighted with the memory of the old couple left dead in their home. An unbearable hollowness filled him like a poison, his occupancy of space and time—of the here and now—seeming somehow ghostly and gratuitous. He couldn't even imagine that going home would let him escape or find refuge from this desolate dread. Minutes later, in the tent, while some headed for showers, some for their bunks, he took his rosary out of his pocket and in desperation began to pray—*Hail Mary, full of grace...* —with a newfound sense that no one was listening. He looked down as he worked through the rosary. On the floor before him were his spare boots, alongside his MICH, a ragged bit of 550 cord, a used plastic spoon from who knows where. Then he stopped. A tiny seed of fury broke open in him, barely discernible yet, but something he might eventually grasp. Not hope exactly, but a handhold.

BOBBY SAT ON his cot, hair still wet, a towel wrapped around his waist, just out of the shower. He took the Asus EEE notebook out of his foot locker and plugged it into a power strip that ran from the generator. The team had its own VSAT modem. He booted it up, leaned back onto a poncho liner draped over a duffel bag, kicked off his shower shoes and pulled his feet up onto the cot. Once the notebook finished booting up he opened his email.

There, among the spam for fake Viagra, thicker dicks and get-rich scams was the subject line, "Sayonara, Motherfucker!" Sender: carolina-groove@gmail.com. Bobby's heart leapt. Something was really wrong here. He opened the message.

"All I can take from you, Bobby. I'm leaving you a little going away attachment. YOU PIECE OF SHIT MOTHER-FUCKER! ROT IN HELL!" There was a video attachment. Bobby looked around, angling the screen away from the interior of the tent, and killed the sound before opening the attachment. The picture was dark and grainy, the camera obviously set down at a distance, and the room poorly lit. It took him a moment before he recognized his own bedroom in their Fayetteville home. Within a few seconds Bobby could discern the action. Carolina was in the bed, hands lashed to the head-board somehow, wearing a blindfold. Her legs were up, though, wrapped around the black man who was thrusting into her as she appeared to make involuntary vocalizations. Bobby gazed into the screen with horrified fascination.

STAFF SERGEANT HOWE, aka "Chlamydia" from the chow hall, was draped in a disposable blue paper gown, her head enveloped in a matching hood with a plastic eye shield. A Mortuary Affairs Specialist, she prepared to wash Gene's body. Gene, completely naked, face up on a stainless steel table, his eyes now a flat, milky blue, had a post-mortem semi-erection with a drop of dry blood plugging the meatus. His mouth was open as if he were about to speak.

The morgue was draped with flags on one wall, one for each nation belonging to ISAF. There were two high lockers for the MAS's to change their clothes. Wall hangers held vari-ous implements, from forceps to plain scissors. There were rolls of paper towel at each end near the hand-washing sinks, rolls of plastic and packing tape, stainless cabinets, an X-ray machine to check dead bodies for debris or booby traps and large black plastic totes to drop in clothing and equipment. One of them was open, with Gene's uniform and gear inside, to be separated after the body has been processed. In another corner was a break area with a snack table and a mini-fridge. A dartboard hung on the wall with six darts in it—three red and three blue.

Howe dipped a large sponge into a bucket of soapy water and started with the feet. When she was done and Gene was dried and packaged and shifted onto a gurney for storage and shipment, SSG Howe hosed down the table. The murky water would be swallowed by the drain in the middle of the swaled concrete floor.

THE SECURE PHONE lit up as it gave out a simple ringtone. Colonel Thomas picked it up.

"Thomas." A long beat. "Roger, I'll turn it on now."

He was red-eyed and unshaven. His uniform blouse hung on the back of his chair. He got up, crossed the room and picked up his cable television remote. He clicked it at the wall-mounted screen, sank back into the chair and thumbed it to pick up TCN International.

There was a loop running with the remains of two smoking, heavily damaged automobiles with Afghani cops milling around. The newscaster was a female, voiced over.

"...Three people were killed, including a French journalist, and at least eight wounded. The bomb, which is suspected to be the work of the Taliban, detonated in the morning, before the streets were filled, minimizing casualties...

"On the scene is George Yowell."

George was dressed in body armor and a Kevlar helmet, facing the camera. He seemed very serious. There was a satellite delay of about two seconds.

"Thank you, Marina. Yes, we're withholding the name of our colleague from France until his next-of-kin have been notified. But this appeared to be a case of wrong place, wrong time. This is normally a very busy street, and it is *right outside our hotel*. Speculation is that the bomb was on a timer and detonated early..."

BENHAM AND THREE other AMF's were eating together in the Afghani section of the DFAC. Their conversation was furtive. Benham remained when the other three rose, carried their trays over to the bus tubs, and exited.

Minutes later

LENNY FORD WAS on the main gate again, baked on hash before 8:30 AM. When the three AMFs in their beat up Jeep Cherokee approached from inside the compound, he didn't even look as they held up their security passes. He just waved then through and popped the top on a Red Bull.

Kabul, Afghanistan
Chinese Restaurant
July 14, 2010
10:18 AM Local

COLORFUL UMBRELLAS PUNCTUATED the bustle of the busy street, giving street merchants a spot of shade. The sun was clear and already earnest as traffic ground its way through thoroughfares choked with exhaust fumes. One could almost taste the diesel smoke. White-and-yellow taxis stood out as specimens of uniformity in the chaos. A battered Corolla with a packed interior was also carrying four children in the open trunk. A cart laden with car tires was wedged into the traffic, towed by a donkey led by a man in a blue *shalwar kameez* and a black cap. Men walked their Chinese bicycles, stopping often to talk. An old woman sat on one corner, waving away flies, selling biscuits out of a tub to other women enshrouded in burqas. Pigeons and sparrows watched and foraged. Children laughed and squealed. A gaggle of girls passed by wearing blue school uniforms with white headscarves.

There was one particular dusty man in country garb who wore a filthy keffiyeh over his head and face. He carried a large bundle on his back, which he plopped down in front of the Chinese Restaurant. He pounded on the black steel security door.

Camp Virtue
July 14, 2010

"COCKSUCKER! MOTHERFUCKER!" HE muttered as he changed the cables on a faulty SATCOM. Virden worked in one corner of the commo hooch, a minimal designation for what was one of the biggest structures on the compound—a giant Quonset hut that bristled with every species of antenna. If electromagnetic waves were visible, it would glow in the dark.

When Virden was on active duty with 3rd Group he learned that the detachment's communicators were always in the spotlight. The higher powers wanted communication more than they wanted mission completion. Often just making the communications work was considered mission completion. When they were cross-training, the other specialties liked doing IVs with the medics, playing with guns with the weapons men, blowing shit up with the engineers, but commo always bored them. *Nothin' sexy about radios, until they fuckin' needed one.* But when the after-action reviews were done, the commanders' main metric was whether or not you had established and maintained commo. If not, guess whose ass was on the line? *The same motherfucker who humped eighty pounds of radios, batteries and antennas, that's who!* It was all taken for granted until you were taken to task. Everyone jacked off about how smart the medics were, but no one cared that you had mastered wave propagation theory, that you could copy code or memorize twenty call signs and frequencies before each mission. Radios don't bleed or make a big bang. So, fuck it, he was sick of it, and when he found he could do the same shit for $140,000 a year, plus his per diem, it was "gone baby gone."

He was running late when the SATCOM went down, and he had to meet Peanut like five minutes ago. Check in with Nanji, get a few things in town. They wanted to get in early and get out. Shit was blowing up all over the country. The last two days were like a rocket-propelled grenade bash for the Hajj. Eight motherfuckers killed in Helmand alone—stay the fuck out of Helmand, and Paktia, too—militias catching hell, car bombs, you name it. Talk was they were going to ratchet down Camp Virtue for a few days; and Nanji owed him an advance on next week's shipment—two girls from Tajikistan.

PEANUT PULLED UP in the Batmobile. Virden came outside slinging a day pack over his shoulder, circled the front of the vehicle, opened the door, tossed in the pack, pulled his weapon out of the seat and got in.

They drove away, flushing up a black-headed jay feeding on a dusty chunk of cantaloupe that lay discarded in the middle of Main Street. Peanut swerved to mash the fruit with a tire. Virden stared up through the tinted ballistic glass, ignoring Peanut's little game.

Post Chapel
Camp Virtue
July 14, 2010

PRO DEO ET *Patria.* So read the sign on the gable above the chapel door, the words curving down and around a shield, gold over blue, looking like a scrotum on a vaguely phallic coat of arms, the shield itself topped by a glans-like knob composed of two wheat spikes arched over a shepherd's staff. Below the stubby phallus was a simple sign, again gold over blue: "Camp Virtue Chapel." The rest of the building—a simple wood-framed quadrangle with a 12/5 bi-pitch roof—was painted tan to blend with the desert camouflage motif of the base. There was a glider swinging on four chains at one side of a short wooden porch for chaplains to put their flocks at ease.

The door swung open just as Baby Doc was about to knock, and Captain Nelson, or *Father* Nelson, stepped out, offering Baby Doc his hand.

"Hi, Hector." Father Nelson was in his t-shirt—chaplains were allowed these little deviations—and so freshly shaved that his cheeks were an angry pink, contrasting unnaturally with his nearly white eyebrows and lashes. The chaplain's pale hair was buzzed almost to the skin, his scalp girded by a line of eczema.

"Father..."

"Have a seat," Nelson aimed his upturned palm at the glider, taken a bit aback by how badly Sergeant Fermin stank, still filthy and unshaven—which was strange, because Hector Fermin was previously the only man left on the Detachment who had stateside garrison grooming standards. As for the rest, with those beards and costumes...

The wind picked up a bit as a C-5 howled through a take-off.

Twenty minutes later, Father Nelson asked, "Of how much of this are you sure?"

"All of it. Pretty sure. The mission, I was there. The other, I'm pretty sure..."

Nelson sighed and leaned forward, placing his elbows on his knees and his hands over his face. He rubbed his cheeks, licked his lips, and then rubbed his hands together.

"You know that you and I are both prohibited by law from discussing mission details with the public. I'm in the Army just like you. On this other, you need to be perfectly sure. This is profoundly serious, Hector."

"What the fuck does *that* mean?"

Chinese Restaurant
July 14, 2010

HE LEFT HIS assault rifle in the seat. Peanut stayed behind the wheel. Virden approached Nanji's front door with only a battle vest, radio and sidearm. Virden banged on the security screen with the side of his fist, making a sound like someone shaking a chain link fence.

"Nanji!" he yelled, impatient with the looming threat that they would lock down Virtue and disrupt his cash flow. The door cracked open and a hand shot out and in to unlatch the security screen, like a lizard tasting the air.

Virden just caught sight of a back disappearing into Nanji's office. Nanji had all the lights out, and Virden was still sun-struck and half blind. He looked back at the bar of sunlight pouring through the open door, swimming with lit up specks of dust.

"You just gettin' up, you lazy fuck?" Virden said as he entered the office, which was also enclosed in an unlighted gloom. He heard flies. Nanji was sitting at his desk looking at the ceiling. Virden blinked twice as if that would restore his dusk vision. A surge of adrenalin washed through him and he felt his scrotum contract and his anus loosen. Nanji's throat was cut. Virden looked down. He was standing in a sticky map of blood.

Virden went for his sidearm and started to yell for Peanut, turning around, only to see a dirty Afghan man, his face veiled by a keffiyeh. The room jumped to the side, then a star blossomed on the side of his head, and then he was asleep.

Peanut was sitting in the truck watching a skinny dog quivering to shit when the radio squelched.

"Get in here right now!" Not even a callsign. *What the fuck?*

Peanut grabbed his rifle and ran, then hesitated halfway to the door, realizing he was leaving a vehicle and a weapon unattended. He ran back, jumped in and pulled the keys, hit the door locks, then ran back into the building, where two shots in rapid succession took off most of his head.

The girls upstairs began screaming. Dale stepped back into the office, looked down at Virden where the rifle butt had felled him, and shot Virden once in his upturned nose, making his eyes bulge. Then he had to run upstairs to reassure the girls. There were seven of them, wet-eyed, huddling together in a corner.

HE DUG HIS dirty uniform out of the sling and left the Afghan clothing scattered on the floor upstairs. He was at first flummoxed by the locked door of the truck, but then realized that Virden's driver must have the keys, went through Peanut's pockets and found them. Once the Batmobile was open, the back door agape, he shouted in Farsi at the gaggle of girls waiting just inside the door.

"*Biaa injaa!*"

The grizzled garage guard leaned his weapon against the wall and averted his gaze, wondering if he still had a job and grateful to still have his life.

Downtown Kabul
July 14, 2010

HAMAYOON DOZED A bit in his shisham-wood rocker. The hangers full of blue burqas on both sides of his shop made him feel as if he were inside a den. His black trousers and blouse made him feel invisible, and the breeze cooled his sandaled feet. He dozed blissfully until he heard the shop bell. That roused him. A customer!

His merchant's enthusiasm liquefied into fear when he saw the apparition. Aquamarine eyes rimmed in red, the begrimed *amrekayan* uniform, the assault rifle. The apparition spoke, in Farsi. Yes, he understood a little. There was blood on the *amrekayan*'s hands as he pulled out an enormous wad of cash—dollars, euros, rupees, afghanis. Leaves of currency fell on the floor as the crazy man demanded seven burqas, small.

Highway A-77, West of Kabul
July 14, 2010

SEVEN BLUE BURQA-CLAD girls walked together down the shoulder of the road. Somewhere ahead was Iran. None was sure what to do except walk. The mountainous terrain ahead looked infinitely open and dangerous. Freed into this uncertain future, dishonored, they knew nothing but an abyss of fear. They prayed together as they walked. A throaty noise rose around the bend in the highway. A truck of some kind, maybe military, maybe not, color green or gray or something in between. The glare off the windshield pierced them like a beam. The truck slowed as it approached.

Nuthatch

ABNER DALE LAUGHED. He wasn't sure why, but the fact that he was suddenly rich with Nanji's cash and roaming around in an Army truck completely outside the lines "struck him funny," as his Grandpa used to say. The opium didn't hurt either. He had found it in one of Nanji's drawers, so what the hell. After he had dropped the girls, he stuck a ball of the O onto the tip of his pocket knife and set fire to it with a lighter. He inhaled the dancing strand of smoke up his nostrils and held it in—imagining he could feel the magic melt outward from his core. He had to bear down to keep from coughing, finally releasing it as he felt the languid flood of warmth.

My God, he suddenly thought as he found himself shepherding the truck through a crowded street. *I'm so hungry.* He hadn't eaten anything but three protein bars since before they had marshaled on the airfield the night before—was that last night? *What an eventful day!* He really needed to eat. *And I'm rollin' in dough.*

Following a column of cooking smoke, he turned right, then left, punching deeper into the crowded marketplace. He wished he had a loudspeaker so he could say "excuse me" as he nudged forward, feeling a kind of generalized opioid-induced affection for these people who were walking, swaying and standing all around him. The thunderous diesel motor clattered, revving and falling. Like an ox wading through a flock of egrets, the MRAP crawled ahead, leading with its square snout, wheels coated in ochre dust, the side windows sealed.

On his left, three AMFs were drinking tea, their Galils slung over their shoulders.

He advanced by short lunges, a meter or two at a time, past the tea shop, with its blanket door and cheap street tables, past makeshift awnings of many colors, past bicycle carts, butcher stands, smoking stove fires, fruit displays, storefronts with clothes for sale lined up on wall pegs, potato crates, plastic wares, pots and pans... past two sheep. Past people, mostly men, who moved reluctantly aside, averting their gazes, as if avoiding the eye of a belligerent bull, as the truck passed. A cacophony of shouts and murmurs, metal banging, horns, roosters, feral boys.

A.D. saw it then, on the street stretching out to the left. A man with a steaming grill the size of a trampoline covered in sizzling meat and vegetables. That was what he wanted. He turned slowly left.

He started to dismount, then remembered he had dropped the rolls of cash on the passenger seat. He pulled the door closed, grabbed a wad of afghanis, and stepped down, leaving his M-4 inside, and closing the driver's door. He was no longer at war. Just stoned and really deep-down, molecular-level hungry.

He was organizing the currency when the first shots hit him on the left side and his legs stopped working. The three AMFs were coming, firing, missing. Train and train, and these guys still hated to aim, he thought; then a sing-song from childhood, *buy ya books and buy ya books and all you do is eat the pages.* Someone screaming. Others running, crawling away. He looked down at a muddy footprint, suddenly infinitely interesting, and when he raised his eyes again, one of the AMFs was looming above him, the Galil's muzzle brake inches from his face. When he laughed, he made a funny wet noise and felt a faraway wintry pain in his side.

"Nuthatch," he said through bloody teeth. Then the kill shot came, in his face. Dale crumpled and twitched, blood pouring out of his head like a spring.

Jahid, Rafik, and Omar looked at one another as if to ask what the *amrekayan* had said. Nuthatch? No one knew. It couldn't matter. Perhaps a prayer. Jahid opened the door of the MRAP, tossed in a grenade, and closed the door. People were far away now, still running pell-mell to escape. The grenade gave a lusty interiorized crunch. The windshields bulged out and spider-webbed, like the truck was a puffer fish.

Camp Virtue
July 14, 2010

NOTEBOOKS IN THEIR laps, Sergeant Barber and Major Carroll sat facing each other in his office.

"Today is a better day for Afghanistan," he read to her. She followed the verbiage with her pencil. "The Taliban's senior intelligence chief, Usman Jahangiri, is dead. Yesterday, in a daring raid by American Special Operations forces..." He stopped to mark something out, write something else. "Last night, in a daring raid by United States Special Forces, Jahangiri was killed near Charikar. He was accompanied by an armed unit. The entire formation of Taliban was killed during the engagement..." She was making the changes, when he stopped again. "This ends..." They both looked up at each other, she concentrating, he looking through her as he searched for just the right turn of phrase. "This puts to an end the terrorization..." He halted again, puffing, and she knitted her brows, sighing in frustration as she scratched through something and waited again. "Jahangiri can no longer terrorize Afghani..." She set her pencil on the notebook. She would wait until he had this figured out. Or not. She took a deep breath.

"Jahangiri can no longer terrorize innocent Afghan civilians," she offered, and he looked up with an expression that conveyed gratitude and apology.

The phone rang. He picked it up. "Major Carroll." Barber watched his expression disappear as he listened. "Got it," he said, hanging up landline, then sitting silently looking at the toes of his boots.

"What?" she asked. He looked up, seeming puzzled by the question for a moment. He started to stand up, then sat back down.

Finally, "Three of our AMFs are bringing a body from Kabul. It might be Dale."

SERGEANT BAINES SAW Major Carroll through the curtain as Carroll entered the press hooch. Today the curtains were exactly six feet on either side of the press podium.

"Get it right, Baines," said the Major as he strode past, Staff Sergeant Barber in tow.

"Yes, sir," Baines replied. "It will be perfect." Carroll had already gone back to his dressing room, where Baines knew he applied a dust of makeup. Quickly, as the door closed on the dressing room, Baines unzipped his trousers and tugged his penis free. The water glass was on the tray to be placed on the podium with the pitcher. Baines ran the head of his dick around the rim of the glass three times, pressing down and wiping as he went. Just as quickly, he placed the glass back on the tray and zipped his trousers.

When he placed the glass, the pitcher and Carroll's notes, he complied precisely with instructions—pitcher left, glass right, notes dead center. Alongside the podium he set up a tripod and mounted a five-foot-high photograph of Usman Jahangiri's dead face, enlarged from Bobby's photograph. The incoming press beheld the picture like a hunting trophy—a trophy more costly now, measured in lives lost.

Within fifteen minutes, reporters throughout the room were murmuring, huddled in clusters near the coffee and the *hors d'oeuvres*. In addition to George, Connie and Ann Marie, more than three dozen reporters showed up today, with many new faces. Cameramen assembled equipment, sound techs tested microphones.

Colonel Thomas strode in and many of them fell silent. He headed straight backstage and halted in front of Baines, who snapped to attention.

"Major Carroll," the Colonel demanded.

"Dressing room, Sir."

Thomas tried the door, but the deadbolt was thrown. He banged twice, hearing an intake of breath and a rustle.

"Just a moment, Sergeant Baines." Carroll.

"It's me, Will. Open the fuckin' door."

When the door swung back, Carroll started to push through, his eyes down. Thomas caught a glimpse of Staff Sergeant Barber, who appeared to be applying lip gloss in the mirror. She threw a nervous glance at the door, then twitched her eyes back to the mirror.

Thomas glared at Carroll, who held Thomas's eyes with an effort, hoping that Thomas wouldn't look down until his erection went away. Thomas looked back for a moment, then dropped his own eyes, seeming to shift gears somehow.

"I'm taking this one," the Colonel said.

Will Carroll was momentarily confused.

"What? Taking who? What?"

"The briefing. I'm doing the press briefing. I need your notes."

Carroll felt the bile rise, but if he had any good instincts, they had to do with his own professional survival. He clenched his teeth and drew a deep breath.

"Sir. Yes, Sir. The notes are on the podium. Sergeant Barber will introduce you."

She was just coming out the door, trying to duck behind them, and looked up as she heard her name.

"What, Sir?"

"You'll introduce Colonel Thomas. He's taking the press brief today."

SERGEANT BARBER APPROACHED the bank of microphones surrounding the podium.

"Ladies and Gentlemen, Colonel Thomas will be out momentarily. Please find a seat and make yourselves comfortable."

As the murmuring subsided and the audience settled in, Colonel Thomas appeared from between the drapes and strode quietly to center stage. He carefully poured a half glass of water and took a small sip, licking his lips to wet them. Baines watched from offstage, slightly disappointed at hitting the wrong target but still having to suppress the urge to laugh.

"Good morning," said Colonel Thomas. There was a smattering of half-hearted good mornings from the assembled journalists. "I'm Colonel Boyd Thomas, the Task Force Commanding Officer, I'd like to welcome you again to our weekly operations briefing."

He stopped and turned to look at the photograph of the dead Jahangiri, willing the audience to do the same. Then he turned back to them.

"Today is a better day for Afghanistan. The Taliban's senior intelligence chief, Usman Jahangiri, is dead. Last night, in a daring raid by United States Special Forces, Jahangiri was killed near Charikar. Jahangiri was accompanied by an armed unit. The entire formation of Taliban was killed during the engagement. Jahangiri can no longer terrorize innocent Afghan civilians, and his intelligence cell has been smashed. This was not a cost-free mission, however. Two brave Special Forces soldiers were killed in action during this operation. Their names are being withheld pending notification of their next-of-kin. On that sad note, I'd like to extend the sympathy of the entire Task Force Bird staff to members of the press for the loss this morning of one of your colleagues in a cowardly bomb attack. Apparently, two American civilian contractors are also missing since this morning. This just underlines why the United States and the International Security Assistance Force in Afghanistan are committed to defeating

Al Qaeda and establishing a new and secure future for the people of Afghanistan..."

Water people

July 12, 2010
Jordan Lake, North Carolina

MONDAY WAS A down day for Deangela, and she had driven to the lake, 15-501 from Chapel Hill to 64, then east, crossing the bridge, then following the back way in to the Pea Ridge Road bridge. Farah came up from Fayetteville, a halfway meetup for one of their ad hoc fishing dates.

Farah discovered the spot years ago, back in the 90's. On a good day there were no more than three cars at her spot—a patch of field between road, water and bridge—that gave a handful of people access to the bank. A creek emptied into the lake where once a deep draw had been. Ten feet from shore there was a drop-off that plunged to 30 feet, submerging the old stumps and stones from the dry land draw and creating a perfect hot-weather habitat for Pomoxis nigromaculatus—black crappie, a panfish that worked well in the fourteen Belizean fish recipes Farah had tried. She southern-fried them too, in beer batter, but dressed them with her own hot salad. She had lived in North Carolina for nearly twenty years now, after all. Fusion cuisine was bound to happen.

Farah was a cane pole purist, insisting that Deangela learn cane-poling, too. "Ya look at dem men wid dey big Mercury engines makin' roostah tails over da wa-tah, five-hundred dollah rod and reels, ah-tificial baits cost twenty dollahs apiece. Ya need a trailah f' de boat, and ya need a truck f' da trailah. Ya not even past da retail phase, den, ah ya? Dey fish all day, get ten pounds of fish, and some nice pictures. All dat t' catch a fish. Not fair to d' budget. Not fair to d' fish. Ya need tens-a-tousand-a dollahs to catch a little fish. We come down heah, spend twenty on gas, drinks and some minnows, we go home wid ten pounds a fish. Way we do it, my opinion, is closah to art." Farah had given this monologue at least twice a year for the last five.

Deangela was competitive when she fished, even though she needed to pretend she wasn't. She was already grasping for a wet minnow from the bucket to bait her hook while Farah was still at her car changing from flip-flops into her eight-dollar fishing sneakers.

To the southwest, against the tops of the pine trees, a line of clouds was encroaching against the otherwise blue sky. As she looked down the bank at Deangela, a puff of wind came in from that direction, stirring the high oak leaves. A cardinal suddenly streaked out of an old, bent pin oak, crossing behind Deangela like a drop of blood skating across the mottled afternoon shadows.

"SOME PEOPLE AH wa-tah people." Water people. Deangela didn't ask for an explanation. She knew it was coming. This was the preface. This has come up—wherever it was going—because Farah had just landed her fifth crappie to Deangela's one. Deangela's mood, on this occasion, was not altogether charitable. Her nose was rubbed in it a bit, because Farah would stop after each catch, pull out the fillet knife, bleed, rip and strip the fish, and drop the fillets onto the five pounds of ice in her cooler. She acted like she had all the time in the world while her incompetent daughter continued to muddle around, feeding minnows to relentlessly attacking four-inch bluegills. Farah would give the line a twitch, setting the hook, skate the catch over the surface to her, lip the fish expertly, then pop out the hook with the hemostat she wore clipped to her dirty white t-shirt.

"People live on da wa-tah, dey ahl tied to the wa-tah, but dey do a tousand different tings."

"This sounds like a Credence Clearwater Revival song."

"Don' be fresh, o' ah jalapeño ya bottom." Against her will, Deangela smiled at this. "Ah'm not a-gloatin' on yah. Ah'm tellin' yah sometin. And if yah drop that bait another foot from da bobbah, yah'll hit da slabs instead o' dem squash seed.

"All ahm sayin', deys wa-tah, and people, and people need wa-tah. But deys a difference in workin' and livin' on da wa-tah, an' cuttin' ahn de faucet wheh ya nevah see de rivah o' da lake." Deangela grudgingly swung her line back and raised her bobber, pitching her lifeless minnow in the water. "Deys mountain people, swamp people, people who work in mines, den days most a dese people heah, wha dey do is two tings. Dey mash buttons and spend money. Okay, so dey mash buttons o' wiggle a computah mouse ahl day. Dey not tied to nut'n real. People got lazah beams fa eyes, loss dey peripheral vision. Dey tied to a batch a numbahs, o' a graph, a spreadsheet o'..."

"Oh!" blurted Deangela, as her bobber plunged out of sight, grabbing her cane pole and giving it a snap with her wrist to set the hook. Just in time, because the pole suddenly bent, and hard, as the fish—something big that strained her shoulder and bicep—dove toward the bank, then stretched out as it headed back out for deeper water. Farah was on her feet.

"Holy shit!" Deangela grunted.

"Ain't a crappie, sweetbread. Finesse dat one. She break ya line ahn ya."

Deangela wanted this fish, whatever it was. She had one aqua-socked foot on the bank, one down in the water, dreading that sudden relaxation in the pole if the line broke. But it didn't. Not yet. The fish pulled hard away from the shore, then gave up for a bit. Deangela gave an exquisitely light rotation to try and turn the fish without breaking the line. It worked. When the fish took off again, hugging the bottom the whole time, it went left toward a hole full of coontail and hydrilla. Farah was saying something to her, but she couldn't really understand it. Deangela stepped into a hole as she waded in, sinking to her hips and almost capsizing, but she held the pole aloft—maintaining that light tension—with her right hand, batting at the water with her left to regain her equilibrium. She wanted the fish in the weed bed to blunt its thrusting power, but she knew she had to keep the line high to prevent tying up in the vegetation. With two clumsy steps, she came back up out of the hole and was wading at knee-height. The fish decelerated in a patch of duckweed, then turned left again, coming right toward her, bending the pole almost double. Farah was shouting that it would break, when Deangela choked up on the pole, re-grasping it halfway up with one hand, and reached for the line with the other. Stepping backward, she held the fish inside the weeds as it approached the shore. Deangela backed up again, hit the little ledge on the bank, dropped on her behind, recovered and stepped back. The whole while she led the fish in, now by pulling the line itself, her pole abandoned at the waterline. Then the snout appeared at water's edge. She had partially beached it, and it was churning the water into mud. Two feet of it from the looks.

"Ah don' know what dat is." Farah was standing right behind her, looking down at the snout. "Hand me yah pliahs." Farah's little hemostats were too small for this one.

Deangela was kneeling now, holding tension on the line to prevent the fish gaining any purchase on deeper, clearer water. She shifted the line from her right to left hand so she could reach the Leatherman holster on her belt, unsnapping it and handing it to Farah. Farah flipped open the Leatherman, gaped the pliers, and squatted in front of Deangela to hand grip the fish hard under the lower jaw.

"Got some fraitnin' teet', dis one," she said, changing her mind. "Oh mah jeez!"

Farah dragged the fish up on the shore, Deangela stumbling behind her to keep the line clear and taut. The great fish heaved with such force that its entire body levitated and gave a quarter spin. Both women yelped at that.

It was green like tarnished silver, and somehow ancient, more cylindrical than most fish, almost a fat snake. It had barbels like a catfish, but smaller, just protruding alongside the nostrils. The long dorsal fin and the short anal fin almost blended with the tail, so far back were they set, and there was a large black spot on the upper half of the tail. The teeth, as Farah had noted immediately, were rows of curved needles, real thumb-shredders. She was surprised these teeth hadn't cut the line.

The fish was gasping, it gills fanning, and one of the eyes was covered with dirt and twigs. Deangela was at once overwhelmed with a profoundly uncharacteristic anxiety.

"Put her back in," she said.

"Ah don't know how to cook dis anyway..."

"Now. Put her back in now."

Farah looked up at her daughter with concern now. The clouds were now filling the sky behind her, and a gust of wind raised one side of Deangela's hair. She had never seen Deangela exhibit fear like this. Growing up, this child had rescued spiders, chased bees, picked up snakes. She could hold a catfish without getting spiked.

Farah squatted, having seized the fish behind its gills, fast and hard to prevent it kicking loose. She fastened the pliers to the shank of the hook buried in the fish's hard pallet, giving the pliers an authoritative twist. The hook popped loose with a little crunch, like someone stepping on a beetle. She stood, leaving the fish on the ground, pushed her toe under the midsection, and kick-pitched the fish back into a few inches of water. It lay for a moment twitching and gasping, then batted the surface and disappeared back into the hazy green depths. A roll of thunder sounded far in the southwest as the clouds overtook the sun. The afternoon went dark, the water turned opaque. The cardinal shot past again, returning to his crippled pin oak.

###

About Stan Goff

Stan Goff (b. November 12, 1951—) is an American writer who has lived variously in California, Missouri, Arkansas, Colorado, North Carolina, Washington (state), Georgia, Tennessee, New York (state), Texas, Panama, and Costa Rica. He now resides in Michigan. He is married to Sherry Goff, and they have seven grandchildren (with another on the way). Goff has been a day laborer, a pizza deliveryman, a grocery bagger, a stone mason's assistant, the organizing director for a twelve-state non-profit, a freelance journalist, a deconstructionist (nothing to do with postmodern studies, it means taking houses apart by hand to salvage the materials), and for most of the period between January 1970 and February 1996 he was an active duty member of the United States Army, both infantry and special operations. He served in eight active conflict areas. Included in his assignments were the 173rd Airborne Brigade (in Vietnam), the 82nd Airborne Division, 1st Ranger Battalion, 2nd Ranger Battalion, 75th Ranger Regiment, 7th Special Forces, 3rd Special Forces, and 1st Special Forces Operational Detachment-Delta. He is now a member of Veterans For Peace.

Other Books by Stan Goff

Hideous Dream: A Soldier's Memoir of the US Invasion of Haiti (2000, Soft Skull)

Full Spectrum Disorder: The Military in the New American Century (2004, Soft Skull)

Energy War: Exterminism for the 21st Century (2006, Lulu)

Sex & War (2006, Lulu)

Borderline: Reflections on War, Sex, and Church (2015, Wipf and Stock)

Mammon's Ecology: Metaphysic of an Empty Sign (forthcoming, Wipf and Stock)

Caeneus: Violent Women in Film as Honorary Men (forthcoming, Wipf and Stock)

Made in the USA
Lexington, KY
26 November 2017